WIN
ARRES

WINIFRED PECK (1882-1962) was born Winifred Frances Knox in Oxford, the daughter of the future Bishop of Manchester. Her mother Ellen was the daughter of the Bishop of Lahore.

A few years after her mother's death, Winifred Peck became one of the first pupils at Wycombe Abbey School, and later studied at Lady Margaret Hall, Oxford. Returning to Manchester, and under the influence of Christian Socialism, she acted as a social worker in her father's diocese, as well as starting out as a professional writer.

After writing a biography of Louis IX, she turned to fiction in her early thirties, writing over twenty novels, including two detective mysteries, *The Warrielaw Jewel* and *Arrest the Bishop?,* now republished by Dean Street Press.

She married James Peck in 1911, and they had two sons together. James was knighted in 1938, and it was as Lady Peck that his wife was known to many contemporary reviewers.

Bewildering Cares, a novel about the perplexing and richly comic life of a parish priest's wife in the early months of World War Two, is now available as a Furrowed Middlebrow book.

BY WINIFRED PECK

FICTION

Twelve Birthdays (1918)

The Closing Gates (1922)

A Patchwork Tale (1925)

The King of Melido (1927)

A Change of Master (1928)

The Warrielaw Jewel (1933)

The Skirts of Time (1935)

The Skies Are Falling (1936)

Coming Out (1938)

Let Me Go Back (1939)

*Bewildering Cares: A Week in the Life of
a Clergyman's Wife* (1940)

A Garden Enclosed (1941)

House-Bound (1942)

Tranquillity (1944)

There Is a Fortress (1945)

Through Eastern Windows (1947)

Veiled Destinies (1948)

A Clear Dawn (1949)

Arrest the Bishop? (1949)

Facing South (1950)

Winding Ways (1951)

Unseen Array (1951)

MEMOIR

A Little Learning: A Victorian Childhood (1952)

Home for the Holidays (1955)

HISTORY

The Court of a Saint: Louis IX, King of France, 1226-70 (1909)

They Come, They Go: The Story of an English Rectory (1937)

WINIFRED PECK

ARREST THE BISHOP?

With an introduction by
Martin Edwards

DEAN STREET PRESS
A Furrowed Middlebrow Book

Published by Dean Street Press 2016

Copyright © 1949 Winifred Peck
Introduction copyright © 2016 Martin Edwards

All Rights Reserved

The right of Winifred Peck to be identified as the Author of
the Work has been asserted by her estate in accordance
with the Copyright, Designs and Patents Act 1988.

Cover by DSP

First published in 1949 by Faber & Faber

ISBN 978 1 911413 91 2

www.deanstreetpress.co.uk

INTRODUCTION

WINIFRED PECK's achievements have perhaps been overshadowed by those of other members of her astonishingly gifted family. Yet her career as an author lasted for almost half a century, and her work has enjoyed considerable popularity. Less than a decade ago, a reprint of her novel *Housebound* (1942) earned enthusiastic notices; Michael Morpurgo, for instance, described it as 'beautifully written ... supremely funny'. When Peck died in 1962, *The Times* said that "she showed a marked talent for sharp characterization, amusing dialogue and an ability to condense a life history into the minimum number of words."

Peck was a versatile writer. She published a life of Louis IX in 1909, when she was 27, and turned to writing novels in her late thirties. Most of her books can be described as mainstream fiction, often written with a light touch that has drawn comparisons with the work of E.M. Delafield and Angela Thirkell. During the 1950s, she also wrote a couple of books about her childhood, but before then she had explored detective fiction. Her work as a mystery novelist, however, has tended – despite its quality – to be overlooked.

The Warrielaw Jewel and *Arrest the Bishop?* are detective novels that demonstrate the quiet accomplishment of her writing, but there are obvious reasons why she did not make a lasting impact as a crime writer. The books appeared more than a decade apart, and she made no attempt to write a series, or create a signature sleuth. The books had long been out of print and hard to find until Dean Street Press, which has unearthed a considerable number of long-lost gems, resolved to give them a fresh life. Their republication also gives a new generation of readers the chance to compare Peck's fiction with the more high-profile detective stories written by her brother Ronald Knox, who was one of the leading lights of "the Golden Age of Murder" between the two world wars, and a founder member of the legendary Detection Club.

The Warrielaw Jewel was first published in 1933, but the events of the story take place in the era 'when King Edward VII lived, and skirts were long and motors few, and the term Victorian was not yet a reproach'. Thus the novel represents an early example of the history-mystery, a fashionable sub-genre today but much less common at the time that Peck was writing. The setting is Edinburgh, which 'was not in those days a city, but a fortuitous collection of clans. Beneath a society always charming and interesting on the surface, and delightful to strangers, lurked a history of old hatreds, family quarrels, feuds as old as the Black Douglas. Nor were the clans united internally, except indeed at attack from without. Often already my mother-in-law had placidly dissuaded me from asking relations to meet, on the ground that they did not recognise each other.'

The story, narrated by the wife of the legal adviser to the Warrielaw family, encompasses such classic Golden Age elements as murder, a trial, a valuable heirloom, and a mysterious curse. The quality of Peck's prose lifts the book out of the ordinary, and in a review on the Mystery*file blog in 2010, Curtis Evans argued that it is 'an early example of a Golden Age mystery that, in its shifting of emphasis from pure puzzle to the study of character and setting, helped mark the gradual shift from detective story to crime novel.'

Pleasingly, Peck makes use of one of the game-playing devices popular with Golden Age novelists, a formal 'challenge to the reader', at the end of the twelfth chapter:

'STOP. THIS IS A CHALLENGE TO YOU. At this point all the characters and clues have been presented. It should now be possible for you to solve the mystery. CAN YOU DO IT? Here's your chance to do a little detective work on your own – a chance to test your powers of deduction. Review the mystery and see if you can solve it at this point. Remember! THIS IS A SPORTING PROPOSITION, made in an effort to make the reading of mystery stories more interesting to you. So – don't read any further. Reach your solution now. Then proceed.'

The mystery writer most closely associated with explicit challenges of this kind was the American Ellery Queen, but the device was also employed by a range of British detective novelists, including Anthony Berkeley, Milward Kennedy, and Rupert Penny. It was a way of making explicit the fact that the whodunit essentially involved a battle of wits, dependent on the author playing fair by supplying (although often disguising) the clues to unravel the puzzle.

Having entered so wholeheartedly into the spirit of Golden Age detective fiction, Peck promptly moved away from the genre, and did not return to it until after the Second World War, by which time tastes in crime writing, as well as much else, were changing fast. *Arrest the Bishop?* appeared in 1949; set in a Bishop's Palace, the story made excellent use of her first-hand knowledge of ecclesiastical life. This is another history-mystery, written in the aftermath of one world war, but relating events set in 1920, not long after the end of another.

As a bonus, the book is also an example of that popular sub-genre, the Christmas crime story. The murder victim is, as so often in traditional whodunits, an unscrupulous blackmailer, and again Peck makes use of tropes of Golden Age fiction such as a timetable of key events, and a list of prime suspects itemising their respective motives, opportunities for committing the crime, and instances of their seemingly suspicious behaviour. The result is a good old-fashioned mystery: Peck's gentle humour ensures readability, and in the twenty-first century the book has added appeal as a portrait of a vanished age.

Winifred Frances Knox, born in 1882, was the third of the six children of the fourth Bishop of Manchester. She had an older sister, Ethel, as well as four brothers. The eldest son, E.V. Knox, became well-known as editor of *Punch*; he was also responsible for a splendid parody of the Golden Age detective story, 'The Murder at the Towers'. Dillwyn ('Dilly') Knox became a legendary code-breaker who worked for British Intelligence during both world wars, while Wilfred Knox earned distinction as an Anglican clergyman and theologian. The best-known of the four brothers was Ronald, a man of extraordinary talents, who was also ordained an Anglican clergyman before converting to Catholicism; he proceeded to carve a considerable reputation as 'Monsignor Knox'. Amongst many other activities, he was a popular broadcaster in the early days of the BBC, one of the first Sherlockian scholars, an expert on word games such as acrostics, and creator of the Detective's Decalogue – ten jokey commandments for crime writers that were adapted into the initiation ritual for new members of the Detection Club. Suffice to say that these supposed rules of the game were honoured, by Knox as well as by his crime writing colleagues, more in the breach than in the observance.

Winifred shared, *The Times* said, 'her brothers' lively wit and sharp minds, and was well able to hold her own in the complicated verse games they played among themselves. It was the family custom to spend the summer holiday in a furnished house, generally a rectory, where they amused themselves tracing the life of the absent incumbent as revealed in the photographs that were hung about his walls. In such stimulating and imaginative company she had every inducement to become a writer, where much of the material the novelist needs lay to her hand.' In almost any other family, Winifred's record as a high achiever could not possibly be eclipsed, but such was the brilliance of her quartet of brothers that even her niece, the Booker Prize-winning novelist Penelope Fitzgerald (whose father was E.V. Knox), made only fleeting mention of Winifred in her book *The Knox Brothers*.

Winifred was among the first forty pupils to study at Wycombe Abbey School, and proceeded to read History at Lady Margaret Hall, Oxford. In 1911, she married James Peck in Manchester Cathedral. James, described by Penelope Fitzgerald as "a small, quiet, reliable, clever and honourable Scotsman", was at the time Clerk to the School Board in Edinburgh. The couple had three children, and James became an increasingly influential figure in both local and central government; when he was knighted in 1938, Winifred became Lady Peck.

By the time Winifred Peck died, her detective fiction had become a footnote to her literary career. It was not even mentioned in her obituary in *The Times*. Present day readers of the books will, I think, agree that this is a pity. Her contribution to the golden age of crime fiction, although modest in scale, is well worth remembering.

Martin Edwards
www.martinedwardsbooks.com

To and For My Husband

—Or more properly the Ablative—

By, With and From My Husband

because

We planned to write this together: we discussed it together: you made any original suggestions it may contain: you only refuse to appear as collaborator because I did what you may justly cal the donkey-work of writing it. But you cannot deny that it is partly your work and that it was you who horrified a guest at J— by announcing at breakfast: "Yes, we'll make it a fatal dose of morphia", that it was you who sent my terrified housekeeper a message: "Tell Lady Peck we must have an inquest". You read, criticized and corrected the MS: you must, in short, admit a certain responsibility for this belated offspring as far as to accept this dedication from

Your Wife

I
WEDNESDAY AFTERNOON

"HOW ON EARTH can any one afford to keep all this up now-adays?"

This was the invariable question of every tourist who, for the sum of half a crown, was privileged once a week to view the grounds of the Bishop of Evelake's Palace. It was not so much the Palace itself, that long low patchwork of Elizabethan brick and Georgian stone, that plum-and orange-coloured centre in the pattern of brilliant flower-beds, shimmering glass-houses and starry shrubs, which inspired the question. Ringed by shaven lawns, the patchwork quilt was set in a frame of grey fragile arches, haggard pillars, broken lichened steps and tombs, bounded by the crumb ling yet inviolate walls of the old Abbey of Evelake. To preserve this grey-gold outer fortification was the responsibility of the Bishop of the See, and a heavy one financially.

"Well, we married Pound's Paste!" was the answer of the butler-guide in 1920, a cigarette poised behind his ear. In that time of domestic upheaval any butler was better than none, and the ex-Miss Pound, as Mrs. Broome, the Bishop's wife, made light of the impertinence when the rumour reached her. "I'll tell Soames he must really keep to his Book of Words," she said pacifically to her horrified informant. "He'll probably understand what I mean and of course it was perfectly true!"

The See of Evelake was indeed one of those which caused perennial difficulty to the Crown early in this century. Twenty-five years before the diocese had been divided and the episcopal income with it. Twenty-five years later the Palace would be handed over to the National Trust.

"We must look first for a man of means rather than a man of God," said the Dean sardonically when the ex-head master of St. Blaze College, Dr. Broome, was appointed. "I am glad to think we shall have a little of both. Ours is the Church of a Compromise!"

"You've got a man of peace anyhow," suggested his inter-locutor. "That is more than you can say of most school masters. Too much peace and too little discipline at St. Blaze in his time, they say."

But the Dean was not to be drawn on the possible failings of Dr. Broome in his former career. "The less discipline anyone tries to enforce in the Anglican Church the better!" was his only reply.

If our Church is one of a compromise so also was the Palace. To the Bishop as he made his way from his low, panelled room to tea in his wife's drawing-room, on a grey stormy December twilight in the year 1920, it seemed a symbol of his life. The original building, long and low, its mullioned windows gazing from its mellow, red-brick walls with the serenity of three hundred years, recalled to him his early life, his brilliant youth, his Oxford successes, his idyllic marriage and rapid rise in the Church. And then—the low graceful passage opened into an amorphous wing, known as the Bridge. "Thrown out by Bish-op Main in 1850, with no architectural pretensions, to house his family of twenty children," said the Book of Words. ("And no such goings-on nowadays," Soames usually added with a chuckle.) Now, to this Bishop, that huddle of pantry and offic-es and rather mean bedrooms above seemed a parable indeed of his years at Blaze, his heart broken by the loss of his young wife, his spirit broken by the covert resistance of the masters, and open rebellion of the boys, against a young and nervous newcomer.

The Bridge passage terminated in a new wide archway opening upon a magnificent white-panelled hall, and it was thus, it seemed to the Bishop to-day, that his new life with his second wife had begun.

"My dear, you must just have that Bridge business pulled down," said Mrs. Broome's Pound relations, who were all by this time established in vast Palladian country houses. But the ecclesiastical commissioners were difficult, the architect half-hearted, and, after all, St. Paul had indicated, said Mrs.

Broome, that a Bishop should have plenty of spare bedrooms, especially at Ordination times. So between them the architect and Mrs. Broome tacked on the excrescence of a more or less Georgian new wing, with a suite of drawing-rooms which Mrs. Proudie might have envied, and luxurious accommodation for guests and servants above. It was a pity, she told her relatives laughingly, that by the time it was finished the Bishop had dug himself into the old wing, and refused to change his own study, or the old bed room suite of long-dead bishops; it was not even possible, in view of the coal shortage, to use the new draw-ing-rooms habitually. But to-day everything was prepared for a large house-party for the Ordination. ("And that means, dear," wrote Mrs. Broome to a Nonconformist aunt, "two young men to be priested, six to be ordained deacons, the Chancellor to license them and Canon Wye to address them. As dear little Sue and myself will be the only womenfolk it wouldn't be your idea of a successful house party!")

"Well, did you enjoy your long walk to-day?" Mrs. Broome rose, as she spoke, from a desk covered with Christmas corre-spondence, as big, welcoming and genial as one of her large gay arm-chairs. This comment on the distances to be covered in the Palace was a well-worn family joke, but perhaps it was not, she considered, very tactful this afternoon, in view of the Bishop's weary countenance.

"It has been a worrying day, a very worrying day," said her husband, moving gratefully to his luxurious chair by the blazing fire and the shining hearth.

"Dear me, I am sorry," said Mrs. Broome, in the voice that somehow always sounded jovial. "Never mind, the Ordina-tion will soon be over, and no one is arriving till about six. Everything is arranged, and I made sure that that stupid Soames had got the name-cards in the bedrooms right—the Chancel-lor in St. Francis, Canon Wye in St. Dominic, as usual"—(it should be admitted that nothing in Mrs. Broome's scheme of comfort suggested the austerities of the patron saints)—"And all the candidates will be in the top story of this wing. Except

Dick Marlin, for he's almost one of the family so I've put him in St. Bede. These three all like the old panelled rooms like you, I gather, though I can't understand why! I'm so glad we needn't use the Bridge bedrooms, as I've got poor old Moira in the one over the pantry to save trouble in carrying trays. I do hope the Hospital will send for her soon, for she's often in such pain!"

"Dear, dear!" murmured the Bishop courteously. Ordinary people had not at that date begun to see themselves as in a State of Conflict. The Bishop would have diagnosed his state of mind as a want of consistent grace rather than dignifying himself as a split personality, but there was indeed a hidden conflict between the stately ascetic divine revered by his diocese and wife, and the terrified heart, haunted by memories, beset by future fears, which beat beneath his episcopal garb. Let it be said at once that few guilty secrets lurked there, as the world would count guilty. The evil genius of the Bishop's life, as a scholar, don, cleric and schoolmaster, had been no thrilling vice, but the possession of one of those morbid consciences which cannot put the past behind them, combined with an imagination which hagrides the mind all the more mercilessly because it has always been so sternly concealed. "The dear Bishop is so sensitive and far-sighted," was Mrs. Broome's version of her husband's character. "The man's a coward and afraid to say so," declared one of the Council of St. Blaze College, after a peculiar exposure of indecision in the Headmaster's attitude. "You've only to say that you tremble for the future if he won't adopt your view, and he'll give way," the Dean would advise his clergy confidentially. From the Bishop's Guardian Angel, who understood the tragedies in his past life, the depth of his devotion for his loved ones and his God, the struggles for trust and for hope, that most elusive of the Christian virtues, we may imagine a far more tolerant and pitying verdict. Few but the angels presumably, and a skilled psychiatrist possibly, could understand the discrepancy between the clean-shaven, finely moulded and lined face, and the cautious self-composed manner, with the heavily lidded eyes of a frightened and hunted child which peered out in side glances. His chaplain, who entered now, held that with his beard the Bishop would represent exactly the drawing of St. Joseph by Leonardo, and some such parallel might be discerned in the Bishop's nature with the thwarted yet exalted saint who bore in his bosom the torment of doubt and dread, of self-suppression, as the world gazed at his so-called wife and that miraculous Birth whose ultimate promise to the world must have seemed very far away in Nazareth.

"I'm sure everything is in the best possible order!" Though he roused himself to speak and smile, his wife's cheerful vitality seemed to the Bishop only as a fire through a glass screen to a cold man. "Where's Sue?"

"Out at the G.F.S. party, but she'll be back soon."

Like most clergy and headmasters the Bishop had a secret predilection for the society of the other sex, and not least for the young and attractive. Sue, his only child by the second Mrs. Broome, had managed to inherit her father's admirable features with her mother's quality of cosy warmth. She was no noted beauty like Judith, his daughter by his first wife, but that young lady's meteoric career through two seasons with her stepmother's wealthy relatives, mild flirtations, broken heart, spectacular wedding and recent far less pleasing, and even more notorious activities, had given him a certain distrust of outstanding charm in women.

"Ah, here's Bobs! That's nice. I'm sure you've arranged everything beautifully for us, Bobs!"

There was no false geniality in Mrs. Broome's welcome to the genial, red-headed young parson who joined them. One of a Bishop's problems is to find a chaplain who is a budding administrator, a competent shorthand typist, and congenial to his family all in one. The Broomes had endured in succession a bullying martinet and an over-competent young business woman during the war. They were, after this, delighted to welcome Robert Borderer, a connection of the Pounds and an Old Boy of St. Blaze, though his powers of organization were as sketchy as his Pitman, because he was pre-eminently pleasant to live with and devoted to the family. (Too devoted to Judith once, but that's over long ago, thought Mrs. Broome sometimes.) Of course, as Bobs himself candidly told them, it was too cushy a job for him, but a wound sustained as a stretcher-bearer and chaplain in France made more active work impossible for the present.

"Not more muddles than usual, I hope," said Bobs, taking a large muffin. "We haven't fixed up about the reading aloud, my lord. We had Jeremy Taylor last September, Latinius' sermons last March. Should we have something lighter?"

"I'd prefer P. G. Wodehouse myself," said Mrs. Broome, absently, looking curiously from her husband to Bobs. It was clear that they were worried, seriously worried over something, and though this was frequently the case with her over-anxious Mark, it took a good deal to worry Bobs. "Or let the poor boys talk for a change! Two of the deacons were here before the war, dear, Dick and Mr. Staples I mean, just when that dreadful trouble over Mr. Ulder hung over us—he was turned out of his headship of the Theological College just afterwards, wasn't he? And the others who are to be ordained deacons looked such babies when they came for the Examination! I'd like to give them all a good time, specially just before Christmas! Oh dear, what have I said? Something is wrong, I can see! You don't mean that this dreadful Mr. Ulder is making trouble again!"

"He has written to threaten me with a visit shortly," admitted the Bishop unwillingly. "But we won't talk about it, please, my dear. Let us—let us consider this problem of the reading aloud by Bobs. I must say I prefer to listen to him rather than to find subjects of conversation."

"But we'll have the Chancellor and Dick and Canon Wye! They're all easy enough! Still, what about a little Tolstoy?" Mrs. Broome tried to retain her habitual cheerfulness, but there could be no doubt that a blight had fallen upon the room at the mention of Ulder's name.

It is certain that some commentators must have suggested that the thorn in St. Paul's side referred to a contemporary deacon or elder who had disgraced his calling and his God. There can be few greater trials for any Father in God, more especially nowadays when the press never fails to give widest publicity to the scandals of the Church. ("Only the birth of quintuplets or the wedding of a film star will ever get Ulder off the front page of the Penny Press," Bobs had groaned once.) And the thorn is all the more painful in the Anglican Church because it is as difficult to deprive a parson of his living as to extract a deep and festering splinter from the human hand. Thomas Ulder had been the Bishop's thorn for the fifteen years of his Episcopate. The last Bishop had just appointed him Head of the Theological College before premature senile decay ended mercifully in the death of the prelate. For all those years vague tales of bad management, financial difficulties, and the dislike and distrust of the candidates who spent a year in Lake Hall in preparation for Ordination, had harassed Bishop Broome. Five years ago definite tales of drunkenness and dishonesty were circulated and Mrs. Ulder left her husband, retreated to their native Donegal, and died. That was just before the first Great War, and it had taken all the efforts of the Bishop, the Chancellor of the Diocese and the Ecclesiastical Court of Appeal to dislodge him. For Ulder was not only a supremely crafty man: his neat figure, pale full face, unctuous manner and beautiful voice gave no suggestion of villainy: he made a good impression on all strangers, and his defence even in the last sulphurous accusations brought against him was almost water-tight. The case had ended in a compromise, largely brought about by Richard Marlin, the only ordination candidate of any promise or personality whom the College had seen for years. Through his skilful negotiations Ulder was persuaded to retire to the remote country living of which he was parson, where the congregation was so small and so old that, as Richard said, they would hardly notice the change in parsons. Even so the affair weighed heavily on the minds of all Dick's theological superiors for they could not escape, as the young deacon escaped, to meet an open and less scabrous foe on the fields of France.

"Oh well, it was a bad business," was all the information Dick gave Bobs. "I expect I made a fool of myself and every one but it wasn't easy. You see, Ulder had all the honour cards and knew how to bluff us anyway every time. We'd all the low cards of procrastination, and cowardice, and failure to take our opportunities in the past. He could throw such mud on the Bishop and through him on the Church for not acting before, that he had to have his foul mouth stopped. He started by demanding a vacant canonry, then a rural deanery, then a good fat living. All I did was to argue him down to Mendle and its twenty inhabitants and five churchgoers. Oh, it was all wrong, of course—it was rather like leaving a unit in danger to save the whole brigade, or so it seemed to me. But the Bishop wholly refused to face the open scandal Ulder would have made."

"How did you get let in for it at all?"

"Because Ulder himself had rather a weakness for me. The horrid fellow knew my grandfather was in Debrett, and I was the only chap there who'd been at Oxford. I tried to make him see that I only put up with the poisonous place because I was set on that curacy at Blacksea" (the one manufacturing and incredibly slummy town in the diocese) "but I expect it was a good thing. By Jove, if good presupposes the existence of evil anyone who put up with Ulder for a year should have seen enough evil to become a saint." And Bobs had submitted, laughing, to Dick's conclusions.

"I've one piece of news for you," said Mrs. Broome now, reflecting that the best way to cure one worry of the Bishop's was to superimpose another. "I've had a telegram to say that Judith is coming to stay to-night—by car, so we won't have to send for her. Yes, Soames, you can come and take tea away!"

There was a general tendency in the diocese, and still more in the Palace itself, to consider Soames a very unworthy representative of that once high office, the Bishop's butler. But, as Mrs. Broome pointed out apologetically, the best butlers of the Kensitas advertisement had been dying out for years or going into retirement, and their young efficient successors were swept away by the war. Soames was, she must admit, bad-mannered, under-sized and given to spots, but he had seen service in the war, he had had some experience under the Headmaster of a neighbouring school, and as a footman in some vague past: he was handy and liked odd jobs; and he was quite intelligent about messages and faces. ("Too intelligent," commented Bobs, "he's the ear for a key-hole right enough!") And, most important of all, he had been introduced by the old housekeeper Moira who, till her recent severe illness, had ruled most household affairs. His dealing with the tea-tray, which suggested a hasty make-do service in a canteen rather than the reverent collection of shining silver on the vast silver tray with its Crown Derby cups, usually tried Mrs. Broome's equanimity, but to-day she was glad that the Bishop must suppress the first dismay which news of his elder daughter's arrival invariably gave him of late years. Silently she passed him the telegram for which he held out his hand. Better let him see its wording at once!—"In dreadful trouble. Coming to you this evening to stay—Judith."

At least the personality of Ulder wavered as that of Judith filled the room. On the wall hung her portrait, known to the artist, as he studied her and was inevitably dazzled by her blue eyes beneath long lashes, her long neck, curling black hair, long white hands and air of exotic mockery, as "The Blue Poppy". "It doesn't show her gaiety clearly enough," held Mrs. Broome, who adored her stepdaughter, except when she worried her father to death with her escapades. "Not dare-devil enough," said her younger sister Susan. "Rose of all roses, rose of all the world," was a Canon's secret lovelorn verdict. A very clear, clever exhibition, thought the cynical Dean privately, of what we hear about as sex-appeal, to a most marked extent. But Bobs perhaps expressed best the overwhelming charm of her personality when, twenty years later, forgetting his quiet, kind wife, he read Esmond's tribute to his Beatrix: "He who is old feels young again as he thinks of her and remembers a Paragon," and putting down his Thackeray, sat lost in thoughts of Judith Broome.

"But it is impossible, quite impossible that she should come here during the Ordination," declared the Bishop, rising as Soames disappeared at last, and addressing the room as if it held his old School. "Good Heavens! Even before her marriage we used to pack her off to save at least one broken heart. I remember clearly after her wedding" (and a vision came to him of Judith, radiant in white satin, pearl tiara and veils, half-dancing down the aisle as if she were the fragrance of her lilies personified) "yes, just after the wedding, she cried: 'No more cathedrals or palaces or Ordinations for me, Daddy darling! Mike and I are practising heathens!'"

"Mike was not the man for her," said Mrs. Broome almost automatically. It was with this phrase that she charitably comprehended the flying scandals culminating in a spectacular action for divorce which had marked her stepdaughter's career. The Bishop, heart-broken at the memory of his first wife's modesty and purity, had refused to allow Judith to the Palace till her decree was absolute. Mike was not playing the conventional gentleman's part, but indeed Judith's affair with Clive Fitzroy, that renowned Guardsman and V.C., would have made it a little absurd. Whether her Clive made her an honest woman or deserted her seemed almost immaterial to the Bishop. His child was in any case, he felt, a child of shame, and nothing in her gay, flippant, infrequent letters altered his view.

"It is impossible to have her," he reiterated, while Bobs sat pale and silent for once, torn between his longing to see Judith and the hopelessness of his love for her.

"But, dearest, she says she is in terrible trouble! To whom should she come but her own father? Besides," added Mrs. Broome, lapsing into her usual common sense, "we can't stop her. She must be on her way in Clive's car by now for the telegram was handed in at Evelake. What is it, Soames?" (How ubiquitous the shabby little butler seemed this evening!) "Another telegram? Perhaps she's changed her plans! Oh no, it's for you, Bobs. Well, dear, I for one shall welcome our little Judith gladly. I think she shall have her old room and I'll move the Chancellor to St. Thomas Aquinas."

"I presume she'll be tired and dine in bed," was the Bishop's dubious note of welcome. "Why change your arrangements for her?"

"Did you ever know Judith tired? Of course I could put her in the Bridge room next poor old Moira—I had a bed made up there in case of an emergency."

"Certainly not," said the Bishop with an emphasis which betrayed his impression that Judith's life had been only too much of a passage way for her lovers.

"No answer, Soames." Bob's face was even more troubled as the butler left the room. "I'm afraid this is really tiresome news, sir, Ulder wires that he is coming out here in the hope of an interview with you and other guests at the Palace to-night."

"Oh, my God!" said the Bishop. It was a prayer rather than an oath he uttered as he fell back in his chair, so clearly prostrated by the news that Mrs. Broome rose quickly yet heavily from the sofa in dismay and went to his side. But the Bishop, with unaccustomed brusqueness, brushed her aside and made for the door with a murmur about his work.

"But he's going to the Chapel, not to his room," said Mrs. Broome, listening to her husband's steps followed by the clash of the Chapel swing doors. "I thought all the trouble with that wretched Ulder was over long ago, Bobs. Has he been getting into fresh disgrace or rousing some old scandal?"

"Hullo, Mummy!" A gay voice from the door saved Bobs the acute embarrassment of a reply. "What's happened to poor Daddy? We met him just now on his way to the Chapel looking as if all his candidates had been drowned or gone over to Rome, at least! Poor Daddy! He didn't even look at Dick here, so you must be extra nice, Mummy! Yes, I picked Dick up, hiking, along the road from Evelake. I thought he was being humble and apostolic!"

"But it was only that my ecclesiastical superiors had got the one and only taxi," added the newcomer. "So instead of following the Chancellor and Canon Wye on foot in proper humility, Sue has whisked me here first. I'd no idea she'd become such a Jehu with a car. The best girls didn't crash along on their own before the war, as I tell her."

"I had to learn when Morris left and often we wish we couldn't drive, don't we, Bobs? We're just 'Fetch and Carry' like the two old maids in some book! But what is wrong with poor Daddy, Mamma?"

"He's a little worried, darling. That tiresome Ulder has wired to say he is coming out to see him and his guests, as he puts it, to-night. You know what a nuisance he has been! And then, too, Daddy is a little upset because Judith is arriving on a visit to-night as well."

"Ju? Oh what fun, how lovely to see her! But—" she paused. Such a very carefully edited story of Judith's affairs had been given her by her parents that Sue, who knew all about it with the simple acceptance of a post-war youth which would never again confuse ignorance with innocence, sometimes forgot how little she was supposed to know. Victorian girls were not allowed to see or touch pitch for fear of defilement. Sue and her contemporaries had learnt to meet it and wash away the stains carefully afterwards.

"Shall I take you to your room, Dick?" Bobs was only too anxious to escape with his old friend, Dick Marlin. They had only met for a few minutes since Dick was demobilized, and returned to the Theological College, and as friends since childhood, through private and public school days and life at Oxford, they must obviously find an early opportunity of tiring the sun with talking. But though Dick agreed warmly he showed no disposition to leave Sue's side in a hurry, and Mrs. Broome showed no wish to speed her guest.

"Don't hurry Dick away, Bobs," she said, her jolly face looking for once a little strained and anxious. "I don't know why it is but ever since I can remember him I've felt safer and happier when Dick was about, yes, even when you were in the nursery, Dick." And it must be admitted that no handsomer tribute could be paid to any young man.

Behind his pair of horn-rimmed spectacles Dick Marlin glanced deprecatingly at his hostess. They were old acquaintances, for the Pounds had purchased his grandfather's place in Wiltshire and restored and renovated the old house to the intense fury of the old gentleman in his new little home across the Park. It was Mrs. Broome who, as a visiting aunt of the Pound family, had befriended little Dick on his rather alarming visits to the old man, and later welcomed him to her own married home. He and Judith had become friendly enemies from the first, and Sue had later sunned herself in the big boy's patronage. "Friend of all the world," Judith called him scornfully, and he deserved the title, for he was one of those lucky people who retain the charm of modesty to their elders, whose intellectual brilliance stimulates without annoying their contemporaries. And he happened to be born with an odd love for humanity.

"Why do you think about other people such a lot?" Judith asked him in her imperious girlhood. "I don't bother about them! I think about myself!"

"They're more amusing than I am, I expect," was Dick's diagnosis.

"And you go on liking stupid people even though you're clever enough to know they're stupid! Why?"

"Perhaps Dick sees their nice side, like the angels," suggested round, cheerful little Sue.

"More likely an extrovert than an angel," laughed Dick. The unknown word had closed that discussion with Judith, but there were many others more stormy as he grew older and paid frequent visits to the Palace. For Judith at sixteen was more than ready to try her prentice hand on a brilliant young Oxford undergraduate, and was naturally annoyed to find his friendship as firm as ever, but quite untroubled by her wiles. If she could not marry a Duke or Earl, or better still a sheikh, she might, she reflected, even marry Dick some day, supposing three or four intervening relations obligingly died and left him a Baron:

if also, she had to admit, Dick showed any signs of wanting to marry her. But all that came to an end of course when she discovered, after her first season, that Dick, crowned with University honours and a Rugby blue, was about to become that most despised creature, a parson.

"But why, Dick, why?" she reiterated, all the more angrily because it was clearly useless to threaten him with the withdrawal of her affection, because he wouldn't really mind.

"I don't suppose you'd understand." Dick was a little weary of adapting his answer to the various relatives, dons, acquaintances and important political friends of his family in language they would understand, but with Judith he let himself be outspoken and simple. "I don't care a hoot for success or ambition or more money than will keep me in tobacco. You know my uncle enraged Grandfather by going out to India as a missionary instead of filling up that stuffy old rectory at Orchard Hundred. And he married a missionary, and, as I remember them both as the happiest people in the world, I suppose I got inoculated with their germs. Anyway, I happen to think that the only work worth doing is to try to help a few other people to God. Oh yes, you can tell me that a year or two ago I was pretty lax about Church and all that, but I've outgrown those teething pains. Now you can fire ahead and tell me what a fool I am, for I suppose I can't pull your hair any more now that you're a full-fledged deb. and the success of the season."

It need not be said that Judith took full advantage of the permission though with the sad consciousness that her words had no effect. Only, as it happened, her parting cuts were justified.

"You'll never stick to it, Dick, never!" she cried, and she was right. Dick was ordained deacon on 14th June, 1914, and in September of that year he had gained a commission in his county regiment. ("Not even the Guards!" wailed Judith.) There was not much interest in academic brains in the army of those days, but Dick's gift of rapid yet thorough investigation into any subject, his intuition, and adaptation to every sort of circumstance and character did not escape the notice of his

Commanding Officer. After a severe leg wound at Loos he found himself shifted into Military Intelligence, and for the last three years had been mixing, in France or at home, in the company of those specialists in crime and treason who might well have under mined his faith in human nature. To love sinners and hate sin may seem an almost impossible task but Dick, like Napoleon, had no use for the word impossible, as far, at least, as ultimate salvation was concerned. Refusing all offers to stay in the Services, or join the G.I.D. after a merely nominal service in lower ranks, Dick emerged from the army to return to the Theological College for a year before his priesthood, more determined than ever to carry on war in Blacksea, that war against sin and poverty which has so often silenced other more tempting music in the ears of world losers and world forsakers.

"Though why Evelake?" asked the old school friend who understood his motives best. "I mean, I can understand dear old Bobs clicking with old Dithers." Such was the reprehensible nickname given to the Bishop by an unnecessarily acute Sixth Form. "He's a decent fellow, and Bobs isn't particularly critical or perceptive and can't take to parish work till he's well. But he's too easygoing and weak for you."

"My own padre isn't, and I shan't come across the ecclesiastical brass hats as a curate. If you want to know, I suppose it's because my wicked, offensive old forebears made their ungodly pile out of sweating Blacksea, and enslaving its people in mines a century ago, that I feel I owe it a sort of debt. Besides, I understand them down there as I'd never understand your cockneys and those North Country chaps, all burrs and blasphemy. I'm set on going to a man like Mayhew who gets on with Dissenters and cares more for principles than frills, more for Christ than the Church."

And so Dick set out on the career which led him now to Evelake Palace for his Ordination.

"There's a poem called the 'Hound of Heaven'," said Bobs, to whom poetry was a book you got for prizes rather than a book you read, a week later, "but you're cut out for the Sleuth of Heaven all right, Dick, my boy."

But this nebulous career was very far from the imagination of Dick as he mingled his pleasure at being back at the Palace, and his solemn thoughts of the coming ceremony, with the reflection that Sue was even more of a darling now than he remembered of old.

II
WEDNESDAY EVENING

THE LIGHT from the shaded electric chandelier fell on the dinner table in the old Palace as Bobs concluded his reading from *Pilgrim's Progress* and sat down to eat his pudding in an embarrassing silence. He had chosen Bunyan at a last moment's appeal from the Bishop for reading aloud of any nature, and had to his horror sheered off Christian's conversation with Madame Bubble only just in time. Judith's eye caught his now in amused mockery as if to remind him that after her clerical upbringing she'd spotted the danger all right. Bobs smiled back bravely, though he inwardly regretted her presence bitterly. He thought he had conquered his old passionate dream; he knew certainly that Judith was as little fitted for a parson's wife as she would be likely to contemplate that role. But that did not seem to matter. The plain fact remained that in any gathering her personality and vitality dwarfed all others. At the head of the table, the Bishop's pallid face, finely moulded and set in those tragic St. Joseph lines, seemed carved in marble, and lifeless as his predecessors on the Cathedral tombs. The Chancellor presented as a rule a picture of a prosperous family lawyer, with his rubicund face, curly white hair, old-fashioned fringe of grey whiskers and jovial laugh, but to-night he seemed to wear a mask. Of course he was still grieving for the loss of his wife: he was present now because kind Mrs. Broome had asked him for Christmas, and he had himself expressed a wish to come earlier and join in the

Ordination ceremonies, but it seemed to Bobs it was anxiety for the future rather than grief which obscured his usual geniality.

On the other side of Mrs. Broome sat the Examining Chaplain. The young people had christened Canon Wye "Torquemada", so thin, black and white was his high, narrow, pointed head, set on a neck so curiously thick, and so emaciated a body, that he was, as Dick said, the living image of a torch at one of his *auto-da-fés*, with flame supplied by his flashing, fanatical eyes. But the torch was not lit to-night: his face was dead and cold. Staples, the other candidate for the priesthood besides Dick, and the six who would on Sunday discard their shabby tweed coats or worn uniforms for very precise new clerical clothes, were all of them, chubby or lean, keen or vacuous, like mere pictures on a wall. Even Mrs. Broome seemed to lose her warm jovial personality as she presided, in the long black satin gown after the fashion of statelier days: Sue in a wispy dress of pale grey seemed a shadow. Only Judith in a long yellow tea-gown, swinging back a priceless ermine cape and perfect pearls a little impatiently, was radiantly awake and alive. ("Not Mike's pearls, you know; someone else gave them to me so I don't mind wearing them," she had just explained to Dick.) Dick himself seemed to Bobs, with a vague memory of legal parlance, nothing to-night but a Watching Brief behind his horn spectacles. Cover her face: mine eyes dazzle, thought poor Bobs, wondering for the hundredth time whether such was the fatal gift of charm and beauty which cost Ceres all that pain to seek her loved one through the world.

"Just open the window for a moment, please, Bobs!" Mrs. Broome's voice recalled the young man with a start.

"If it's not too much for you, Chancellor? Our steam-heating really parboils us at times!"

"Quite, quite! By Jove, snow! A white Christmas after all, I'd say, for it's been a heavy sudden fall."

Bobs lingered at the lattice. Yes, the snow had fallen and transformed the winter night. The moon fell on blanched lawns, and beyond them laid capricious fingers on the ruins of the Guest House and Infirmarium, visible from this side of the house. The walls lay dark and ominous but a white radiance fit up here a broken roof, there a fragile rose window and desolate turret stairway. Behind them the bare trees and shrubs stood like a ghostly concourse of those Carthusian monks who had paced the cloisters to the first Matins of Christmas long ago. There, beyond the frame of the luxurious rose-velvet curtains, far from the sparkling fire and table behind him, lay the true life of endurance, asceticism and world-denial, thought Bobs, fanciful for once.

"Oh, Father darling, at last I can talk to you!" Judith moved to a chair by her father, as Dick left it to join Bobs at the window. She lowered her clear gay voice to a murmur quite audible to Bobs and, obviously from their sidelong glances of interest, to most of the table. "That funny reading! And did you hear darling Bobs skip Madame Bubble? I must tell you all about my spot of bother." (So this was Judith's version of terrible trouble, thought Mrs. Broome.) "So tiresome! Clive felt we must have a little conference about What Next? So we thought we'd be terribly wise and careful, so darling Clive suggested …"

"My dear Judith!" The Bishop came to life with his best headmaster's voice. Some of his prefects and most of his Staff had recognized it as a stucco facade in the past, but all his energy was in it now. "Not here! Not at the moment! This is not the place for any trouble you have to confide to me!"

"But, darling, in a moment you'll be interviewing all these dear, dear boys in your room, or praying away in Chapel, or signing papers with darling Chancellor Chailly! You know I'll never manage to get hold of you and it's urgent! Listen, please!" Her voice sank to something more like a whisper as Soames and the parlour-maid cleared the table, and arranged apples and port ceremoniously. "I'll whisper." (But the whisper was sadly penetrating.) "So Clive settled on Blacksea, for he felt sure no one we'd ever known or heard of could possibly track us there, and not the place for a King's Proctor to week-end in, you'd say! And who do you think we met in the hall, just as we were leaving? Why, that ghastly repulsive parson who gave you all that mountain of worry—Elder—no Ulder, wasn't it?"

"Did he speak to you?" The Bishop could speak now, for Dick and Sue, Bobs and Mrs. Broome, had galvanized some sort of conversation into life round the table.

"Spoke! He came straight from the visitors' book to address us as Mr. and Mrs. Mortimer, but we thought that was the last of it. But, oh, darling, far from it! Clive left me in my flat on Monday, of course. We are both terribly careful about Curzon Street, in case we're watched—I always think those funny *earthy* women going into the Garden Club are detectives, you know!—and there, next morning, was a letter from this dreadful creature threatening to expose us to the King's Proctor unless we simply unloaded our bank books on him. Darling Clive was really angry!"

"Probably!" interposed the Bishop dryly.

"He said it was blackmail, of course, and all sorts of other things beginning with B, much worse! And that he'd go straight to the police. But of course he can't, and that wretch knows he can't. If it all became public I'd never get a divorce from Mike, and I really must marry Clive and settle down. It's really urgent!"

If the Bishop grasped the appalling implications which Mrs. Broome would have drawn from those words, he could not have been more dismayed. He could only look at Judith in dumb misery, while she, evidently relieved by confession, began to peel an orange adroitly, flashing a smile at Bobs and Dick. The word a-moral had not yet become fashionable, and there was no shred of extenuation in the poor Bishop's mind for the utter frivolity and laxity of his own daughter. But the horror of Ulder's appearance in the story blinded him momentarily to the scandalous behaviour of his child.

"So Clive said the best thing we could do was to come straight to you and consult you, because you know the old wretch and may keep him quiet! I mean you could unfrock him for blackmail straight off, couldn't you? I'm sure the Chancellor would love to, and I'd love to tug off his horrid collar myself, only I expect it's greasy and scurfy! But I wasn't sure if you'd like me to bring Clive here, as you have to be rather *collet monte*. I explained to Clive, so he's staying at the Mitre, and I can let him know just what you think we should do."

"Judith dear, we're going." As Mrs. Broome had no success in catching her stepdaughter's eye politely, she had to raise her voice authoritatively. "Now mind you men join the ladies for coffee as soon as you like, Mark dear, for it's nearly nine and Compline time." Dinner, she reflected, had taken terribly long, partly because Judith was inevitably unpunctual, and partly because Soames had waited so badly and looked so nervous and ill at ease. She must really speak to him to-morrow!

"What's wrong with them all?" asked Dick in a more confidential whisper than Judith's, lingering with Bobs at the dining-room door.

"Ulder, I suppose," murmured Bobs. "The Bishop had an enormous letter from him which he kept to himself. And the Chancellor and Canon Wye went to confer with him the minute they arrived, and were with him till dinner was announced. You can hear the Chancellor's voice above a thunder-storm, you know, and as I was finishing letters in my room I kept hearing the name Ulder again and again. Heaven knows what's up! I thought Ulder's teeth were drawn. He's threatening a visit in a wire we got after tea—an immediate visit. He'll hardly come out to-night, I imagine, but the wire was from the P.O. at Evelake."

"Of course if he'd had a drop or two—" Dick paused.

His gaze had been wandering over the group in the hall, vaguely contrasting the scene with the bare ascetic clergy-house awaiting him at Blacksea. Mrs. Broome stood by a table laden with coffee cups and silver jugs, for with her hospitable soul she loved to pour out coffee and extract confidences simultaneously from what she called the Bishop's Boys. Firelight from the vast hearth shone upon great pots of orchids, poinsettias and azaleas, upon the dark and fair heads of Judith and Sue, and their shimmering frocks. Beyond a group of candidates the Chancellor and the Canon were conversing, the prosperous lawyer and the fanatic churchman as sharp in type as if drawn by Bunyan himself. The Bishop, very pale and lined by the glow of the chandeliers in the main part of the hall, was moving to his own room, with the courteous excuses of a born host. And then, as he paused for a moment to look at the long low refectory table where letters and papers were laid out, the 'whole setting, clear, picturesque and mannered as any scene of a drawing-room play, was broken by the sudden sound of the great door bell. No one moved or spoke as Soames entered through the baize door from the servants' quarters, just beyond the wide oak staircase, pushed back the tapestry curtains to the vestibule, and switched on the light outside.

A Georgian bishop had added this entrance hall and surrounded it with inappropriate busts of Caesars. Even those close curled heads and beards seemed to shiver in the gale which swept in the wind and snow. Behind Soames was visible a short, clerical figure, relieving himself of a black hat and old-fashioned ulster. There was no need for Dick to glance at the horrified faces around him to realize the truth. Like every older person in the room he had known since the first loud clamour of the bell that the guest was the Rev. Thomas Ulder.

There are some few men who possess undoubtedly an aura of evil, visible even to those who profess no psychic powers, and Thomas Ulder was one of them. His personal appearance had not been attractive in old days but five years of sloth and self-indulgence had revealed the ugly contours of his narrow brow and heavy chin till they resembled a pear in shape; his figure had widened on the same lines; his intemperate life had resulted in watery eyes and a twitching face. In the five years of his retirement he had deteriorated, as Irishmen can do with extraordinary celerity, but it was only when he focused those eyes on you, with the secretive stare of all creeping, slimy things and when his too oily manner stiffened into threats, that the sensitive shuddered as if turning over a stone which conceals maggots; and felt, in Bunyan's phrase, threatened by an evil, a very evil thing.

Christians must always differ in their attitude to evil, Dick supposed tolerantly, as he noticed that the Bishop's first reaction was evidently to retreat through the narrow open ante-room into his own study. Just in time the prelate recognized that he was too late for he could hardly pretend not to hear the unnaturally loud and hoarse voice with which Soames heralded the visitor. Mrs. Broome advanced hesitatingly, Judith sank suddenly on to an oak settle, half concealed by a great pot of azaleas. All the rest of the company stood as still in their places as if they were trained members of a Greek chorus (or was it a picket on the alert?) except Bobs who moved forward as if to intercept the Bishop.

"Ah—ha, my lord, I have caught you!" The hearty yet curiously careful manner and voice showed Bobs and Dick at once that their visitor had primed himself well for his arrival. "I thought this might be a lucky hour and day for me!"

"I see no one without an appointment, I fear, Mr. Ulder." ("Poor Dithers has the jitters," the Sixth Form at St. Blaze would have diagnosed from the Bishop's voice.) "I asked my Chaplain to tell you that I give none during the Ordination week-end."

"I think you will make an exception for me." Ulder grew bellicose, but restrained himself with a sudden unpleasant smile. "I brought my kit with me in case I had to stay. If every one here is reasonable I shall get off to-night and I will not detain you long!"

"Let me turn him out, sir!" Bobs moved forward in impatient anger, but Ulder brushed him aside. For a minute he stood looking round him in malevolent triumph, holding out his hand to Mrs. Broome. Then suddenly he caught the back of a chair, staggered and groaned. Next moment there was a heavy crash and fall, and before that motionless circle of spectators the parson lay motionless and livid, while lilies from a vase fell, like a grotesque wreath, across his chest as the water dripped on his unconscious head.

In any accident one notices how almost immediately the spectators divide themselves into an inner group who try to give aid, however inefficiently, and an outer ring who tender plentiful advice. It was Bobs, Dick and Mrs. Broome who knelt beside the prostrate figure, while behind them suggestions of "Straighten his legs" … "More air" … "Brandy" … "Water" … "Ring up the doctor" … rose in chorus. Only the Bishop's contribution struck Dick a little curiously as they loosened Ulder's collar. "Is he dead? Is Ulder dead?" The words suggested a certain awe and alarm, but also a vast relief.

"Dead! Not a bit, sir! Dead drunk more likely!"

"No, Dick, there's something odd about his heart," said Bobs. Last time they had knelt together like this was over the victim in a rugger scrum, but between that day and this the two men singly had seen too many wounded and dying to ignore certain symptoms—"Isn't his pulse a bit odd too, Mrs. Broome? I think we should get the doctor at once."

"Shall I ring up?" Sue had recovered herself now and was stooping over Judith who for once in her life, Dick noted, actually looked a bit upset.

"Yes—but wait, darling! I think he may be here any minute, for he promised to look in on Moira and try to give her some light sedative so that she'll sleep before the hospital ambulance comes to-morrow. Mrs. Lee will tell you if he really is on the way, so do ask her, darling. Do you think we should move him, Bobs?"

"Where to, Mrs. Broome?"

"Well, a sofa on this floor anyhow! We'll have to put him in the St. Ursula room on the Bridge later, for luckily it is all ready, and then with the pantry just below it's so convenient for an invalid's trays," she added, her house keeping instincts reasserting themselves, though it seemed a little doubtful to the others, gazing with horror on that stricken, immobile, sallow face, whether any trays would be needed. "Ah, there's a car in the drive surely! How lucky! It must be Dr. Lee!"

"Well, well, easy to see where he's been lately!" Dr. Lee, as he bustled in, small and sturdy, and as hasty in his speech as in his pronouncements, had, whatever his limitations, that great medical gift of making a major disaster seem for the moment, at least, a minor everyday occurrence. The tension lessened a little, though the doctor's face grew more serious as he bent over the patient.

"Give me a hand, Bobs, will you? That's better! Well, well, how he dared to indulge with a heart in that state! Not too nice, Mrs. Broome, not too nice at all! I'm afraid you'll have him on your hands to-night!"

"Of course he must stay till he's better!" Mrs. Broome glanced at her husband who was making no offer of hospitality.

"I don't know about that. Might be as well to take him off in the ambulance to-morrow with Moira. Ought to be under observation. Heart's not in good case, not at all. He's a sick man, and if we pull him through, he'll have to change his way of life, altogether. It's the water waggon for him!"

"Could we not get him into an ambulance now?" asked the Bishop.

"Couldn't send one out to-night. It was all I could do to get along on chains. This fall of snow's been very heavy, and the cold would finish him. We have the new ambulance booked for Moira, and that's worth waiting for. He won't want attendance to-night, I hope. I'll give you something, Mrs. Broome!" The doctor fell upon his country-practice black bag, that pharmacopoeia of cures. "First, something to bring him round, but we'll get him upstairs before that, for I expect he'll have pretty acute pain. Now where's my nitryll? Ah, here we are. I'll take this up with me."

"And something for the night that I can give him," urged Mrs. Broome, accustomed as she was to the little doctor's deafness and forgetful ways.

"Yes, yes, I'll leave this with you. Now where are we? Here we are! Not the whole phial, I think—dangerous, and I may need some at Holt's ... going on there ... will be no joke in this snow. Now where are those containers?—chemists send me some, Mrs. Broome ... come in handy!" The doctor fumbled for cotton-wool and stuffed it in a glass tube, talking all the time. "Six I'll give you, but one every six hours is the maximum dose, remember. There you are, half a grain each, and remember they're dangerous! Now then we must get the patient upstairs! If four of you lads will give a hand up these abominable polished stairs. As bad as these long passages! Glad I don't live in a Palace!" As the doctor's voice and the heavy footfalls of the bearers died away in the distance the group in the hall stood in stunned silence till the tall clock chimed out nine times.

"Compline," said Mrs. Broome automatically. She and Sue were on their knees retrieving the broken vase and its contents. "But, oh dear, perhaps to-night, Mark, with Bobs upstairs ... ?"

One of the penalties of high ecclesiastical office must obviously be the impossibility of owning to a disinclination for Church services. Even as the Chancellor said firmly that he didn't feel like Chapel after all this, and wanted a talk with the Bishop as soon as possible, Canon Wye was offering his services as Chaplain in place of Bobs, and the Bishop assenting with an attempt at gratitude. "We will consult together afterwards, you, I and the Canon," Mrs. Broome heard him say as he moved away, his head and shoulders bent. Why did her dear Mark seem almost an old man to night? Although some of Judith's remarks had escaped her stepmother, she had gathered at dinner that Mr. Ulder's visit was connected with her stepdaughter's escapades, and she briskly invited Judith to a good talk with her alone (certainly the confidences were unlikely to be fit for Sue's ears).

"Quite soon, darling, but I promised to go and see poor old Moira after dinner," replied Judith. And of course, thought Sue, with the tolerant clear-sightedness which distinguished her, though Ju really is fond of old Moira, she isn't looking forward to a talk with Mummy. Naturally she prefers men in her confessional!

"I must see about some night things for the poor man, if Bobs hasn't already," said Mrs. Broome, ringing the bell. "Soames, I suppose that Mr. Ulder had no luggage with him?"

"That butler springs up like a jack-in-the-box," said Judith distastefully as she went upstairs with Sue. "I believe he listens at keyholes all the time, for he couldn't have got from the pantry in that ridiculous Bridge so quickly."

"Doris says he's a nosy-parker and a know-all," smiled Sue. "Listen to him now!"

"Yes, madam, and I was surprised," Soames was saying, "seeing as how he was not expected for the night. He passed some remark about never letting his things out of his sight!"

"Well, take it up and just leave it till the doctor goes—in fact I think I'd better get out anything he wants later myself. He must not be disturbed."

Soames went to the vestibule, and Mrs. Broome sighed a little as she left the hall. It always seemed so deserted at the exodus of the party to Chapel. The open doors of the Bishop's and Chaplain's rooms and the old library revealed desolate stretches of dark oak faintly irradiated by wood fires. Judith and Sue had vanished up the stairs, evidently wanting to be alone together. She felt a wretched weight of solitude and depression as she walked down the passage to the Bridge. On the right of the entrance was the big door into the Chapel and a murmur of intoning voices. Beyond, two narrow staircases enclosed the pantry and offices, and one of these Mrs. Broome ascended now. She would visit Mr. Ulder in the nearer room, St. Ursula, look in on poor old Moira next door, and then finish the evening in her own warm, vast, modern drawing-room. Sometimes she felt the Bishop's spirits would be benefited if she could coax him out of the old part of the house with its low roofs, twisting passages, mysterious little stairs and creaking boards. But the whole family preferred the old gracious Elizabethan rooms, and all that Mrs. Broome had been able to do was to pack them with every conceivable modern convenience. The old drawing-room was now Sue's gay sitting-room; in the old library, rows of desolate, wire-guarded old volumes and yellowing busts lurked harmlessly behind Mrs. Broome's bright chintz-covered chairs and sofas. The Bridge wing she had never been able to transform satisfactorily. It was too shoddy, ugly and cramped, and to-night she remembered, as she always remembered when she was tired and depressed, the rambling attics above the Bridge bedrooms and the old wing, full of the junk of departed predecessors. They could only be cleared after the Bishop had glanced through the rubbish, to ascertain what, if any, were diocesan fixtures, and that was always to be to-morrow and never to-day! And then the sensible woman gave herself a mental shake. She was merely letting the house obsess her because she wished to avoid the far greater worries connected with Judith, Mr. Ulder, and her poor old sick housekeeper, Moira. It would be far better to face these squarely!

"Is that my pet at last?" Old Moira's quivering voice reached Mrs. Broome as she turned the corner of the narrow stair and saw Judith rush into her old nurse's room. Poor old Moira! She was indeed capable of returning from the grave to see her adored charge. Judith had been second fiddle to Sue's nurse when the Broomes arrived at Evelake, and Moira, inherited from the Bishop's predecessor as housekeeper, had at once taken the seven-year-old child under her wing. Perhaps Mrs. Broome had too weakly tolerated a distraction from Moira's passion for bullying and upsetting the staff, for certainly she had been one of the adorers whose incense had tended to veil Judith from criticism and self-criticism alike.

Dr. Lee opened the door of St. Ursula and admitted Mrs. Broome cautiously. He had just, it is to be feared, commented on the room's name to Dick, in view of the scandals connected with his patient—"though perhaps eleven thousand is an exaggeration," and his smile encouraged Mrs. Broome till she heard a low groan of pain from the bed.

"It's passing off," Dr. Lee assured her, "passing off. There has been acute pain, and he has been restless enough to make me glad of these two Rugger toughs, but you can go off now, boys!"

"Should we have a specialist?" asked Mrs. Broome doubtfully. The two so-called boys looked, like all untrained male attendants who have had to watch physical suffering, as if they wanted to be sick quietly; women are luckier for they merely feel faint. Dr. Lee was a good sound country doctor, but he was old and he was deaf, and would his stethoscope record to him what she vaguely diagnosed to herself as the murmurs of the heart?

"I'll get Dr. Gonne to see him in hospital to-morrow," Dr. Lee assured her. "He's first rate in these cases. I could have given Ulder that morphia I gave you to ease him, but he refuses to take it till he's seen the Bishop. Wants to see Canon Wye and the Chancellor as well, but dissuade him if you can. I've given him an anodyne which won't send him off to sleep as he insisted on keeping awake, but be very careful now with the tablets I gave you, Mrs. Broome. Only one at a time, even if the pain recurs, and no more till after a six-hour interval. But I don't think it will be necessary. And no stimulants on any account, though he's asking for them! Not on any account. You'll be within earshot and his bell's working? Excellent. Now, sir, you're feeling a bit easier, aren't you?"

"Yes, yes!" Mr. Ulder's voice was thin and weak but resolute. For the first time Mrs. Broome glanced at the bed, trying to conquer her nervous distaste for the scene. All the rooms in this Bridge wing were lighted by only one narrow window, set high in the wall, for old Bishop Main was a sincere advocate for keeping his sons at home. The Broomes had bought the ugly suites of fumed oak bedroom furniture from their predecessors, and not even Mrs. Broome's attempts to brighten them with chintz and low rose lights redeemed them from the air of unoccupied apartments in a boarding house. Between the dressing-table on the left side of the room beneath the window, and the wardrobe on the right by the fireplace, the narrow bed faced her, and from the bed Mr. Ulder's malevolent face and silky voice greeted her.

"Is that Mrs. Broome? I must apologize for troubling you. But I must see the Bishop as soon as possible. You are sure, Dr. Lee, that this abominable stuff won't send me to sleep first? Plenty of time for sleep, plenty of time!"

"Is that Moira laughing next door?" asked Dr. Lee incredulously, as he turned from the bed to close his bag, and Mrs. Broome was thankful now for his deafness, as Judith's clear, gay voice recounting her own story and the adventures of the evening was perfectly audible to her step mother. "Miss Judith's a better doctor than I am!"

"Of course everyone was disappointed that Ulder didn't pass out altogether," Judith was saying as Mrs. Broome softly opened Moira's door for the doctor. "You could see it in all their faces, and I know I was myself."

"Have you told your mamma your lovely secret, dearie?" Moira, lying grey, frail and spent as a dead leaf on her pillows, was too preoccupied by her own discomfort to take in many ideas at once, it seemed.

"Darling, it won't be a lovely secret, it'll be a nameless child if that old devil next door can't have his mouth shut!" Mrs. Broome gasped in consternation at this further complication in Judith's tale. Had the girl, or had she not, confided this to her father at dinner? "Hullo, Mummy! I'll be off, Moira, and leave you to flirt with Dr. Lee, but I'll see you in the morning. Leave a little rat poison with us, Dr. Lee! Hullo! What's that?" She paused at the door. "Oh, it's Soames with the Ulder kit! Leave his things just inside the door, Soames, Mrs. Broome says, but don't go in and disturb him by unpacking! See you soon, Mummy dearest! Good-bye, Dr. Lee! I'll be seeing you soon for some new sort of dope. I've nearly finished mine, and it doesn't seem to give me much sleep these days anyway!"

From the Chapel came the faint sound of men's voices chanting:—"Save us, O Lord, waking, and guard us sleeping!" but except for that very necessary petition, for the faint distant sounds from the kitchen quarters, and the whistle of wind and swish of falling snow, the Palace was very dark and still as Bobs and Dick went downstairs to take refuge in the old library, and sink down gratefully with their pipes by the fire in the plump, comfortable armchairs.

"This is a bit of all right after Chaos and Old Night in the Palace," said Dick gratefully.

"Funny home for us," meditated Bobs. "Oh, I don't mean this. I mean the Church of England which seems a bit of a drug in the market to-night." He rose suddenly and limped down the long room through the intercommunicating door to the Chaplain's room, returning in a very baggy old Harris coat of loud design. "That's better! How I hate my clerical rags!"

"Uniform, after all!" said Dick, vainly endeavouring to clean out his pipe. "I must marry soon to have a wife's hair pins ready for this job! Uniform, and thank Heaven clergy have no buttons to polish. Though I must say my lamp of faith burns lowest when I see the parson in the advertisements of gents' outfitters!"

"Yes, but uniforms of what sort of army?" asked Bobs with unusual bitterness.

"Same as any, I expect. At least we can't criticize our Commander-in-Chief. The Staff must have rotters as well as good men; the regimental officers differ a lot. It's difficult to make the average Tommy see that he's fighting in a war of sheer survival against all the evil in the world, but if you can get at him he'll do his job. It's funny when you've been in M.I. to see how exactly the other Churches represent military allies. You've all the same enemy, you admit politely, but there's the devil to pay in differences over strategy and policy."

Dick and Bobs had known each other so long and intimately that each knew when the other was ready for the confidential conversation into which they drifted now, though they exchanged no high phrases about ideals and vocation, as they grunted out remarks between their pulls at their pipes. Early in this century, under the influence of Anglo-Catholic divines of unusual gifts or charm and warmed by the fire of the Christian

Socialist, and the first glow of the Students' Christian Movement, both had taken orders. Bobs, simple soul, met with the joyful consent of his family, and the puzzled approval of his Oxford tutor, who felt that the Church after all was the only future for a Fourth Class man; Dick came by way of Military Intelligence and Settlement work, activities which had brought him to the conclusion that personal religion was the only possible hope of happiness for any individual soul, and that the Church Militant rather than the Civil Service was more likely to help that end. Now together they looked over that past across the gulf of the war, and Dick's attitude was as clear-cut and cheerful as his hatchet face behind his horn spectacles. They could talk things out, for the exodus from Chapel led to no disturbance. Bobs cocked an ear as steps sounded outside, but relaxed.

"The Bishop's taken Chailly and Wye to his room for a consultation. That's O.K. Go on, Dick ..."

"All that's the matter with you," Dick summed up at length, half an hour later, "is that you don't like your job here."

"I don't, but I'll say this, it's cured me of any ambition ever to be a Bishop!"

"But you aren't fit for regular parish work till your leg's sound. The doctors give you hopes of a cure in a year and meanwhile you must make the best of a routine job. It's just a war sentence, a medical board, Bobs, and after a bit you'll join me at Blacksea, won't you? And meanwhile can't you take a hand in movements like Life and Liberty and Toc H, which get overlooked in parish routine—for there'll be routine enough anywhere, I expect! Lots of spiritual spit and polish and dress parades in the best of Churches."

"Yes, I'm doing that!" said Bobs more cheerfully. "But"—relapsing—"it's having to do with people like—"

"You only come across a prize specimen like Ulder once in a thousand, my boy."

"I didn't even mean him alone. I don't want to be disloyal," said Bobs, proceeding naturally to be so at once, "but I can't help noticing the cowardice of our—our leaders. I love the

Bip, but he'd do anything to avoid a row. Canon Wye is good at getting up a scrap, but he funks the issue. With the Registrar and the Diocesan Board generally one lives in a sort of Trollope atmosphere of stuffy offices, crammed with seals and tapes, red-faced, casual, prejudiced lawyers catching at eighteenth-century regulations to prove some unimportant point and afraid, yes, afraid to take action against a man like Ulder, because of the scandal. There's some crisis about his visit, Dick, I'm sure. The Bip pocketed his letter and, as I told you, he and the other two big-wigs were closeted together. Hullo, that's the Bishop's bell! Wait a minute! Yes, Dick, as I told you …" Bobs had limped to his room and came back perturbed. "The Bishop wants you for a consultation with the Chancellor and Canon Wye. You're marked for M.I. and an adjutant's job in the Church all right, my son!"

III
WEDNESDAY NIGHT

"To GIVE LIGHT to them which sit in darkness" were the words which echoed oddly in Dick's mind as he entered the shadowy study. It was an absurd and topsy-turvy idea for a humble can-didate for the priesthood to entertain of his fathers in God, but under the low hand lamp by the dismal fire the Bishop, more like a death mask of St. Joseph than ever, the saturnine still-ness of Canon Wye and the obvious perturbation in Chancellor Chailly's rubicund face, suggested a huddled party of alarmed pilgrims in the Valley of the Shadow of disgrace. If only Dick were a Greatheart instead of his very everyday self!

"We have sent for you, Dick, because we feel the need of advice, and you have been in our dealings with Ulder from the first. You know—" and here the Bishop felt obliged to recapit-ulate the full story of Mr. Ulder's exposure and disgrace. Dick's thoughts wandered a little, but he woke with a start as the Bish-op fumbled among his papers and handed one to the young man. "I received this communication only this afternoon. I had no time to think of the proper course to take, no time at least for any decision with my friends here before dinner, and now this wretched Ulder arrives! You realize doubtless that he has come to give us fresh trouble. He feels himself in so strong a position that he had the insolence to expect my hospitality and bring his luggage. No doubt he was thrown out of the hotel at Evelake! And now, how can I help myself, how can any of us? To some extent we are in his power. Yes, read this":—

"MY DEAR BISHOP,

I am writing to ask that your Lordship will be so good as to give me a private interview on a personal matter which I venture to believe is even more important to you than it is to me.

As you may know, I have not been happy in my work since the unfortunate events of five years ago, and I gather that there is a movement afoot to secure my resignation from my present small charge. My own desire is to leave the scene of so much injustice and so many cruel suspicions and make a fresh start in America, not necessarily as a clergyman. But there are financial difficulties, and it is these I wish to discuss with you in, I hope, a spirit of mutual accommodation. Under certain conditions my resignation would be forthcoming and this would ease your official position and that of the churchwardens. And in your case there might be a personal reason why you might feel it desirable to provide some substantial inducement to persuade me to leave this country and forget all I have suffered and *all I have known* here."

"I received an appeal of the same nature," said the Chancellor, crossing and uncrossing his legs uneasily. "But with me he was even more explicit. Two thousand is the price of silence."

"He named that sum to me in a letter couched in similar terms." It seemed as if Canon Wye's thin lips could hardly bear to open on so unsavoury a subject.

"But, forgive me, sir, nothing could be clearer. He's threatened blackmail in three different letters. He won't have a leg to stand on in Court, for of course you'll all hand these letters to the police?"

"Impossible ... impossible ... think of the scandal in the Church." The three might have been singing a catch, thought Dick as the words poured out.

"Very little, indeed, my lord. In such cases the names are never divulged."

"Everyone will recognize Ulder's diocese," pointed out Canon Wye.

"Still, even so he'll get far more mud than he throws!"

"What will that matter to him in America?"

"Well, that's true, I suppose, but if he's prosecuted for blackmail he'll never get there!"

"I can't trust to the secrecy of the Court," intervened the Bishop, his forehead sunk on his hand. "Dear old Verrall, whom you'll remember, Dick, died a year ago and a fellow called Mack was appointed Chief Constable from the ranks, by this deplorable new scheme. He is a violent Dissenter, no mere agnostic, but a real enemy of the Church and Cathedral and all they stand for. He would gloat over the flaws in our case and give it all possible publicity."

"I don't agree, my lord. I've heard a lot of him and I'm sure with him it would be justice first always, and prejudice a long way behind. In any case he could have no animus about the personal affairs of you and—and your daughter. Mack—and the outer world—will no doubt criticize the original hushing up of Ulder's affairs, if it gets into the news, but that sort of thing is soon forgotten, and our Church has never claimed to be infallible."

"We can't let it go to the Courts." The Chancellor reiterated his remark, deaf to Dick's arguments.

"I agree that it's out of the question," snapped Canon Wye.

"He must be silenced," agreed the Bishop.

"Well then, my lord," said Dick rising, "there's no more to be said. You mean to pay up and be fleeced for the rest of your lives?"

"Ah, but he's going to America!"

"There's a mail," said Dick dryly, "and a British scandal-loving public in the States, all ready for a plausible Irish tale-teller!"

"But can you not think of some other expedient, you who have been so much more in touch with crime and criminals in your recent career?" asked Canon Wye.

"Yes, sir, but that was different!" Dick faced the three older men firmly but respectfully. "In any action I was given all the facts as far as they were available. If you'll forgive me for saying so, I don't feel the same in this case. You must each of you have further reasons for yielding to these preposterous demands."

"It was a shot in the dark," Dick told Bobs much later, "except as far as the Bishop was concerned—Judith saw to that. But I felt that the other two were scared for their own reasons, not only for the Church. And my bluff worked!"

That it certainly did, for after gazing enquiringly at his friends, the Bishop said heavily: "Well, well, you're right, Dick, and it pays a tribute to your insight. Gentlemen, I suggest that we should all lay our cards on the table!"

Meanwhile upstairs poor Mrs. Broome kept watch. Her drawing-room seemed too far from the invalids, so she established herself in the sitting-room, which, with her own and husband's bedrooms, formed the most charming suite on the first floor of the old wing. She was worn out after a long interview with Judith in which all her feelings as wife, stepmother, churchwoman, President of the Evelake M.U., G.F.S. and Purity League were outraged. She must talk to her Mark, and her Mark did not appear. The whole house hold seemed indeed to be walking backwards and forwards past her door to the Bridge, but she did not like to look out and seem to spy on her guests. Once she was sure of the Bishop's step, but it was the Chancellor whom she saw at Ulder's door. Then she heard the sound of clinking glasses: that was Soames putting out the ten o'clock tray of drinks on the table in the Bridge passage: it was the hospitable custom to leave one in this neutral territory between the old and new wings, but she wished she had arranged differently to-night, in view of the two invalids—if the candidates talked loudly over their nightcaps of whisky or beer on the way to bed, she must really go—but no, it was all right. They were evidently a nice, abstemious set, or perhaps they had been warned of the invalids, for they were going almost at once to their new wing bedrooms, quietly enough. Now the Chancellor was leaving Mr. Ulder's room!—and, oh dear, how he banged the door! As if he were in a bad temper. Soames was still fussing about, but surely everyone would be in their rooms in a minute, and she could at last go to settle poor Mr. Ulder off for the night. But, even as she thought so, she heard the quick martial step of Canon Wye outside her room, and yet another knock on Mr. Ulder's door. It was really monstrous that they could not leave the invalid alone! She had changed out of her black evening gown into a really old-fashioned tea gown, a trailing affair of purple velvet and lace, worn only in the family circle as a rule, but she really must warn the Canon not to make a visitation!

"Canon Wye, I really think Mr. Ulder—Oh dear, what are you doing?" Mrs. Broome faced the Canon with some severity as he stood over the tray outside St. Ursula's open door, taller, thinner and more inquisitorial than ever in his black cassock.

"Ulder asked me to get him a drink—he feels tired." The Canon, a confirmed celibate, froze into anger at Mrs. Broome's implied rebuke.

"But, my dear Canon, he must not have it! The doctor said that on no account was any stimulant to be given him to-night, certainly not before his last dose! And I am quite sure that Dr. Lee would say the poor man should be left in peace!"

"He sent a message that he must see me. I will not stay with him more than five minutes, Mrs. Broome."

"Well, I shall come in five minutes then, and settle him for the night. Where is the Bishop?"

"Talking to the Chancellor in his room, I think: they suggested that I should join them shortly."

Five minutes! It was not worth her while to collect the papers which she had left in the drawing-room, decided Mrs. Broome. She would go on with her list of diocesan Christmas cards—they were late already and it was a duty which she took seriously. She had only just reached the rural deans when she saw that the time limit had come and rose briskly. She must remember, when her invalids had settled down, to fetch the list of these addresses from the drawing-room.

Canon Wye was not the person to instruct the candidates in the visitation of the sick, she reflected with annoyance, as she heard Mr. Ulder's door bang noisily and met him striding, tall, self absorbed and fierce-eyed down the passage. Nevertheless, true to her hospitable tradition she stopped to bid him good night, and was enquiring into his comforts and the condition of his fire when to her horror she saw another figure steal swiftly up to Mr. Ulder's door. It was Judith of all people, Judith who had emerged from her room and ran to the invalid, intent no doubt on some desperate appeal or some urgent cajolery. How like the foolish child to imagine her wiles would have any effect! How like her, too, to ignore every instinct of propriety and decorum! Mrs. Broome almost ran in her haste to get her step-daughter out of the room and smuggled away before any one could see her, and then stopped dead in the Bridge passage at a sound above her. Someone was moving about at the head of the stairs which led from the Bridge to the passage of the new wing where the candidates slept. One of them was certainly on the alert and he might unluckily have seen her step-daughter.

"Is anything wanted up there?" she called sharply, as a faint scuttle showed that the unknown watcher was retreating.

"Oh no, no thank you, Mrs. Broome!" The red-haired, untidy head, sharp face and blinking eyes of little Mr. Staples appeared round the corner. ("A Christian perhaps, but a gentle-

man never," had been the Chancellor's unchristian comment
on this candidate for the priesthood.) "I just thought I heard a
door banging in the wind and that I—I had better close it in
case it kept people awake."

"All the doors will be shut before we settle down," smiled
Mrs. Broome a little perplexedly. "I'm sorry you were disturbed. Have you everything you want?" She was speaking in
a lowered voice, but trusted that its sound would reach Judith
and make her retreat. She had had enough of explanations and
scenes to-night!

"Indeed, indeed yes—every comfort—every luxury—only
too much when one remembers ..." But Mrs. Broome's memory that Mr. Staples was said to be Red in his sympathies made
her move on with a hurried good night. And only just in time
too, for, as she approached, Judith rushed out of St. Ursula, and
began recklessly filling up a glass from the whisky decanter.

"Judith!" Mrs. Broome was so seldom roused to anger that
her reproofs were usually effective, but she had not expected
her subdued word of admonition to have such an effect. Judith
started and dropped the glass, which fell into a thousand splinters, and pattered away at full speed in her feathered mules, her
turquoise satin dressing-gown flying round her.

Had she really managed to rouse Mr. Ulder at all, wondered
Mrs. Broome as she looked softly into the invalid's room. It was
only as she stood by the bed that she caught a faint murmur
of: "Whisky!" Should she give him some stimulant after all, for
his pulse was alarming? And what about the doctor's pilule? He
seemed about to sleep—but no! Suddenly an agonized groan
came as she reached the door, and putting on the bed lamp, she
saw the sharp face wet with sweat, the ugly mouth and secretive eyes twisted in agony. She had placed the tiny bottle on
one of the shelves of the ugly Victorian oak dressing-table, and
in a moment she had shaken out a tiny capsule, and, lifting the
patient's head, persuaded him to swallow it with a little water.

"There, there," she said encouragingly. "It will ease you
quite soon, the doctor says! Yes, hold my hand, or, stay, let me

rub your heart gently! Does that ease it?" She wiped his fore-head. "And let us try a whiff of these salts," for a terrible spasm shook the patient. "Ah, that's better, I can see! Really better!" For the face was relaxing. "Now lie quite still and I'll stay with you and say something!" Mrs. Broome before her marriage had engaged frequently in visits to hospitals and was of the sim-ple faith which knows no false modesty. Only it was a little difficult to offer prayers for repentant sinners, for, as that look of quite anonymous agony passed, Mr. Ulder's face resumed its usual mocking, inquisitive, sardonic stare. "The Lord is my Shepherd—"

That most personal yet most universally applicable psalm, came naturally to her lips, and really as she spoke of the Valley of the Shadow her patient's breathing did seem to grow easier and his hand relaxed its hold of hers. "Good night," she mur-mured as she saw Mr. Ulder's eyes close and his body relax. His head was turned a little into the pillow now, and something in his attitude made unimaginative Mrs. Broome see him for a moment as he must have been in his innocent childhood. "God bless and pardon and keep you," she whispered as she prepared to go. She never told any one but her husband of that moment, but she was glad to remember it years later, when the shadows closed round her own life.

"No one shall come in now, I'll make sure, and you shall have a splendid rest," were her last words as she left the bedside. Those bright observant eyes were still following her, but the drug would do its work soon. She even fancied that she heard a word of thanks to cheer her as she opened the door, and found herself, to her surprise, face to face with Soames, at Moira's door.

"Having heard a crash, madam, I came upstairs to remove any traces of an accident," said Soames glibly, before his mistress could speak.

"But were you in Moira's room?" Mrs. Broome was puz-zled at such unusual diligence, but the glass had certainly gone and her glance fell on a dustpan full of broken pieces at the top of Soames' stair. Perhaps he was to prove biddable after all, in spite of his shortcomings to-night, but he had no business to disturb Moira.

"Yes, madam, she called out to know what the smash was and to clear it up, and I happened to hear in the pantry. I just looked in to tell her all traces had been removed."

Mrs. Broome turned and made her way to Judith's room with a lump in her throat. How little they all truly appreciated the faithful devotion of Moira and her kind! Would she herself, on the threshold of a severe operation, trouble about a few pieces of glass in the passage, rouse herself from a drugged sleep and organize a clearance? Nothing would have been further from her thoughts, but then these Moiras of a vanishing generation with their deep narrow sense of external order and propriety had no share in her own mental and spiritual anxieties over those they loved. To Moira Judith was perfection and above criticism, whereas to her stepmother she was a tragic insoluble problem.

Long years of experience should have taught Mrs. Broome that the problem would certainly prove elusive now, but hope springs eternal in the breasts of Presidents of Girls' Friendly and Young Women's Christian societies. She entered Judith's room with loving words of caution on her lips, only to find, of course, that her bird had flown. Sounds of laughter in Sue's room next door made her accept defeat inevitably when she looked in. For how could she tackle the question of Judith's divorce or Mr. Ulder's blackmail when the girl herself was sitting on the fireside rug like a child of twelve, chatting with Sue who, in bed in her white nightgown, her cheek distended by a chocolate, the *Daisy Chain* of Miss Yonge on her quilt, looked more like a child of seven? Mrs. Broome recognized with shame that she was being drawn into most frivolous conjectures of the two girls about the probable night wear of the old tabbies (as Judith would call them) in the Cathedral Close, before she pulled herself together and turned away.

"I must have a long talk with you to-morrow, Ju dear," was her only tribute to her earlier designs. "And you should go to bed now and let Sue go to sleep!"

"But what about you, poor Mamma? You look so tired," said Sue.

"I'm just going to finish addressing some of those Christ mas cards till your father comes up. He is sure to want to talk to me. The list was in the drawing-room, wasn't it?" The passages all lay still and dark before her as she left Sue's warm sweet-scented room for the new wing. But she was so tired that really, she told herself, her reliable nerves were on edge for once. It seemed to her, as she passed the Bridge, that she heard footsteps retreat hastily up the stairs, as if some candidate had been lurking about, and when she reached the drawing-room she had the uncomfortable sensation that someone was in the big room, so dimly lit by the one far light which she now turned on, and by the embers of the dying fire. She, usually so imperturbable, only just managed to repress a scream as her instinct was proved right. A sudden squall and howl of wind blew over her desk as she retrieved her list and she swung round to the big west window to see Soames emerge from behind the dark velvet curtains. Was she never to be free from him to-night!

"Soames! What are you doing here now?"

"I was just closing the window, madam."

"But you opened it after I came into the room!"

"I could not bolt this one properly, so I opened it to bring it down firmly, madam!"

"But they should have been done long ago, before dinner!"

"They were, madam, but I remembered I had difficulty with this bolt then, and came to make sure."

"I see. Is there anything the matter with you to-night?" Soames' explanations were again perfectly plausible, but his voice was so squeaky, his face so sallow that Mrs. Broome's thoughts flew to influenza at once.

"No, thank you, madam. I may perhaps have been a bit upset over this here Ordination. I mean"—Soames pulled himself together after such a lapse into his native speech—"I mean that it was a new experience, and of course we had not Moira's assistance in instructing us in the usual routine."

"Poor Moira!" said Mrs. Broome mechanically, considering what a pity it was that Moira always got on so much better with men than women servants, for of course most of the staff were women. "I hope we shall soon have her back quite well again."

"If the gentleman—Mr. Ulder—is going to the Hospital by the same ambulance, at what time shall I take up his breakfast, madam, and what would be suitable for him?"

"I think perhaps nine o'clock," said Mrs. Broome, reflecting, as so often before, on a household staff's perfectly inexplicable means of gaining information. How should Soames know that Mr. Ulder was to be taken to hospital; except indeed by eavesdropping? "Yes, a light breakfast at nine o'clock—eggs, toast, tea, I think, and his things must be ready by nine o'clock."

"The Chaplain told me not to touch his bag, a big one, as it's all ready for a voyage."

"I see—and Soames!" Mrs. Broome paused. It seemed an opportunity to speak to the butler of his shortcomings, of his holding dishes out to guests on the wrong side, blowing down the backs of their necks in an onion-scented hurricane, piling dishes up and banging the doors. But the poor fellow looked so wretched that she forbore and contented herself with a kindly "Good night."

At last she was back in her bedroom and could hope for peace at last. She had stolen on her way into the rooms of both her invalids, to find that all was still, and went to her window with that longing for even the frostiest air which any sick-room inspires. It was hard to hold the catch for the snow was coming in wild gusts now, but even as she looked one blast seemed to blow itself out, and for a moment she saw, across the white velvet of the lawns, the black spectral arms of the pillars and ragged walls of the ruins and the snow-tipped dark branches of the great elms beyond, raised as if in desperate appeal for the troubles surrounding the Palace. Then, shuddering, she returned to the fire and tried, in her own old-fashioned phrase, to say her prayers. It was not easy, for her ears were now over-sensitized to sound and the passages seemed full of steps and footfalls, however severely she told herself that it was only the wind playing havoc with old beams and panels, low windows and wide doors. It seemed an eternity before at last the Bishop entered.

"My dear!" Mrs. Broome jumped up, alert and anxious anew. "You came from the Bridge, didn't you? Don't tell me you woke poor Mr. Ulder again! I settled him off to sleep a few minutes ago, and he has had far, far too many visitors! I don't know what Dr. Lee would say."

"Dr. Lee telephoned Bobs to say he was caught by the storm attending a confinement at Mrs. Holt's," said the Bishop evasively. "As he is so near as that he hopes to look in to-morrow at nine to see his patients, for he doubts if the ambulance will ever get through the snow."

"How kind of him! But were you with Mr. Ulder again?"

"I just looked in," admitted the Bishop, "a second ago!"

"And was he asleep?"

"Yes, yes, he was sleeping when I left him. Don't worry, my love! I am sure he will sleep well to-night."

"I only wish we could," thought Mrs. Broome. A long miserable discussion about Judith was no good prelude, and far into the early hours she tossed and turned, knowing that her husband lay taut, silent and wakeful in his bed, while she herself listened still for sounds, listened and rebuked herself for her imagination, as she did so. Twice she was so sure that she heard a creak, and then a swish, in the distance that she crept to the door, but each time the passages lay before her as dark and inscrutable as the avenues of death itself. There was not a sound but the scuttle of mice and creak of woodwork, no cry nor whimper but the moan of the wind. "He must be asleep," she was telling herself, when sleep came to her at last.

IV
THURSDAY MORNING (9-11)

"SO, ASSEMBLED TOGETHER for this most solemn moment of your lives of self-dedication, may you, and all of us here who are as it were spectators in this great Tourney, free our minds from all worldly troubles, cares and anxieties."

Mrs. Broome sighed restlessly in her seat in Chapel as her husband gave this exhortation. She was tired after a sleepless night, and the long early service which preceded the address: to be candid, she habitually found the daily prayers before break-fast the time when the programme for any day's duties beset her. The Chapel, a small neo-Gothic excrescence of the 1850s, never seemed to her inspiring, and how could you help think-ing of your household when you were all boxed up together, even on an ordinary morning? And now to-day, as she sat in the front pitch-pine pew of the tiny nave, here was the Chancellor beside her, fidgeting restlessly, his nerves evidently on edge, Sue pale and listless after the scene last night, Judith, present most of all by her absence, thought Mrs. Broome disconnectedly, a weight of such care to her stepmother as defied devotion. Be-hind her, having joined the congregation as Matins began, was a very poor showing from the servants' hall, though the Bish-op had urged their special attendance. Soames was presuma-bly setting and carrying trays upstairs, leaving his self-righteous and rather hysterical helper, Doris, the parlour-maid, to take his place. They were short-handed, for after the last war the domestic situation was serious, though not as final as that of 1945. Mrs. Briggs would be coming from the lodge, fat, com-petent and serene, to help in the dining-room as usual, but she didn't see her way to coming up in time for Chapel any longer, she explained, and Mabel and Irene, the upper and second housemaids were absent, leaving their place to their ultra-re-ligious, sentimental 'tweeny with her adenoids. Cook refused attendance—"what with this miserable bacon and alligators' eggs they say"—though her kitchen- and scullery-maid gladly evaded her to attend any service, but they really were of very inferior appearance and upbringing and so ready to titter in Chapel! These fell into the Bishop's category of worries, but Mrs. Broome was to-day faced by more serious anxieties. There in the Choir sat the Bishop and Canon Wye, gaunt, miserable, haunted men, in their canopied stalls. Bobs' cheerful face next the Bishop was haggard and strained, and little Mr. Staples, sallow and nervous, never stopped fidgeting. Dick, remote and absorbed, even the row of nice, young, chubby deacons seemed keyed up to some crisis in her imagination: even the rather repellently coloured and bearded evangelists in four narrow lancets above the altar seemed to look down with eyes of suspicion. How, when the names Ulder, Judith and Mark, her husband, repeated themselves in a dark pall of fear and dread in your mind, could you conceivably follow your dear husband's mellifluous advice? "Anyhow, things *could* be worse," she told herself, seeking the last ditch of the habitual optimist.

She was only too right. As the Bishop laid down his papers and Bobs rose with his prayer book, the Chapel door was flung open and, heedless of that still solemn congregation which turned surprised at such violation, in hurried, nay rather bounced, Mabel, the head housemaid, every trace of her normal soft-footed propriety and decorum vanished.

"Oh, madam," she wailed in a whisper that rang through the Chapel, "please come! You must come at once! It's Mr. Ulder! Soames took in his tray just now, and he gives such a call a minute later, and Irene and me rushes in, and oh, madam, we're nearly sure—the poor gentleman!"

Even as Mabel finished her speech by raising one hand to Heaven, in the dramatic manner common then to a class which dislikes the very name of death, Dick, for all his surprise and horror, found himself thinking that most of the congregation present would have hesitated to feel so sure of Thomas Ulder's future destination. Then he caught Mrs. Broome's glance of appeal, and in her horrified helplessness recalled himself from that enforced tolerant acceptance of death inevitably acquired in war, and followed her and Sue as quietly as possible out of the Chapel.

"You said Dr. Lee was held up at the Holts'," said Sue, shivering but capable. "I'd better ask him to come across at once if he can, hadn't I?"

"Certainly! I expect Soames was exaggerating! Servants always do!" Mrs. Broome's role in life as a shock-absorber made her fling out the suggestion, though she spoilt the effect by adding—"And don't come upstairs on any account!"

The lights in the Chapel had been so dim that the Bridge staircase, under the snow-covered cupola on the roof, seemed as massively, glitteringly white as a heap of florists' wreaths on a hearse. But in Mr. Ulder's room everything was grey and still. Soames had not drawn the curtains, and the bright circle made by the bedside lamp only just revealed the dull, drab Victorian wallpaper, the massive furniture, the dead ashes in the grate; and that which lay upon the bed was wrapped in the greyest, darkest shadows of all.

"Yes, he's gone!" Dick answered the question which Mrs. Broome was too perturbed to ask. "But not long. I fancy that an hour ago we might have been some use, but I don't know. No, no," as Mrs. Broome began to reproach herself tearfully. "How could you tell? Obviously it was best to let him sleep as long as possible."

"He does not look as if it was that dreadful pain at least!" The Bishop's wife pulled herself together and joined Dick by the bedside. "I suppose it was a sudden heart failure."

"Or that!" The two had paused for a minute's viaticum over that poor lonely soul which had winged its flight so recently, but now Dick's eyes were awake and keen as he pointed to a tumbler by the bed and sniffed it. "Didn't the doctor say he must have no stimulant?"

"But he hadn't last night! He asked everyone for it, but I forbade Canon Wye and—and someone else to give it. And he had none, and no glass was here, when I settled him off for the night!"

"Is the tray still there?" Dick looked out of the door. "Could he have helped himself?"

"The tray wasn't there first thing this morning," said Mrs. Broome positively. "I listened at this door and Moira's for a moment after my bath, and certainly I would have noticed such a slovenly bit of neglect. I am sure he could never have got to the door—every movement was liable to bring on that dreadful pain, and he made no attempt to stir from bed!"

"Dr. Lee, madam!" Mrs. Broome turned at Soames' entrance and announcement with as much relief as if she hoped the doctor might almost bring back the dead to life. It was left to Dick alone to note Soames' movements.

"Leave that glass!" The butler had picked it up as he passed the table after drawing the curtains and blind, and now, with the respectful surprise of one stopped in a mechanical duty, left the room.

"Well, well, I feared as much!" The little doctor was as brisk and fresh as ever after his disturbed night, and shake down at the Holts' farm, and his matter-of-fact manner was somehow a balm to poor Mrs. Broome. "Better so, indeed! I doubt if he'd ever have given up d—, I mean lived an orderly, quiet life. Alcohol's a tremendous temptation to a man with a heart like that. He'd never have been able to do much at the best. I see, Dick, he couldn't keep off the bottle even here. When did he get hold of it, Mrs. Broome?"

"We don't know. Was it that—?"

"Oh no!" The doctor was bending over the bed now in a more thorough examination. "Very inadvisable after the injection I gave, but still—Besides he took it last night, I imagine, and it can't be more than an hour or so since he actually went off—and peacefully too, from his looks. I should have expected signs of pretty acute pain, I must say."

"What about his eyes?" Dick asked as the doctor bent down again. He had a startling fear of his own from a cursory glance, and hoped the doctor would dispel it.

"By Jove, yes!" At Dick's words the doctor had put on his glasses, and looked more keenly—and why had he spoken, Dick was to wonder all that day, since his words alone had roused the doctor's attention. "This is odd, very odd. Mrs. Broome, how many doses did you give Mr. Ulder?"

"Just the one!" Mrs. Broome was more perturbed by the doctor's flurried manner than his question. "That was at about— oh, half-past ten or eleven last night, and I never went into his room again as he did not ring his bell. The Bishop looked in and thought he was sleeping peacefully at about twelve o'clock, but I suppose by then——" She shuddered as she remembered the Bishop's words to her, "He will sleep well to-night!" They had been only too true.

"Then he got hold of it himself. You see the pupils narrowed to a pin-prick, Dick?" (It was precisely this which Dick had noted when he spoke.) "Sure sign of morphia poisoning. That explains why he looks so peaceful, poor chap. He must have had an attack and decided to end it all, for I warned him not to dose himself. Where is the phial I gave you, Mrs. Broome?"

"Up on the top rung of that hideous dressing-table," said Mrs. Broome agitatedly. "Oh dear! Oh dear! I should never have left it in the room. I do blame myself! Did he take it, doctor?"

"Here we are!" The doctor unscrewed the cap, held it up to them, to show that only cotton-wool remained in the receptacle. "You gave him one, Mrs. Broome, so there were five tablets left. It was more than I usually would have given, but I feared you might be snowed up here for a few days so that I couldn't get to you. Five's a big dose, but whether it would have had this effect——"

"I expect he was in agonizing pain and hardly knew what he was doing," suggested Mrs. Broome.

"No, you can see he wasn't in any pain when he was last conscious. And I warned him very seriously of the danger of helping himself to morphia."

"I should never have left it in his reach!"

"Now don't blame yourself, Mrs. Broome, it's hard to believe he could have reached it up there. In fact, it's hard to believe he was just dosing himself—it looks to me far more as if he had intended to end his life."

"What about the whisky?" put in Dick.

"We'd better not touch that glass, but I'd say there were grains of morphia in it—see that sediment? The drink wouldn't finish him, of course. I only warned him of it because it would retard the effect of the morphia. If he'd decided to end everything he might well have put the dose in the whisky and gone to sleep for ever. But what perplexes me is that I doubt if it was a fatal dose!"

"Suicide! Oh, how ghastly!" moaned Mrs. Broome.

"He may have had a doctor's prescription of his own," suggested Dick. "And added that, if he meant to make sure. Shall we have a look at the room?"

"He seems to have very few things about," said Mrs. Broome, as the three explored the vast wardrobe and many drawers of the dressing-table. "I imagine Soames unpacked his night things. Mr. Ulder told us not to touch that big bag. He wouldn't need it till he got to America."

"America? That fellow off to America in the state he was in?" cried Dr. Lee. "And Heavens, what a sporting outfit!" as Dick opened the bag to reveal flashy plus-fours and garish shirts. "This is all the oddest business! Nothing there, Dick, I'm sure!"

"He must have had a hand-bag as well." Dick was looking even more puzzled and perturbed than the doctor. Ulder would never have parted with the papers which incriminated his victims and these were nowhere to be seen. He went over to the fire and stirred the ashes gently.

"Did you leave a big fire burning, Mrs. Broome, when you last visited him?"

"No, indeed. I thought any light would worry him and made sure it was practically out. But what do you mean about another bag, Dick? His night things are out, you see, his brushes and so on."

"Those are all Bob's—and his pyjamas. Bobs got them last night so as to put him to bed as soon as possible—and we'd no idea then that he'd brought any luggage, of course. Why did he?"

"Soames reported that he said he never let his possessions out of his sight. He told the Bishop he meant to stay if—if he could not settle some question with him, but you know he was—well, hardly himself!"

"Then there must be a hand-bag somewhere," repeated Dick urgently.

"But why does it matter so much?" Mrs. Broome spoke impatiently, for what did these things matter to poor Mr. Ulder? The other world was not a junction where you demanded your baggage.

"The bag may have contained another bottle of some morphia prescription," replied Dick abruptly. "It must almost certainly have contained some letters or papers or some personal traces if he was just leaving home for good. No one would remove it from this room, surely, without his knowledge. Why should he have removed it himself, and where did he put it? Was he really in a fit state to get up to that shelf, find morphia, fetch himself a whisky and conceal his bag somewhere, doctor, and why on earth should he?"

"He may have asked Soames to put his bag somewhere— or Doris—I think she's outside, so I'll go and ask her!" Mrs. Broome still felt Dick's insistence a little tiresome as she went out into the passage calling the maid.

"Does she realize that suicide, or even a dose taken inadvertently, means we must call in the police—and at once?" asked Dr. Lee in a lowered voice. "Get the Bishop's leave for that, Dick, as soon as you can."

But Dick did not answer at once. He had bent over the bed in search of any trace of another medicine bottle or tablet, and now all such thoughts were swept from his mind by a piece of crumpled paper, just protruding from the pillow which caught his eye. It was only a rough slip, but bending over the cold, still body, Dick could just make out a short list:

Bishop (he read)	£2,000
Chancellor	2,000
Judith	5,000
Wye	2,000
Staples	50, etc

"Better break it to her that we must notify the police," murmured Dick, as Mrs. Broome returned, distraught, and Dick had to look up and try to hide his horror at his discovery for the moment.

"Mabel was with Moira, and the poor old soul is in a dreadful state! Mabel says she has even got out of bed and walked about in her agony, and you know she hasn't stirred from bed for weeks. Can't you give her something, operation or no operation, doctor, for how can we tell if the ambulance will ever get out at all to-day!"

"I will! I will! Just get your spirit kettle going with some boiling water and I'll give her a shot at once! But one moment, Mrs. Broome. You are aware that as this is almost certainly a case of suicide, whether by accident or intention, we shall have to notify the police and I fear we shall have to expect a visit and enquiry from them."

"Oh dear, oh dear!" cried poor Mrs. Broome, distracted. "Why did he want to kill himself here? Oh, how wrong of me to say that but—well, it seems such a *pity* to choose this house and the middle of an Ordination! Dick, dear, you must break it to the Bishop and do all that has to be done. You and Dr. Lee will help us in every way you can, I know!"

Every way you can! thought Dick. Just for a moment the temptation to take that appalling list and destroy it was overwhelming. Ulder was dead—why should his evil deeds live after him? Of course Dick could not and would not commit such a breach of his moral and professional code, but still—

For one dreadful moment as the doctor fumbled at his bag Dick let his mind dwell at last on the possible suspects. Motive and opportunity alike seemed to point skeleton fingers at such preposterous figures—Judith—the Chancellor—Canon Wye—the Bishop himself! No, a million times no, he told himself, while the cold question: Who else? began to creep into his mind like the freezing wind outside.

"Why on earth was Ulder here? What do you think of all this, Dick?" asked Dr. Lee.

"I couldn't say before Mrs. Broome, but how and why should Ulder have finished himself off like this?" answered Dick slowly. "He was making a new start in life, and it wasn't humbug about his going to America, with that big bag full of fantastic lay clothes. He came here of his own accord—he was in no new disgrace. If he had reached up for that container he'd have burst his heart, I imagine, and we can see he wasn't even driven to it by pain. And as for the bag—well, I must admit to you in confidence that he would never have asked anyone to remove his papers, or let them out of his sight for a moment!"

"What were these missing papers?" asked Dr. Lee abruptly. As a good old-fashioned churchman and a confirmed gossip, he knew all and more than all there was to know about Ulder's expulsion from the College. "Were there any of importance? Blackmail?"

"Looks like it," said Dick laconically, pointing to the paper under the pillow. The doctor put on his spectacles quickly enough as he bent over the list, and looked up at last as if he had seen a ghost or the devil himself.

"I suppose," he said, in a voice Dick hardly recognized, "that we must leave this here, that we can't let the whole affair be buried?"

"You don't mean that, doctor! If you really mean to suppress evidence just sit down and sign a certificate of death from natural causes!"

"Really, sir!" spluttered the doctor. "Honesty—my honour—my oath!"

"Just so, but it's as bad to tamper with evidence of any kind. It might always boomerang on the innocent, and, if any one here poisoned Ulder, he probably wasn't sane at the time—he must be a lunatic, you'd say, not fit for a position of trust."

"Any one ... but who's any one?" The two men stared at each other. "But, my dear Dick, if you knew our Chief Constable now you'd understand how damnable this all is!"

"I've heard of him," said Dick, "and that he'll enjoy a scandal here! But I'm sure he'll keep his prejudices to himself."

"I'm not," said the doctor, as he went off to the next room. "Oh well, go ahead and tell the house party here that we suspect suicide and no more, and ring up the police. But I hope to goodness Sergeant Tonks comes alone, for he's a good churchman and as stupid as they make them too! If he falls for suicide—it's no affair of mine!"

"There'll have to be some arrangements about—" Dick pointed to the bed.

"Yes, yes, I thought of that. Look here, I'm going to give that poor old soul next door a good shot of morphia now, in case the ambulance isn't here anyway till midday. Tell the police to try to make their examination at once and then the ambulance and mortuary van with the body can get off together—safer if together in case there's a breakdown. They'll want an autopsy I expect. Never thought to live to see one on a parson, but the damn world's upside down!"

The doctor's world had turned upside down and his language with it, thought Dick, as the poor little man bustled away to the next room. Dick felt far indeed from his own normal self as he too walked to the door and locked it behind him just as steps re-echoed along the passage, and the silence was broken by the voices of the Bishop and Canon Wye as they hastened from the Chapel to the room. It was a mercy, reflected Dick, that Bobs had mesmerized them all into staying put in the Chapel till the Service was finished, or they would all have been all over Ulder's room, Bishop, Canon, Chancellor, Staples, Soames and all! And one of them, the realization fell again like lead upon his heart, one of them surely was hurrying here because he must know most, and dread most, the discovery of what had passed in that room that night. Well, as it was, that person had better hear the suspicion of suicide at least, and Judith might as well take it too, he decided grimly, as the girl came out of Moira's room with tumbled curls and flushed face, the scent of flowers clinging to the rustling dressing-gown which revealed her slim, exquisite form in its primrose silk pyjamas. Dr. Lee and Mrs. Broome had just sent her away, it appeared, and Soames followed her, carrying away Moira's breakfast tray.

"What's wrong?" Her light tone voiced the question which no one dared to ask. "Mabel called me with some story of murder and sudden death, but I was too sleepy to make it out and I've been with Moira since! Thank Heaven Dr. Lee is giving her something at last!"

"My lord, may I please telephone for the police?" Dick forced himself out of the maze of horror and incredulity, in which his suspicions wandered.

"Is it necessary in a case of natural death?" asked the Bishop, "for I assume Dr. Lee can sign the certificate in view of poor Ulder's condition?"

"Not in this case. Ulder did not die of heart disease, but of morphia poisoning."

"Self-administered?" Canon Wye's question was as sharp and brittle as the icicles on the windows.

"There must be some enquiry about the method," answered Dick evasively.

"Poor Lee miscalculated his dose! Is it necessary to expose him?" The Bishop's voice and hands were trembling as he spoke. "Why think it self-administered?"

"I'm afraid it is not our province to decide whether his death was accidental or intentional," replied Dick. "Perhaps you would rather see Dr. Lee, and then telephone yourself, my lord? He is with Moira."

"Yes, yes!" The Bishop moved to Mr. Ulder's door—"And meanwhile I must pray by this poor mortal—"

"I'm afraid the doctor wishes the door locked and the room left as it is. The police are always adamant on that point!" Dick's face was as bleak as his voice. Did ever Ordination candidate before forbid a bishop to enter one of his own rooms?

"But that's absurd!" The Chancellor came up, bristling and burly. "We must look through Ulder's papers, find his present address, and notify any relatives."

"There are no papers," replied Dick briefly.

"May I ask who put you in charge of this affair?" If, thought Dick, Canon Wye had a thumb-screw or stake handy, or, failing such happy method, an examination paper on which to plough Dick, he'd be for it!

"I'm not, sir! It was pure chance that Mrs. Broome beck-oned me to come upstairs, and that Dr. Lee asked me to have a glance at things with him. I've no more to do with it."

"Oh, but indeed he has!" Dr. Lee and Mrs. Broome emerged from Moira's room in time to hear the end of the conversation and the doctor spoke. "He's a good head and done military intelligence and all! As good as a layman!" Long acquaintance with the Church had only confirmed the good doctor in his belief that all clergymen were unbusinesslike.

"Dear Dick is so helpful," chimed in Mrs. Broome. "And now I really think we should all leave this part of the house quiet for poor Moira, don't you, Dr. Lee?"

"Certainly. No one can do anything in there." The doctor pointed at St. Ursula gravely. "Dick here knows all the facts and should get on to the police at once. The sooner the formalities are over the better. I'll wait as long as I can myself, and I'd like to see Mrs. Broome and this young fellow settling down to some breakfast with all of you. There's a trying day before your good lady, Bishop, and I wouldn't mind a good cup of coffee myself."

In any trial of will the one person who is sure of himself usually comes off victor. It must be fancy, thought Dick, that al-ready the Bishop, Chancellor and Canon Wye were eyeing each other so oddly, and that Judith had so suddenly disappeared. But certainly what seemed like a united front against his interfer-ence had broken up, or else the human instinct for bodily suste-nance, after being what Judith called "so hard at it in Chapel for so long", was predominant. And to some at least Ulder's death must mean unutterable relief that was another odd consideration—if only the papers had really disappeared. And one—but here again Dick thrust aside the thought—one might even now be in possession of the papers, having abstracted them from the missing bag, and be rejoicing, yes, actively rejoicing in the apparent acceptance of a theory of suicide.

The telephone arrangements in the Palace were, as Bobs always said, entirely lacking in the spirit of the confessional. The main line was in the hall and by picking up the receiver here any one could overhear either the Bishop's conversation from his desk, or Bobs' from his room, or Mrs. Broome's from her boudoir. Any listener was liable to be discovered eavesdropping at any moment, of course, but the entrance hall was likely to be free from interruption till breakfast was over.

"I want to take a call here to the police, Soames," said Dick, catching the butler on his way to the pantry from the hall. It would be safer to explain to Soames that he knew he was liable to be overheard, Dick decided. "Bring me a cup of coffee and a roll or something from the dining-room, will you? It'll take some time to get on."

"The police, sir?" Evidently Soames was taken aback, but then after all you do not expect police in Palaces. "Is—is anything wrong?"

"Not quite a clear case," answered Dick negligently. This rather slimy little wreck of a fellow was, he told himself, about the only person in the Palace who had no connection with the dead man, so why, as the shifty eyes evaded his, should he wonder if the butler had any part in the affair? Wishful thinking, probably, as he still did not dare to think of the other possible criminals. Certainly Soames was curious, for he hung about arranging a tray with Dick's breakfast first on one table in the hall, and then on another, till Dick dismissed him curtly. Still, curiosity wasn't crime and in any case Soames could hope for little satisfaction. After infinite delays at the village post office, while Mrs. Jones was comfortably finishing her breakfast and calling on a stupid operator in Evelake (for the day of dials had not dawned in the countryside), Dick's information to the police station was curt enough, if urgent. As a stunned voice stuttered in reply Dick rang off, finished his coffee and, tray in hand, flung open the baize door to the servants' passage.

There, as he suspected, stood Soames, polishing a door handle vehemently.

"Hullo, Soames! I was just bringing back this tray. Thanks a lot for it. I didn't feel like joining them in there," he nodded his head towards the dining-room. "A bit upset, and I expect you were. Can I speak a word to you, by the way?"

Did Soames realize he was being edged to the pantry? He certainly seemed unwilling to leave the passage, but Dick walked on unconcernedly. He had no reason to expect any enlightenment in this quarter, but he always liked to discover the he of the land, and he wished to disentangle the muddled geography of the Palace. This passage, long and narrow, wound along till it intersected the wide entrance to the Chapel, beyond which lay the pantry and Soames' bedroom and offices. "Just beneath the Bridge bedrooms! I say," said Dick casually, "did you hear anything unusual last night, Soames?"

"Indeed I did, sir. People popping in and out of Mr. Ulder's room at all hours, that's to say, till eleven o'clock at least. It kept me awake."

"So you couldn't get your tray down till pretty late, I suppose?" Dick's eyes rested on the tray of whisky, lemonade, siphons and glasses as he spoke. Soames was clearly enough in a fidget of nervousness but Dick wished him to feel unobserved.

"I—I didn't get the tray down till this morning, sir." (So he and Mrs. Broome differed then!)

"Not many glasses used?"

"No, sir. These candidates, as they call them, seem very abstemious. Not much like an officers' mess."

"You were in the Army then? France?"

"Yes, sir."

"Anywhere near my old regiment, I wonder? The 40th Brigade, Eveshire Yeomanry?"

"No, sir. I was R.A.S.C. Mostly base work." Soames imparted the information grudgingly. "Anyway I was invalided out, shell shock, in '16."

"Hard luck! Nasty business! Did it take you long to get going again? A friend of mine still gibbers if a lorry passes."

"I am not aware of any symptoms now, sir." Had this chap been reading Wodehouse as a guide to butlers? for occasionally he would throw out such Jeeves-like sentiments with oily rectitude, in startling contrast to his usual sulky, aggressive manner.

"Good show!" Why was the fellow edging towards the tray? "By the way, you didn't give this unlucky Mr. Ulder anything to drink, did you? I ask because he was calling out for it, I believe, and it would be difficult for you to refuse it."

"I never gave him anything, sir!" Soames began defiantly and went on cringingly. "I never set eyes on him except to open the door and carry his kit upstairs."

"Ah yes! That's what I really wanted to ask you about. Mrs. Broome thinks he must have had more than the one big portmanteau in his room now. She and the Bishop want to find his address and the address of any relation, if possible, but there's nothing of that kind apparently, nor any trace of ordinary night things. Mr. Borderer lent him all those, but he must have had some somewhere. And papers you'd say! Hullo!"

The exclamation escaped Dick as Soames dropped a heavy decanter to the ground and, with a muttered oath, went down on his knees to retrieve the scattered pieces. It was quite a minute before he looked up with a flushed face.

"I've no sort of idea, sir. I may have carried up one case or two, I really couldn't say. Being the only man here I was carrying up bags for all you gentlemen all evening and was fair off my head with the work. I couldn't tell you about any luggage except yours being an officer's kit and the Chancellor having that odd green baize bag of his. The work's too much for me here, and I shall have to tell Mrs. Broome so, if we're going to have these to-dos every few months!"

"Tough luck! Had you an easier job before?"

"No complaints on either side, sir." Soames was evidently determined to say nothing of his past. "I came here with good references."

"Yes, yes! And I can imagine that the luggage was a tough job. I'll suggest to Mr. Borderer that we candidates are asked to carry up our own kit next time. I wonder if it's possible that you put a bag of Mr. Ulder's in another room by accident?"

"Oh no, sir. Everything else was upstairs by the time he came. It was much later when I took up his. Mrs. Broome said to leave them inside the door and not to unpack."

Did Soames notice that plural, as Dick did, though he made no sign? It might or might not be to cover his admission that the butler went on hastily and almost savagely, "Excuse me, sir, if I say I don't understand what all this questioning is, nor why this talk of the police, when the gentleman had a bad heart and was under the doctor's care anyhow."

"Well, you heard me tell the police there was a question of suicide, didn't you?" said Dick equably. As well to let this fellow know that his snooping was observed! "I am only asking about the luggage because the Bishop wants some clue to Mr. Ulder's relatives. I've nothing to do with any questions which the police may ask about everyone in the house."

Suddenly Soames' whole personality changed. He was no longer a truculent, surly ex-soldier but a skinny, abject little specimen of the slave class of an effete civilization (so Dick and Bobs had termed such people in their hot Christian Socialist days). Leaving his tray and the broken decanter he sidled up to Dick with that desperate fawning humility which Dick had seen too often in lags in the Settlement and regiment.

"Say, sir, please speak a good word for me. I'm doing my best and I did at the Academy, my last place too, and never set hands on a thing I shouldn't. I've gone straight, but what's the good of

it? Once you've been in you're always up against it. Talk of new
starts! Whatever bobby ever let you have a new start?"

"Then you got into trouble in the Service Corps? And again
in Civvy street? Pinching, eh?"

"Nothing worth much," whined Soames. "And me shell
shocked for my country, too!"

"Drink? Cigarettes? An odd watch or two and a few pound
notes? Well, well," as Soames nodded miserably, "I'm sure you'll
find any Court would take your health into consideration if
you ever came before one. I advise you to tell the police this
story straight out when they come. Far better than lying and
letting them worm it out as they probably will. Best of all, have
a good look round for that bag, for otherwise this case can be
no concern of yours. Very easy for you to have put it down
somewhere and forgotten it. In this room, for instance, or your
bedroom?" He glanced through the half-open door into a lit-
tered bedroom which suggested the early stages of a jumble sale
in the East End. "Well, I must be getting along."

The back passage down the old wing to the pantry in the
Bridge was very long and narrow and Dick walked slowly.
More than ever he was confirmed in his suspicions that the
butler had picked up Mr. Ulder's bag as an unconsidered trifle
for his own use this morning. A sneak thief—and Soames bore
that stamp openly to Dick—would not let the presence of a
corpse baulk him of a job; no doubt Soames had told himself
that the reverend gentleman would have no further use for it!
The fact of the theft was only important in view of the papers
which the bag must contain, for Ulder would never have hoped
to extract money from his victims without very definite documents with which to threaten them. Would Soames understand
them? Dick thought not. He could not see Soames as either a
murderer or blackmailer: he had neither the guts nor any conceivable motive to murder Ulder: he had probably not the guts
or education for blackmail. But all the same Dick would give a
good deal to get his hands on that bag.

But was Soames so harmless after all? At the door to the hall Dick looked swiftly round, and in that moment had to revise his views about Soames. Never, he thought, had he seen such a malignant look of hatred and suspicion on any face. He might after all be no mere thieving coward but a force to be reckoned with.

"Sue! Do you remember anything about Ulder's luggage?" It was like Sue to cross the hall just when Dick wanted her, looking like a spring nosegay peeping out of the snow!

"Let me see." Sue crinkled up her low, wide forehead, pushing aside her pretty, curled pageboy hair. "There was a big, flashy bag, I remember. And I *think* a shabby, bulgy, black bag, the sort our Nurses used to take milk bottles and sandwiches in on journeys. Doesn't Soames know?"

"I expect he got muddled with all the traps yesterday—it seems to be missing."

"Let's hunt for it," cried Sue, who had been noted for a passion for hide-and-seek in her youth.

"Later, perhaps! I'm thinking of a spot of Chapel! Yes thanks, I've had lots of breakfast." (Sue was the sort of darling who would think of a man's bodily needs instead of bothering him with questions.)

"But you must help Father to interview the police when they come. Father sent me to tell you so. He says he must have someone with experience."

Dick assented politely. He was aware by now that his activities in the war would always seem to outsiders that of a sort of glorified policeman. Nor could he very well explain that till this day he had no experience whatever of suspecting Church dignitaries of murder.

V
THURSDAY MORNING (11–12)

SERGEANT TONKS was sitting at the bleak desk of the Eve-lake Constabulary, a pile of files beside him and the *Daily Wail* crossword before him when the telephone bell rang. The office was slack, very slack, as was usual before Christmas. Evelake, a backwash of what seems now a forgotten world, depended largely on the Church for its material as well as spiritual activities. Children were regular at school in view of treats: mothers and spinsters of every age had an eye on blankets, coals and Christmas trees. Even poachers were less active as tips flowed freely from squires at the sacred season: publicans were saving their best liquor for Christ mas, and reprobates their money for a burst, now that whisky had reached the appalling price of 12s. 6d. a bottle. Road accidents were few because motors were few, and as for serious crime—"Why, no bobby will ever get experience here," complained the new Chief Constable when he learnt that the Judges almost invariably received their pairs of white gloves at the Evelake Assize. If the Inspector were here he'd be fussing about forms, but such things, Tonks judged, could wait for the duration of his illness. This was the first glorious dawn of crosswords, when they were an occupation rather than relaxation, and it was a tax on Biblical research and natural history to work out a king of Bashan or ancient city in two, and a bird in three, letters.

"Drat that telephone," Tonks said, relinquishing his pursuit of a fabulous bird. He was a middle-sized, middle-aged, respectable family man who had looked like a grocer when he was acting as verger, and a verger when serving behind the counter. Such had been his avocation before the war led him into the police force—as its junior members volunteered for service—and as the Palace dealt with the shop, now carried on by his wife, and his respect for ecclesiastical authority was profound, he was, as he told Mrs. Tonks, knocked all of a heap when he took the message from the Palace.

This was no case for him, was his first reaction. Sudden death at the Palace was bad enough, but suicide! "And there may be more to it!" the voice on the telephone had added almost in a whisper. Now indeed Tonks regretted Inspector Jay's absence. For Jay, if not one of those quick, attractive know-alls you read about, had had long experience in London, that sink of iniquity, as Mrs. Tonks called it, and could and did stand up to the new Chief Constable, Major Mack, as man to man. And Mack would be in on this from the word "Go", thought Tonks, his hand already on the telephone. Clearly he must ring up the Major at once and ask for help in the job. For he'd have to take Simon and perhaps Lace as well, and that would mean leaving Corn in the office, Corn who'd never yet taken a telephone message without muddling it! And ten to one Mack would take on the Palace case himself, short handed as they were, for how he'd rejoice at anything like a scandal in the Church! (Fair wild he'd been when that choir-boy proved an alibi for a mere theft of apples!) He'd never stop to think it wasn't his place, nor mind demeaning himself, as Mr. Verlaine would never have dreamt of, by turning to ordinary police work again. Why should he, when it was just the regular police work he had grown up in? But what a fuss he'd make over it all, and if there was one thing Tonks couldn't abide it was fuss!

"I'll be with you in ten minutes." The Chief Constable's vigorous Scottish burr on the telephone, the excitement in his hasty answer, justified all Tonks' fears. "Have you chains on the police car?"

"Yes, sir. I had Corn put them on this morning."

"Good. We must take him with us, or send him on at once on his bike or tell Lace to follow later."

"He'd be quicker in the car, sir, it's a good three miles. That leaves Simon in the office, sir, and he's not too—"

"Office be damned. This case is urgent. That remark about 'may be more to it' shows they'll be at work hushing things up already. Trust a surplice to conceal a cassock! I'll be round at once."

The constabulary car was a roomy old Humber, but it seemed restricted enough to Tonks as he sat beside the burly Chief Constable. Mack was indeed one of those Scotsmen who occupy a good deal of space in the world. He had a prominent chin and equally pronounced convictions. Prejudices bristled about him, like his wiry hair, in all sorts of unexpected places, including prelacy, pacifism, the modern girl and all foreigners except the Dutch. He had a sound education and little culture: someone has said that Scotsmen may be divided between good shots and good fishermen, that is to say, men of action or philosophers, hard or sentimental, bellicose or pacific according to the type to which they belong. Mack belonged emphatically to the former category, and was, therefore, elated to-day. In Tonks' view he was hardly a suitable guest, at the best of times, to roll through the majestic lodge gates and up the lime avenue of the Palace, nor did his mighty pull at the iron chain of the bell strike Tonks as seemly. He could not tell that the motto, "Neminem averto", carved in stone above the door, reminded Mack grimly that his wife had not, apparently, been considered good enough for an invitation to the Diocesan Garden Party. That imagined slight weighed down the scales of Mack's distrust of prelacy and parsons more heavily than he realized, for Mrs. Mack referred to it far more frequently than Mack himself reflected on theology, nor could the husband and wife know that Mrs. Broome for months had meant to atone by an invitation to dinner, an attention, alas, delayed too long, and unknown, of course, to the predestined guests.

Bobs was standing in the hall as Soames flung open the door of the outer hall (making a dash to cover afterwards in the pantry) and Bobs, looking more flushed and school-boyish than ever, in his efforts to combine the appearance of the police with the solemnity of an Ordination, annoyed the Constable by his first word.

"The Chief Constable? We are glad to see you so soon, sir. We did not expect you yet with the roads in this state. The Bishop is conducting a service in the Chapel for the Ordination candidates, and asked me to excuse him if you did arrive, and take you upstairs."

"But I must see him at once!"

"He'll be out in a few minutes!" Bobs was too well accustomed to impatient interview-seekers to resent Mack's imperious voice. "Dr. Lee is still upstairs, waiting for the ambulance for an invalid in the house. His car's stuck and he hopes for a lift back with her. Here is Mrs. Broome who was first to—to view the tragedy, and can tell you more than the Bishop."

"Indeed I will. I'll do all I can. It is such a relief to see you!" Mack looked more belligerent than ever as the Bishop's wife came across the hall, trim and composed, a sheaf of lilies in her hand. Did these idle rich have nothing better to do, with corpses and invalids on the premises, than to pluck nosegays? "I do hope so much the formalities will soon be over, for it is all so trying for my poor husband."

"Yes, I expect he wants everything smoothed over!" Mrs. Broome started at the undisguised hostility in Mack's voice. "He had some practice at that with this wretched fellow Ulder before, I remember!" Of course, Mrs. Broome also remembered now the report that the Chief Constable, then newly on duty at Evelake, had resented bitterly the compromise which had saved Ulder from the arm of the law. "But you can't evade public enquiries on this occasion, you know. Please fetch the Bishop," he turned to Bobs, "I must have this story first hand."

"Of course! So fetch Mabel, please Bobs. She made the discovery. And please get a message into Chapel to ask Dick to join us at once. He was with me and the doctor, you see," she went on, turning to Mack, "and such a help! The Bishop did not come up from Chapel till some time later. And indeed from first to last I am responsible, for it was to me that Dr. Lee entrusted a dose of morphia for this poor man! Judith, what are you doing?"

Mrs. Broome and the two guardians of the law were in the dark, old passage when the exclamation broke from the worried lady. Before them, radiant in her scarlet frock, the eerie snow sunlight making a gold wreath of her lovely hair, stood Judith, her hand still on the handle of St. Ursula's door.

"I thought Dick was still here and meant to take him down for some breakfast!" (Such thoughtfulness was indeed unusual, but perhaps the shock has roused the child to think of others, thought the optimistic stepmother.) "But the door's locked, and no one answered. Hullo, Tonks! Fancy you here! You've always been so sweet about winking when I was driving dangerously that I'm sure you'll soon settle everything. The Chief Constable, Mother? Oh, how grand! I never met one before. Don't give Tonks a black mark for what I said, will you? I'm sure you'd do the same for me."

But charm is only too often wasted on the North British and Mack moved on indignantly. Mrs. Broome was pausing at the door, her former dread and pity taking refuge in a silent prayer for the vanished soul, but to Mack her agitation seemed only as inexplicable as Judith's apparition. "Very queer goings-on here," he had decided even before he entered the shaded room.

"No, not on the bed, please, Mrs. Broome." The doctor came bustling in and greeted Mack. "Yes, yes, leave the lilies here and I'll see to them later." (Lilies for the police indeed! Flowers for the Judge! thought Mack, who had recently enjoyed a brilliant novel by that title.) "Ah, and here's the maid who found the—the corpse, Chief Constable. I'm sure when she and Mrs. Broome have told their stories you'll let them leave us. I want some words with you alone—unless, indeed, we can have Dick up, Mrs. Broome." (And who's this nosey parker, Dick? wondered Mack privately.)

The doctor fidgeted impatiently as Mabel and Mrs. Broome repeated the well-known story, only patting Mrs. Broome's shoulder reassuringly as she grew agitated over her mistake in leaving the bottle in the invalid's room.

"Quite natural, quite natural, what every home nurse of my patients does."

"I never even dreamt of his trying to get out of bed," said Mrs. Broome, almost tearfully.

"No, no, of course not! Now you should go and lie down a bit, I think: it's all been too much for you. If you've no more questions for the moment, Major Mack?" And it seemed to Dr. Lee that the catechism which the two women had already undergone was even longer than the so-called Shorter Catechism of the Major's native land. One thing was that Mack could hardly question the veracity of the Bishop's wife, for her story proved only too conclusively what a focus of interest this room had been last night. All these clerical visitors to Ulder: her daughter at his door, and the Bishop's visit the last she knew of: the whisky glass brought in against orders: the missing bag. Nor did she even try to disguise the dismay of the party at Ulder's arrival, and their dislike of his activities. A nasty tale, the doctor reflected almost incredulously, as Dick appeared and Mrs. Broome rustled away.

"Well, what are you doing here, sir?" Mack turned scowling at the sight of yet another parson in place of the recalcitrant bishop.

"Mrs. Broome sent for me, sir, but as you've finished—" Dick turned back to the door at once but Dr. Lee intervened.

"Nonsense! You must stay, Dick. Major Mack, this is Major—well, Mr. Marlin now, late of the Intelligence Department and Secret Service. He helped me to make an examination of things here this morning and I'd like him to eke out my information."

"Never heard of you," said Mack gruffly.

"Naturally not, sir. As a matter of fact I heard a good deal about you when I was in the 2nd Royal Scots mess for a few months. The Colonel told us yarns about your doings in the Boer War and the name stuck in my mind because I recognized it. You wouldn't remember an English family at the hotel at Auchenfoyle in 1902—no, 1903 it was, I think? You played golf with my father once, over at Nairn, and beat him, though he was a three handicap. The only time you took a rod you brought home a round dozen of two-pounder trout, and when you went off to shoot or stalk on Echinore with the game-keeper I used to hang about that porch with the fuchsia bushes round it hoping you'd offer to take me too! And at the very end you did take me, and it was on the day you brought down a royal."

"By Jove, so I did. My last day on Echinore. And, of course, I remember your name, sir! How's that charming mother of yours? I remember telling my missus that if all English ladies had families like hers I'd tolerate the Southerners."

"She died, sir, just before this war. I can feel glad for her sake now at times, for two of my brothers didn't come back, but it's a hard job for my father to carry on."

"And what are you doing in this show?" asked Mack, as after a grunt of deep sympathy he looked with disfavour on Dick's clerical collar. "After the Army too! What were you in?"

"I got a commission in the Evelake Yeomanry and was knocked out. When I wasn't passed fit for active service I was put into Intelligence. Now I'm going on with the commission which the war interrupted—in another militant army, you might say!"

"Church militant, eh? Well, there's plenty of the militant side in this extraordinary business. Look here, now I come to think of it, weren't you mixed up in another Ulder business some years ago?" Memories of a Jesuitical curate who had managed to extricate the Church from any exposure of its laxity and dispose of Ulder from the Theological College returned to Mack and he began to bristle fiercely again. "What a show that was! What a scandal that the Bishop—"

"Put yourself in his place, sir. Think of the countless critics and enemies of the Church, and their joy over such a titbit of scandal!"

"No use going back on that now," said the doctor impatiently.

"No, indeed, since they managed between them to put an end to the scandal once and for all! At least my man gathered that from you. I suppose, Marlin, that it's not a clear case of suicide. Now then, let's go into it all. I've got the main plot from Mrs. Broome and I must say she didn't seem to be holding anything back. Correct me where I'm wrong. Ulder arrived, pretty drunk, and had a heart attack. Lee who was on the spot for another case handed out a tube of morphia with strict injunctions to give one dose only and no alcohol. Ulder recovered enough to insist on an interview with the Bishop, another with that

Canon Wye, a Jesuit in disguise if ever there was one, and Chancellor Chailly as you call him, though why Chancellor when he's just an incompetent old family lawyer beats me. One or two servants including the butler were about; that fly-by-night daughter of the Bishop seems to have popped in. What's at the bottom of all this? Why was Ulder here at all?"

"You must ask them," said Dick slowly. "The little I know I've heard in confidence."

"Of course I'll put them through it. Well, to go on, the wretched man is left alone at last. After the dose of exhortation from all these parsons he decides to make an end of it, swallows the rest of the dose, mixes himself a stiff one and—passes out. That it, doctor?"

"Yes, it—it might be." Dr. Lee hesitated. "But honesty compels me to say that I can't see him getting up and reaching for the dose and walking to the door in the state he was in. Nor can I believe that the whisky or the amount of morphia I left would prove fatal. You'll have an autopsy, I suppose, and that should set us right on that point."

"Of course, of course. Well, go on!"

"Ulder was alone here all night and we have no knowledge of course when he took the whisky or the morphia. I think we'll find when you've examined that glass that the morphia was dissolved in the drink—hot toddy, I imagine. Alcohol would of course retard the action of the morphia. I'd say myself that death only occurred two hours ago at most—say, about eight this morning."

"Well, let's see this phial-container! Take care of finger prints, sir! Use a handkerchief!" So the Chief Constable's thoughts were already turning seriously to murder, thought Dick, as he stretched for the phial on its shelf. "Hullo! Why are you looking at it like that? What's wrong with it?"

"It's an odd container," said Dick, looking apologetically at the doctor. He had no wish to expose the kind little man's haphazard ways and short sight, but the discovery he made as he stared at the little bottle in his hand was too arresting for him to conceal his feelings. "You remember, sir," he said to Dr. Lee, "you spoke to us of a patent kind, tried out for and discarded by the R.A.M.C., and distributed to chemists and doctors gratis? And that this was one of them and had therefore a cap at each end?"

"Cap to open at each end? What was the idea?" asked Mack.

"I fancy it was to make it easy for a severely wounded soldier to get at his morphia issue. They were made with that object, I believe," said Dr. Lee, looking extremely uncomfortable. "Well, what's your discovery, Dick?"

"Why, just this!" Dick held out the tube exposing five round little pellets of morphia ringed on a bed of cotton wool. "Here's the dose you left intact at this end. It was the other end which was empty!"

"Then Ulder never touched the stuff I gave him," cried Dr. Lee, sitting down heavily at the dressing-table. "Well, I'm—yes, I'm—I don't know what. All along I wondered how so little had finished him off, but now I understand. But how did he get hold of the morphia which did finish him?"

"I suppose he may have got hold of some before." Mack made the suggestion but already his mind was clearly turning to very different hypotheses.

"If he did, sir, how did he dispose of it?" asked Dick. "We hunted the room pretty thoroughly, because Dr. Lee thought he must have got hold of an additional dose, as well as these pellets, to cause such symptoms."

"You shouldn't have done that. Oh, don't apologize, and stop groaning and cursing yourself for your carelessness. We're getting into deep waters, very deep waters indeed. If Ulder didn't take it himself someone brought morphia into this room and administered it."

"Unless he had some of his own," Dick reverted hopelessly to his one hope. "His doctor might have given him some for his voyage."

"Voyage? What voyage?"

"He was going off to America to begin a new life, he said himself," said Dick reluctantly.

"How could he go to America when everyone knows he's been in a sea of debt since he left your precious College? And if he was set on a new life why end up instead?" Mack walked across to the bed, drew back the sheet and stared at the bland wax mask before him. "And now," thought Dick, "the game's up all right!" for Mack straightened himself up with the crumpled piece of paper and its incriminating list in his hand.

"'Bishop £2,000—Chancellor £2,000—Judith £5,000— Wye £2,000—Staples £50.' What on earth is all this? 'Bishop £2,000!'" He moved to the window and stared at the paper, his eyes alight with curiosity and excitement. "You saw this, Marlin. I'm damned if it can mean anything but—"

"Yes, it's blackmail all right, sir," said Dick steadily for the second time that hour.

"What do you know about it? Out with it."

"All I know has been told in confidence. You'll hear from— from the people mentioned. I can't say more."

"Don't think you can cover this up," said Mack fiercely, yet almost exultantly.

"I don't! Remember, sir, I'd every opportunity to destroy that paper."

"I wonder you didn't—to save your Church scandal again. Scandal indeed! I'd like to know where all this will lead! A search in all the rooms for morphia to begin with!"

Dick shrugged his shoulders. No need of admitting the temptation! He could only hope it would percolate to Mack's mind that clergy as a class were law-abiding and honest. He had no wish to break the silence which brooded over this room where, in the presence of Ulder's lifeless body, the very essence of evil and its awful consequences in other lives seemed to live after him.

"What's that?" Mack broke that long pause to swing round as a clear voice reached them.

"Well, my poor Moira, good-bye for a few minutes."

"Mrs. Mortimer with the invalid next door," volunteered Dr. Lee.

"Can every word be heard from one room to the other? It's a partition wall I see? Could this old woman have heard what went on in here last night?"

"I doubt it! Listen! Mrs. Mortimer's at the door, close to this wall, you see. Moira's bed is on the far side."

"And the door's open," said Dick as Sue's voice reached them now. It had not the timbre of Judith's, but her words were clear:

"Does Moira know you're here then, Judith? Mother sent up to say you'd better come away. She, poor dear, doesn't know if you are with her or not."

"She doesn't! She hasn't moved! I was coming away anyhow." As the two girls walked away down the passage Mack roused himself.

"We must keep this paper and lock up the room and leave it as it is. You spoke of sending the body in by the ambulance? Must go to the mortuary, of course, and we must arrange with Jones for an autopsy as soon as possible. And then, before suspicion is aroused, we must search every room in this warren for morphia of any kind."

"I suppose any sleeping preparation may contain some, doctor? We should collect all we can find?"

"Well, hardly!" The doctor shook his head. "None of the barbituric groups nor even luminol would produce the same symptoms. In ordinary life I'd say any usual sleeping tablets could be exempted, but this war has made a difference. All sorts of dope has been put privately on the market, not a doubt of it. Those mercy tablets they gave the troops have been on a sort of secret market, I've been informed, and used for patent preparations. I doubt their sale in a place like this, but in London you can get any drug you want if you know how to go about it. Look at the cocaine rings, for example. I should say you should get any sleeping draught you come across analysed, unless indeed, you find any container of morphia itself. But have you the right to search private rooms straight away, sir, before the case has even begun, as you might say? If this bag turns up we may find that Ulder had some himself all along."

"And put an end to his own life just when he'd got his hands on over ten thousand?"

"All his victims may have refused. He may have seen no future," suggested Dick.

"They may, but I doubt it," said Mack fiercely. "We've seen already what the Church will do to save scandal. Now time's passing. Look after the things in here, doctor. Now, sir," he turned upon Dick, "you've got to help me. I can trust you, since you were honest enough to leave this bit of evidence about," he waved Ulder's note. "Must have been a horrid temptation to destroy it! You get hold of the big wigs and say I must interview them in turn, the Bishop first. Meanwhile I'm locking all the doors on this floor. When's the next prayer meeting?"

"Chapel at eleven, sir!" Dick could not help a smile and Mack clapped his back.

"You're too good for this show, Dick. Yes, I shall call you that, for that grin of yours reminded me of that day on Echinore. When they're all shut up, Tonks and Corn must comb out every room. We must get on the track of this bag too. There must be important evidence against Ulder's victims in it, he wouldn't come without bringing evidence to support him. What rooms are on this floor in that new wing?"

"The pantry is below, sir, and I wanted to speak to you about the butler, Soames. I think he's worth attention. Only been here a few months, and I could swear he's seen the inside of a cell in his time. Says he was invalided out of the R.A.S.C. with shell shock at Rennes. I'm prepared to swear no German aeroplanes ever reached it, and I should fancy he was dismissed the Service for quite other reasons."

"That's all very well," said Mack impatiently. "I expect he is a bad egg, most butlers are nowadays." (Mack detested men-servants on principle.) "But have a little sense! What conceivable motive could such a fellow have? We'll make enquiries about him of course, but it's a weary business getting through to the Yard from this dog hole. Did any of your corps go into the C.I.D.?"

"One great friend of mine, Herriot. He's a detective inspector now, I fancy."

"Well, look here, you get on to him, and tell him to get a line on your friend's army record and doings since. Ten to one he's taken another name by now, but, of course, all you clever young men think nothing of needle-spotting in haystacks. But I can see well enough you're only starting this hare to take me off the scent for bigger game, but you won't. I've my duty to do, however strange the consequences. Any reason for suspicion?"

"I can't see how any one else would have stolen a bag. It seems so stupid. Of course it probably contained incriminating papers but why didn't—well, any possible sufferer from Ulder's activities—just abstract the papers and leave the rest? Soames equivocated about the luggage he brought up, that was clear, and he's the look of a sneak-thief. Not of a murderer, I admit. I don't really suspect him but I feel he comes in the puzzle somewhere."

"Well, it's murder we're investigating, not bag-snatching. What's this fellow on the list for a mere £50—Staples is it? Oh well, no one is going to bump a man off for £50."

"Fifty down, you see," Dick pointed out. "Staples is an Ordination candidate, was under Ulder, like me, five years ago, left when war broke out."

"What was he in?"

"Well, he was a conchie and was, I fancy, in jug for a bit and then took up some sort of essential work. I've hardly seen him yet but he's a very good chap, I'm sure. I can't imagine what Ulder had against him but I've no doubt £50 would mean as much to him as £2,000 to the others and Ulder may have planned some small regular contribution for him. But though he's a bit excitable and half Irish, I believe, I can't imagine—"

Dick's voice died away. Before all the suspects so obviously in Mack's mind, his imagination was even more powerless.

"Well, Tonks shall start off with his room and your pan tries, and, yes, Mrs. Mortimer's room, and Corn shall see what gossip he can get from the servants and make a list of them and find their references. Ask the Yard's help, do you suggest?"

"No, certainly not, not at present. I'm hoping to get a man from Blacksea to work in our Evelake office so that I can keep the men on the job here. But it's such a confounded haystack of a house to search in, and for a tube about the size of a needle too."

"What about old Moira's medicine chest? She has probably more dangerous drugs in her cubby holes than any one else."

"The old housekeeper? That's true. I must put them on to her room at once."

"You can't possibly search it till the ambulance takes her away for her operation!"

"I suppose not," admitted Mack unwillingly. "Well, I'll tell them to do it thoroughly the minute she's taken away, and keep a look out on people passing in and out. They'll spot it at hospital if she arrives with her own drugs, and I'll tell them to let me know. But if any one managed to get anything out of her room last night they couldn't get it back this morning for she's not allowed to see any one, you say. Now I suppose I must get down to interviews. I want you to come and take notes for me, Dick. (Can't keep to Marling with every one here Dicking away!)"

"But look here, sir, I'm here as an Ordinand, not as a sleuth. And surely it's most unusual to take notes at a preliminary interview? You can't give the Bishop and the rest a preliminary warning, and a chance to send for their lawyer, before you've seen them, and got your own impressions and their version of last night quietly."

"Now, my dear fellow," said Mack almost persuasively, "there's one thing you've got to get into your head at once, and that is that murder has been done in this house and that everyone is suspect, everyone, however many mitres and cassocks he wears. But, of course, I don't want to antagonize any one. That's why I want you to come and take notes quietly and unofficially. I'll explain it's pure routine, just a matter of getting things clear in my own mind."

Dick gave a reluctant consent. Better he should jot down remarks quietly than that Tonks should sit staring at the Bishop and licking his pencil. But another protest he must make.

"You talk of searching rooms, sir? But surely you can't do that without a warrant? Except, I imagine, Moira's, when she has been removed. That would be permissible, but as for the rest—"

"The police must use their discretion in cases of murder," said Mack sourly. "How can I get a search warrant from the nearest magistrate ten miles away? I'm going to call it a search for the missing bag and papers and tell Tonks and Corn to keep their eyes skinned for poison while they're on it. I'll ask leave, you know, and if they refuse one can always put on a bit of pressure—let them see that implies they've something to conceal. I'm going to have a look round that Mrs. Fly-by-night Mortimer's—Judith, as they call her—for myself. She's the criminal type, you know, low wide forehead and lobeless ears! I can't help wondering if there might be collusion between father and daughter—"

"What about Staples, sir?" asked Dick impatiently. How had this impulsive, prejudiced old fellow ever risen one step in the police force?

"The fifty-pound entry? Not enough motive. I'll tell them to search his room, and you have a preliminary talk to him. I haven't time for everything. Now, come on, Dick, to the Bishop's room! And remember I want you to study every one's reactions very closely. So far, you see, it's only supposed to be a case of suicide. Now they're going to hear the truth, so keep your eyes open!"

VI
THURSDAY MORNING (12-1)

APPARENTLY MACK was justified in his belief that the clergy were too ignorant to object to notes being taken of their statements at this stage. The Bishop obviously welcomed Dick as a friend and ally against this stout, fiery opponent of the Anglican

Church, and Dick settled himself miserably in a corner of the big room, with pen and note book five minutes later. If the portraits of the preceding bishops, if the very calf-bound volumes on the long rows of shelves which lined one side of the room had eyes and ears, what would they think of the plight of their successor? The Chief Constable sat forward uncomfortably in a high armed chair by the fire: the Bishop had swung round from the swivel chair to face Mack, his back to the light, a pale, bent, yet courtly St. Joseph. Some predecessor in the See had employed a local artist to make imaginary portraits of the holders of the diocese, and opposite Dick's seat hung a forbidding representation of that Bishop Odo of Evelake who in the year 1210 was brought to justice for the murder of the. Dean on the altar steps of the Cathedral. He had got off indeed by his violent championship of King John against the Pope—but here and now!—Dick pulled himself together. He had been taking down mechanically the answers to Mack's enquiries about Ulder's arrival which could bring no new light to their problem. But now the Chief Constable was beginning to move more swiftly.

"I understand, my lord, that the deceased came here without an appointment, and indeed, in defiance of your wishes. Will you tell me what his object in seeking you was?"

"It was a most unpleasant one." The Bishop raised his arm to the desk and shaded his eyes. "Now that he has gone to his account, his sins, his crimes, had best be forgotten."

"That depends on the way he went to it," said Mack slowly and emphatically. "Bishop, you saw him twice at least, I understand, in his bedroom, during the course of the evening?"

"I paid him a visit as my guest, about nine-thirty," replied the Bishop. "I had occasion then to reprove him for the manner of his life, but as he was not readily impressed, and I laid full stress, I trust, on the infinite mercy of God, I cannot honestly blame myself for driving him to the dreadful step he took. Later on, about eleven o'clock, I looked in, but he was sleeping, as I thought, so I left him undisturbed."

"You noticed nothing unusual on that second occasion?"

"Why, no, but I did not turn on the light as I judged from his heavy breathing that he was asleep."

"And previously you had exhorted him to repentance? Was that the main purpose of your visit?"

"It was—to some extent." The Bishop moved uncomfortably.

"And had he come here merely to receive your exhortation?"

"There were other reasons, but as I said, he is dead and the memory can be buried with him."

"Not if we have reason to believe that his death took place in very curious circumstances! Bishop, I must ask you to be frank. What was that business?"

"Really—" the Bishop glanced despairingly at Dick but gained no reassurance there. For Dick seemed suddenly to see, as with some sixth sense, not what the Bishop did or said, as much as the impression made by his attitude on the Chief Constable. Up to that minute Dick had not even contemplated the possibility of the Bishop's guilt; he did not do so now, but an inner voice began to comment on every remark the Bishop made. "Really," the prelate began feebly, "it is no concern of yours now, Major Mack."

(*"He is fencing. Why doesn't he come into the open?"* Dick's voice suggested.)

"But you would agree it was my concern if we had some suspicion of foul play. I will be frank with you, sir. We have found one of Ulder's papers, which shows he was here for one purpose only, that of blackmail. We have on this paper the names of his victims, beginning with your own. Was he in possession of any other incriminating documents?"

"No, no!" For a moment Dick thought the Bishop would faint, for he sagged over so heavily in his chair. "I cannot understand all this. Pray make yourself clear."

(*But could anything be much clearer than those words Foul Play?*)

"Well, sir, I'll speak out. We doubt if Ulder committed suicide. We have reason to think he was murdered."

"But who—who?" gasped the Bishop. *(But surely how or why would be the obvious questions of any one to whom the pronouncement came as an overwhelming shock!)*

"That, Bishop, we don't know yet?" said Mack fiercely. "But we shall discover it, never fear!"

"But surely everything pointed to suicide?" Dick hardly listened while the Chief Constable tersely related the reasons for his suspicions. His eyes were fixed upon the Bishop's trembling hands. The fire flickered on the amethyst of the pastoral ring; the fingers and knuckles stretched tautly and nervously, livid in the uncanny snowlight from the window, as if they were striving to seize and manipulate the whole dreadful situation. If only the Bishop would show a little surprise or horror, thought Dick despairingly. Who can blame Mack if he thinks he is watching a criminal being unmasked?

"Then whom do you suspect?" asked the Bishop at length.

(But why should an innocent man stammer out these words? Why not protest, as Dick had, that such a crime was unthinkable as far as the house-party was concerned?)

"Someone in this house will be found to have morphia in his possession. Somewhere we shall find Mr. Ulder's missing bag and the incriminating papers," answered Mack weightily. "That person will obviously be open to the gravest suspicions."

"Someone—some enemy of Ulder's—might have got in last night?"

"I've considered that possibility, Bishop, but it's an untenable hypothesis. How was any enemy—and I admit he seems to have had enough of them—to know he was coming here last night? He only thought of staying at the last moment, I gather? His room was booked at his hotel and he only had his luggage with him because he never let it out of his sight, or so he told your butler, I believe? How was any one outside the Palace to know that he would be taken ill, and given enough morphia to make a second dose, even a small dose, fatal? Dr. Lee is of the opinion that it must have been administered not long before midnight. Up to that hour, as far as I can gather, the house party was crossing and recrossing the corridor outside his room and looking in for these most curious interviews. Mrs. Broome and the servants assure me that all doors were found locked and bolted on the inside as usual this morning. Could any one have climbed in at his window, having forced it open, by the way, in that snow-storm, and left no traces on the carpet or furniture? No, it was not an outside job. That's certain. And now, my lord, I think you see it is necessary I should ask you what hold Ulder had, or fancied he had, over you?" Dick put down his notebook and strolled away to the window, unreproved, as the Bishop stammered out his daughter's unedifying story. He had no wish to hear it again, or Mack's comments and questions. To Dick, Judith was just a freak in this setting, one of those exquisite will-o'-the-wisps, born without a soul to beckon men after them. One could only blame the irony of Fate that she had been born in this setting. At least she was showing some concern about her own fate, and that of her future child, and that was an advance in morality for her.

"And now I must go—I must go and pray in the Chapel!" The Bishop tottered from his seat like an old man.

"Well, not a word, please, about this conversation till I have seen your colleagues. Dick, help the Bishop!"

That apparent consideration was, of course, to see that the Bishop reached his canopied stall without speech to any one.

"Damn it, Dick!" Mack was pacing about the room on Dick's return. "I forgot to ask him about the papers you say Ulder must have brought with him. To get hold of them was motive enough! Go and get the Bishop back to tell me what they were."

"Is it necessary, sir? I saw them all last night. The Bishop, Canon and Chancellor took it into their heads to consult me— I'd been in the Ulder trouble before, you see."

"A Daniel come to judgment! Well, go ahead. I must tell my men at once what sort of papers to look for. Whoever finished Ulder off, took them, bag or no bag!"

"Ulder proposed to show the Bishop the signatures of Clive and Judith Mortimer, which he'd torn out of the Blacksea Grand Hotel book—a clean page as it happened. Also a signed statement from the chambermaid that one set of luggage had the initials C.F. and the other J.M. stamped on them. The woman also picked up a letter addressed to Colonel Fitzroy. She will recognize them anywhere on oath. And then there are letters dealing with the old affair showing how the Bishop condoned Ulder's faults to avoid scandal. Ulder had sworn to destroy them all."

"Couldn't show them anyhow or he'd have been prosecuted for theft and so on, surely?"

"No, that's why he waited till he was leaving this country, I imagine."

"And Canon Wye? Same sort of thing? I must tell the men."

"The same and—and a newspaper cutting. But he will tell you himself. Probably there will be smallish packets of letters in envelopes. And the Chancellor the same, but his might be larger. I can't tell you more, sir. I was told in confidence."

"Good enough," grunted Mack when he had sent the message.

There had been tragedy in the Bishop's departure, but there was none in the scene which now took place. Canon Wye answered the Chief Constable's summons at once, and he stormed up and down the room like a caged lion.

"I have nothing to tell you, sir. The man was a disgrace not only to the Church but to humanity itself. I can only wonder that man, let alone God, tolerated him on this earth so long. Why should I regret his killing himself? He should have been put down with poison like a rat long ago!"

"So that's your view!" sneered Mack. "The view of a preacher of the Gospel too! Well, well, it will be no surprise to you to hear the truth, and I think in view of it you'll see that your business with Ulder is my business too!"

What would Mack make of Canon Wye's demeanour, as Mack briefly recapitulated the conclusions of the police? To Dick it seemed as if Torquemada himself, tall and incredibly

thin in his black cassock, with fierce eyes and tight lips, were
listening to the account of a heretic's end with business like
satisfaction. He made no sound of pity or horror, and merely
stood staring from the window at the snow-covered lawns and
phantom arches of the old Abbot's gateway, when Mack ended
his tale. But when his interlocutor shot out the question:

"And now, Canon, you'll tell me perhaps of Ulder's business
with you?" Wye turned round in a fury.

"You'd have known it shortly in any case, I had determined
to take Marlin's advice and communicate with the police. I told
Ulder so last night. It was fantastic that he should consider he
had any hold over me at all!"

(Then did Canon Wye know that the papers were destroyed?
If not, how could he, thought Dick, expect the Chief Constable to believe this defiance? There had been no such desperate
challenge in the Canon's manner when he laid Ulder's letter to
him before Dick in this very room last night. Dick had a good
visual memory and once more the threats, in erratic type on
cheap note-paper, danced before his eyes. "Dear Canon Wye,"
so the letter had read roughly, he remembered, "you may be
surprised to hear from me but I am winding up my affairs here,
as I propose to pay a long visit to America. I can no longer
endure the sense of hostility and suspicion which pursued me
even after my triumphant vindication five years ago: this has, I
know, been rife in high quarters. And yet which of us has not
some secret failing which he trusts to time to conceal? Are you,
my dear Canon, blameless? It has come to my notice (after, I
admit, a little research on my part) that you were the anonymous author of a work which roused the righteous indignation
of the orthodox, ten years ago? I refer to *The Questioner*. I remember among the many hostile reviews one which stated that
the author, a heretic if not an agnostic, could never hope for
preferment in the Church. The Deanery of Starre is vacant and
I have heard your name mentioned—what a pity if your secret
became known and thus deprived you of promotion, and the
Church of an earnest believer in high places. May we meet to

discuss the whole question? I need but remind you of the proverb that 'silence is golden' and you will understand my point. Yours truly, Thomas Ulder." P.S. £2,000 is a good round sum.)

"And you discussed this with Ulder last night? You threatened to prosecute him for blackmail? Did you imagine when you heard of the suspicion of suicide that you had driven him to his death?"

"No! I was surprised that he had the courage to end himself. I gave him a week to leave the country before I made any move, and he had booked for his voyage."

"And he only threatened you with his old story of exposing the incompetence and cowardice of the clergy as I see it, as most laymen would see it? He had no personal hold over you?"

"To some small extent." (The Bishop's very words and almost as untrue, thought Dick—it was pretty ghastly to discover how truth was the first bit of Christian ballast to be thrown overboard in a crisis! And Canon Wye had not in his composition one streak of that moral cowardice which his old pupils had discerned unfailingly in the Bishop!)

"Well—" with a sudden glance at Dick the Canon realized that secrecy was impossible. (Or was it, hoped Dick, that he meant to speak out before he remembered that Dick of course knew of the letter.) "He had a hold over me I already admit. Fifteen years ago as a young priest I was assailed by doubts. I immersed myself in science and philosophy—those temptations of the devil to those who call themselves liberal and progressive, as I did then. I was foolish, nay wicked, enough to publish my speculations in a book entitled *The Questioner—Is There Any Answer?* I did not use my own name, and enjoined the strictest anonymity on my publishers, for well I knew it would lay me open to the charge of heresy."

Was it a slight shock to the Canon that Mack had never heard of the work which had fluttered Anglican dovecots so severely in Dick's youth? Probably now, in 1920, it would not cause such a stir: there were only too many others who had questioned the validity of the records of the Virgin Birth, the

Miracles and the Resurrection. But at the time it had been a major scandal in the Church and the origin of a lengthy controversy which led many, valued for their intellects and influence, into the Church of Rome. It was written with an acidity, a hostility towards revealed religion, and so deep a disbelief in the honesty of its conventional supporters that the very name of *Questioner* was anathema to those in authority. It would be hard for Mack to realize that the Canon's confession seemed far more shocking, even degrading to his audience last night, than any fault of Judith's.

"They are not my views now: they have not been so indeed ever since," continued the Canon. "I sought an interview with the Dean of St. Ruan after reading his criticism in the *Literary Supplement*, and he changed my whole outlook. He bade me start anew and hold my peace about the authorship of the book."

"To save scandal again?" suggested Mack acidly.

"I refused to allow any further editions or any sale to America: what money I had made I gave to charities. It was no small atonement for I have no means of my own."

"Hmhm!" The Scotsman was obviously impressed by such a financial sacrifice. "Well, sir, I really don't see why you had anything to fear from Ulder after such restitution. No bishop would unfrock you"—he glanced distastefully at Wye's cassock—"or sequestrate your living because of a youthful indiscretion if you can call it so. And—damn it all, a book is—well merely a book!"

The Canon had reached the fireplace in his fierce parade of the room, but he turned now and strode away to the big window at the other end. Across the long glimmering oak floor, against the white snow and black trees, he stood gazing out at the ruins for a long minute as if he too were a leafless tree in the snows of adversity.

"We call those ruined choirs peaceful," he broke out. "How many of those old Abbots burnt their hearts and faith out in scheming and struggling to gain their high post? By that sin fell the angels! It was not necessary to speak out my thoughts last night on this topic. What was it the Bishop said: 'Such a revelation might prejudice your chances of preferment, my dear Canon'. … Only later, most tactfully later, the Chancellor said that he had heard my name mentioned in connection with a vacant Deanery. You, Marling, said nothing, of course, but I saw you looking at me as a young man looks at his elders when they have made a mess of their lives, with pity, oh yes, but a touch of contempt too. At the time of my conversion, for only so can I describe the blinding light which struck me after my visit to the Dean, I asked no more than to serve as a humble priest in the Anglo-Catholic Church. And then preferment came, ambition awoke, and I knew myself 'the most offending soul alive'." (How these tags of Shakespeare haunted the poor fellow, thought Dick.) "It even led me to come to you with a lie on my lips—that I had, I mean, no personal animus against Ulder. Now you know the truth and I will leave you to draw what conclusions you will. All I have to tell you of last night is that I visited Ulder, that we had a stormy interview, and that I refused to consider his terms, partly because I could not raise such a sum, partly because I had no reason to believe he would keep his word or leave off his activities from America—why should he?—and partly because my conscience forbade it. I told him I would give him a week to get away, and after that prosecute for blackmail. I left the room knowing that he could ruin me, and hoping that he would never recover from his illness. That was at about half-past ten or a little later. And now I will leave you!"

"One moment, sir! Have you any drugs with you, sleeping draught or so on?"

"Neither I nor the curates in my clergy house touch them!" snapped the Canon as he strode away.

"Another case of going to pray in Chapel, I fancy," said Mack dryly, ringing the bell. "That fellow wouldn't stick at a murder if he had convinced himself he was doing God service! Jael and the butter knife, you know," he added vaguely, as Soames appeared, and was sent off to fetch the Chancellor. "So that little rabbit of a butler is your fancy, Dick? I can't see him in the role, though of course poisoners are a class of their own. But why pick on him without any conceivable reason for the crime? For I can't call a bag of night kit a reason for murder, and he couldn't have been wise to the fact that at least five other people here wanted Ulder out of the way. But you go off and make contacts with your C.I.D. friend—do them no harm to have a spot of work at the Yard. And say your prayers if you must! They need them here! Better not take notes for the Chancellor in this interview anyway."

"What shall I say if Herriot asks if you need their help, sir, as you're so short-handed?"

"Tell 'em nothing," said Mack testily, as the Chancellor entered the room.

"Well, sir!" Mack's voice showed his relief at a change from cassocks and clerics. Though he would hardly have admitted it, he felt it most improbable that a layman and a lawyer could be guilty of so sordid a crime as this murder. He watched the Chancellor closely, indeed, as he broke to the newcomer the result of his investigations and the suspicion of murder, and murder by someone in the Palace. The Chancellor exhibited, it seemed to him, just the amount of surprise, shock and bewilderment which he would expect from a wholly innocent man. Of course, Mack reminded himself conscientiously, no crime, not even murder, could seem as appalling and bewildering to a lawyer as to one of these parsons who had, he considered, been wrapped in cotton-wool all their lives. But Mack all the same began to feel a certain resentment as the Chancellor, his legal rubicund mask unperturbed, rapped out a series of questions to him, instead of answering meekly, extracting a far clearer *aperçu* of the affair than from the tortured clerics. Was he not a little too much master of himself and the situation? Was he not too clearly proving his own case and his own alibi? Better turn on him with a few questions, and see how he liked them for a change!

"Now, sir, I'd like your help in clearing up some points. When did you last visit Mr. Ulder last night?"

"About nine-thirty when the others were all in Chapel. May I say that if you are attempting to throw suspicions on me"—the Chancellor's cheeks grew purple and he pulled out those neat whiskers—"I should like to summon my solicitor here at once."

"Well, you can, of course, but I'm not asking for anything but a story from you as a witness so far. If you won't answer me I can only suppose you have your own reasons for sup pressing evidence." (Mack hurried on quickly feeling that this old gag would hardly impress a lawyer.) "We know that Mr. Ulder was attempting to blackmail you."

"Oh, you do, do you? Did the Bishop tell you?"The Chancellor rose and paced up and down in anger.

"No, sir. A paper was found."

"Papers?" (Was there a note of surprise in the angry voice? Had the Chancellor reason to believe he had himself disposed of all the available evidence?) Mack reserved his opinion, for the Chancellor now plunged abruptly into his story:

"Yes, he had a hold over me and I'll tell you about it. Five years ago when we patched up that affair at the Theo logical College, I sat down and wrote the whole story, and my whole opinion about it, in the most open terms, to a friend in the office of the Ecclesiastical Commissioners. I thought it only right that the facts should be on record. I wrote it by hand in my own office, and put it away in a pigeon-hole to think it over, in an envelope labelled 'Thomas Ulder'. Oh, I know it wasn't business-like, but I was short handed in the war, overworked and hard driven. I wasn't sure of a few points so I determined to go up and make enquiries for myself. No doubt the news of that got about, and Ulder followed me, making enquiries on his own. He had a ferret's power for nosing things out if they concerned himself. Anyhow, the long and short of it was that when I got back the first news my new girl clerk gave me was that a clergyman had called, asking if there was any letter for him, and he had pressed her so warmly that she had looked everywhere for him, and she was so sorry but she hadn't been able to come across anything, though she had hunted through ever so many files in the outer office. Need I tell you that she had left him comfortably seated by my own desk, and that when I looked in it my letter had disappeared."

"But that's five years ago!"

"Just so, so I supposed my idiot clerk had made some mistake or I'd destroyed the letter in a hurry. I worried over it seriously for a time, and then concluded it was all my mistake. But I can tell you I never wrote another version of the affair after the fright I had! For you see there was the whole case against him in black—and no white at all—and the reasons we'd had for suppressing the affair."

"But what were those reasons? All the rest was common gossip when I came here, but I never did understand why you didn't prosecute him, and never shall—drunkenness—immorality—theft too, I suppose?"

"That last was the trouble. He was treasurer of three or four wealthy societies, and he had been quietly abstracting funds for years. And the boards to whom he was responsible were so unbusiness-like, and so easily gulled, that they had never found out—old colonels, maiden ladies and such-like who trusted him and couldn't add two and two, and the old Bishop and some of the Cathedral people who never had time to attend meetings or look into things. It was that young Marling who got on the track of it, when Ulder was rash enough to ask him to make up some accounts for him at the Theological College. I suppose by that time Ulder had got to believe he could fool all the people all the time. Well, I said at first, 'Prosecute and be damned', and then I saw what it would mean. Dirty scandal, and a terrible financial loss to the funds concerned, for who would subscribe to them in the future? So we patched things up, got up a subscription fund for the societies between us, and made Ulder put in a fair sum too, by Jove, to escape prison. Then we turned him out of the College and left him in his living, of which he had the advowson."

"That was abominable! Couldn't happen in Scotland!"

"Yes and no. It's one of those parishes where dissent has so strong a hold, and Ulder had been so hated, that there was no congregation left. A scheme was already on foot for amalgamating it with the next parish, Orley, and then came the war and no more was said about it. I fancy our Father in God here was thankful not to come up against Ulder over it, as we certainly should have. Well, pressure has been brought on the Bishop by the Chapter, who incidentally bought the advowson from Ulder at a price, and the Bishop has had to make a move to revise the scheme. That, I imagine, is why Ulder was on the war-path. For years he has evidently been poking out and amassing evidence against every one of us who, like myself and the Canon, had a chink in our armour. No doubt he collected every bit of scandal he could about the fair Judith and her folly, and this has brought things to a head. If he can quash her divorce and she can't marry her present lover, she'll be left with a child by him on her father's hands. Oh yes, it's as serious as that! Did the Bishop not make it clear? I should not have mentioned it had I known. Dear, dear, I'm very fond of the Rt. Rev. Mark, but moral courage is not his strong suit!"

"I can see that the Bishop and his daughter have every reason to be relieved that Ulder has gone out of their lives." Mack spoke mildly in the effort to lay a trap. "But I cannot really see what harm he could do you after all these years."

"His idea was to publish my letter in a penny rag as soon as he left the country," said the Chancellor, his face lined and sagging again. "No names, but the circumstances clear as daylight. Can you imagine how I'd stand in my profession after my letter was printed, admitting my collusion in a case of this sort—condoning misappropriation of funds, publicly exonerating the man while privately I was exposing him to my intimates? Let alone my accursed carelessness in my correspondence. And I've a son coming home from India to go into partnership with me!"

"So you were going to pay up?"

"I hadn't decided. I told Ulder I must think things over. It wasn't only my concern, you see. I told him I must get expert legal advice before I reached any conclusion, and he told me he had no time to spare, and the letter to the Press would go in a week, unless I produced securities. I never slept a wink trying to decide, I can tell you, and I was no nearer a decision this morning."

"Didn't you take some sleeping draught to get you through the night?"

"Why the devil shouldn't I?" The Chancellor was just indignantly evading the question when Mack put another.

"And you did not get your letter out of Ulder by persuasion or perhaps by force last night?"

"I did not, though I was tempted to. He only let me have a glimpse of it and then covered it up under the bedclothes. He was a sick man. What could I do?"

"Did you notice where he kept his papers?"

"A bag of some sort, I imagine. I didn't notice. Look here, sir"—the Chancellor grew very red and indignant—"I think I've given you all the assistance I can. If you want any more answers I insist on asking my partner to come here, and act on behalf of every one whom you choose to suspect."

"I'd be sorry to seem to go beyond my powers," said Mack pacifically. It was safe, he considered, to lay before the Chancellor the whole question of the missing papers and the possibility of a missing bag. For by general agreement the Chancellor had been the first to pay his visit, and certainly the papers relating to the other victims must have been still in Ulder's possession when the Chancellor left. "I've told my men to look round everywhere for the bag and the papers at once, so perhaps you wouldn't mind giving us a hand," he ended up.

"A search? Have you a search warrant?" said the Chancellor, as Dick had foretold.

"No, but I've told my man to send for one. The Bishop and Canon made no objections to a search. Come, sir, surely we can count on your co-operation!"

But that was the last thing he could count on, decided Mack, as the Chancellor grunted non-committally and made for the door. The house was resounding now with the noises which Mack was soon to recognize as the end of a service in Chapel, the creaking of swing-doors, the hushed reverent voices of the ordinands rising to a cheerful hubbub, followed by another hush as their ecclesiastical superiors passed through them to the library or the Bishop's room. Well, if Mack was sure of anything, it was that the suggestion of murder would soon go round, so he had better hurry upstairs to catch this—was she Mrs. Mortimer or Mrs. Fitzroy or Miss Broome?—he hardly knew—this Judith was good enough—and see if Tonks had come across anything suspicious in his cursory view of the bedrooms in the old wing.

"Come in, Mabel! You'd better finish up quickly!" Mack steered his way by Judith's voice. "Just those frocks, and be careful of that Reville velvet, and leave out the red hat and mink coat. I must go and explain to Mrs. Broome that I simply must get out of this mausoleum as soon as they've taken poor Moira away. Oh!" she swung round as Mack drew attention to his presence by a portentous cough.

"I thought you were the housemaid! What on earth are you doing here? Most compromising! I think I'd better call my friend Tonks!"

"You can unpack those bags!" Mack, justly ignoring such unworthy suspicions, pointed at the expensive suitcase and gold-fitted dressing-case. "No one can leave this house without my permission."

"I shan't unpack, because I never do that for myself," replied Judith composedly. "And why mayn't I go?"

"Because," said Mack with calculated shock tactics, "Madam, a murder has been committed in this house, and I have to question every one who was in any way connected with the victim, Mr. Ulder!"

"He was no connection of mine, and I'm not surprised to hear he was murdered." If Mack had hoped for a womanly collapse, for tears and hysterical admissions, he was bitterly disappointed. Either Judith had got the truth out of her father or Dick, or else she had the best of reasons for knowing the truth already, decided Mack, for she neither changed colour nor looked at herself with one shade less interest in the glass, as she fastened on her little scarlet hat. "I thought he was supposed to have over-dosed himself, but I suppose you big police hats like to have a good run for your money? What happened?"

"He died of morphia-poisoning—a fatal dose was administered to him late last night, and you were one of his last visitors, Mrs. Fitzroy."

"*Not* Mrs. Fitzroy yet, I'm sorry to say, though of course"— she brightened—"everything is all right now, and I'll be able to ask you to my wedding in a month or two! Better call me Judith like every one else, for I do feel a little anonymous. Who gave him the morphia?"

"We are searching the house for any trace of the poison." Mack glared angrily into the big eyes gazing with such assumed innocence into his. "And I myself would like to see the contents of these boxes."

"Why, of course!" Judith seemed, he thought, to recoil momentarily at a sudden thought, but she recovered herself quickly. "May I just run and tell Mummy I'm not going after all—see my hands are quite empty, and there's my bag! I'll be back in one sec! Mabel! Mabel!" She ran out into the passage. "Come back and help me like a lamb! The police are going to search all my things—isn't it dread? And you must show him where I put all my poisons! Mummy!" Her pretty voice resounded from Mrs. Broome's boudoir opposite. "I'm not going after all! The big god policeman says I mustn't—do you think he's taken a fancy to me, for I'm sure I could fall for him in quite a big way! May I take one of Daddy's big silk hankies, darling?" The voice sounded a little more remote now. "Because I must have something to cry into when he arrests me, mustn't I? Don't come! I know just where they are! I'd hate you to move from that sofa after the morning you've had. You didn't poison Ulder by any chance, did you? No, not quite Girls' Friendly tactics! And of course, Sue darling, no one would ever suspect you, as you're a blonde, let alone that you were about the only person who didn't drop in on Ulder for a quiet cup of poison last night! Well, good-bye! I'll see you both on the steps of the gallows, I expect!"

"I never can make up my mind," said Mrs. Broome desperately from the sofa, where she lay, supposed to be resting, trying to address envelopes, and doing nothing but weep softly, "whether darling Judith is mad or bad or both."

"Neither, darling, I expect!" It was best to leave it at that, thought wise little Sue, and confine herself to soothing pats and chat and suggestions of hot milk. By all the symptoms of nursery days she recognized that Judith was immersed in some plot—on the track of some great idea. And whether beautiful erratic Judith's plots and ideas would be effective in a case like this, Sue could not tell. Only one thing was certain, that the more ghastly any situation might be, the gayer and more flippant would her stepsister become. She could only hope that Dick, this new, old, already dear friend, would not misjudge her. And that he would deliver them from this appalling sense of mystery and fear which hung over the house like the snow drifting in at every open window, and the echoing tread of strange men on the old varnished, uneven floors of the Palace.

VII
THURSDAY—LUNCHEON

THERE IS A dreadful moment in bad dreams when we half wake, trying in vain to speak, and fall back invariably into a worse nightmare. That was the sensation of most of the house party during luncheon on that ill-fated Thursday at Evelake Palace.

The prelude introduced the theme crudely enough. The party were assembled in the old library, the gong had sounded, and Mrs. Broome was about to lead the way in, when the noise of the loud crunching wheels of two heavy vehicles was heard in the drive. No one spoke the word "ambulance", but Mrs. Broome disappeared, shutting the door behind her, as if locking the party in till her return. After a pause men's steps were heard on the staircase, and, after a long interval, they returned, uneven under a heavy load, and the door of the hearse was slammed. Then the feet of the ambulance men who were to take Moira away sounded on the stairs. The Chancellor attempted a remark to the Bishop, to find the prelate's eyes shut, his lips moving in prayer. Bobs, on his own responsibility, stepped forward, as he heard the great hall door close, and hustled the guests into the dining-room. Any occupation, if it were only with knives and forks, was better than that listening in silence. There was at least some noise in this room, for Soames, sallower and more shaky than ever, seemed to knock over every plate and glass he touched. Twice he disappeared while Doris, with haughty disapproval, carried on her work unmoved. Some of those present would never, thought Dick, smell the odour of boiled cod or taste the tang of cloves in steamed apple pudding, without living through that meal again.

Bobs, having bolted his fish and got back some energy with a good draught of bitter, seized on the *Pilgrim's Progress* by his place, opened it haphazard, and began to read. He was not lucky with his *sortes virgilianae*, noted Dick, for though the passage was appropriate it was hardly inspiriting for the suspects at the moment. *"Now there was not far from the place where they lay a castle called Doubting Castle, the owner whereof was Giant Despair."*

The steps echoed on the stairs again: Bobs' voice grew purely mechanical. The doors of the ambulance banged for the last time; the two vehicles were started up, the wheels crunching on the avenue. The dead man and the dying old woman had set off at last on what was certainly the last drive of the one, and almost certainly of the other.

"Yes, Major Mack! You must come in to lunch." Mrs. Broome opened the dining-room door and beckoned to a figure in the hall. "You'd prefer it elsewhere? Really I am very sorry but the house is so upset to-day that it would be most kind if you would not insist on a separate meal. And such a pleasure to have you," she added, with the ghost of her usual hospitality. "Your men are dining in the servants' hall."

Every one knew that, for sounds of merriment, most alien to the dining-room party, had reached them now and again when the service door was opened. "A man do help to make a meal go," Cook had pronounced graciously, but it seemed hardly likely that Mack's presence would add to the gaiety of the dining-room. With a scowl he sat down between two candidates of obvious innocence, and bent disgustedly over his plate.

"Then with a grim and surly voice" read Bobs, *"the giant bid them awake and asked them whence they were and what they did in his grounds. They told him that they were pilgrims and had lost their way."*

"Darling? is that you!" Judith's clear voice rang out from the telephone in the hall. "Listen, it's no use coming for me to-day as we arranged when you rang up after breakfast. The most weird, appalling things are happening here. That wretched parson didn't do himself in, but got himself murdered!—Yes—M for mother—U for Ulder—yes, murdered. And we're all suspected, every one of us, and none of us may leave the house. No, no, darling, of course I didn't do it! I might have if it had occurred to me, of course, because there's no doubt it's all a happy release for us, isn't it? … What? … What? … A lawyer? … Oh yes, dear old Chancellor Chailly is here, and you've only to look at his darling side-whiskers to know that you're legally represented all right—except of course that he may possibly be the murderer."

"The Giant therefore"—Bobs raised his voice—*"drove them before him and put them into a dark dungeon, very nasty and stinking to the spirits of those two men,"* but every one's ears were strained for another voice outside. Who would not prefer Judith to Bunyan?

"Yes, Father, the Canon and parsons and all are suspected! But perhaps I'd better not tell you all about it here. Yes, you come out and see me this afternoon if you can in the snow … no, perhaps better not, as poor Papa doesn't approve of us, does he, and he's so much to fuss him! Better wait till to-morrow, and ring me up again to-night. … Oh, I'm bearing up! It's all rather shattering in a way, but it's dreadfully funny too. I've had my boxes searched—oh, only because I was running away to you! … Oh yes, the Chancellor is going to raise Cain about it, for he says the police had no right to without asking my leave, and Mack never did—just rushed at my pretties! But you see this policeman is a big noise, the Chief Constable, so I didn't know I could say: 'Villain, I defy thee!' And I had the loveliest fun. I put him through it all right. I shook out all my frocks and explained to him about the cut and style, and what I'd paid for them! … I thought he'd have a fit. Mrs. Mack favours five-guinea reach-me-downs, I gather! And my frilly things and pretties! I didn't spare him one, and how he goggled!

… Oh dear, here's Mums come to stop me, because she says they can hear every word in the dining-room, and Mack's choking over his fish-bones. I thought he'd quite pass out when he saw those black chiffon pyjamas … all right, Mummy, I'm coming. Good-bye, sweet, and be good, and don't you go murdering anybody! … Hullo, Tonks! What's up with you? You look as if you'd swallowed a mouthful! Have you found another corpse?"

With that Judith flashed into the dining-room, cast her lovely smile on the company, made a face at the pudding, and declined fish. It was left to Bobs to read on while the company watched Mack leave the room to interview Tonks, and return to summon the Chancellor away with him, with a wholly ominous expression. *"Moreover, my brother, thou talkest of ease in the grave, but hast thou forgotten the Hell whither murderers go,"* concluded Bobs, as the dreadful meal ended at last.

There was a break after lunch during which the candidates were at leisure to exercise themselves, or relax in the comfortable sitting-room set apart for their use in the new wing. The Chaplain's room was by convention barred to them, save by special appointment, but to-day they could hardly be blamed for drifting in, one by one, to ask what was up. Their curiosity had of course been partly gratified by the talk of the staff, by questions from the police, by Judith's artless prattle, and by prayers for the soul of Thomas Ulder in Chapel. But when one, Jim Wright, of that curious type who always is on the spot in every accident or row, appeared to ask what Mack was doing in the Chancellor's bedroom having a first-class row, Bobs had no answer. His one desire was to get hold of Dick and hear all his news, but Dick had been summoned upstairs to two very angry combatants.

There could be no doubt that the police had gone beyond their province. It was true that a general consent had been given to a search for Ulder's missing bag and papers. It might be reasonable that, as the Magistrate lived ten miles away across country on roads made inaccessible by the snow, Mack was justified in making preliminary investigations. But the fact remained that he had, at the moment, no legal warrant, and that he had forgotten to ask leave before he set himself to search Judith's room. Still less had he for the further step which his men had taken. Tonks and Corn had been bidden to make a more thorough investigation upstairs, directly after the servants' hall dinner, while the house party were still at luncheon. It was over the result of these operations that Mack and Chancellor Chailly stood facing each other now like angry bulls, while Dick stood miserably regarding the curtains of the fourpost bed and the tapestry hanging on the wall of the low Jacobean room: these had been acquired by Mrs. Broome at Jumieges, they were probably fakes, but they only too suggestively represented the murder of Holophernes.

"My rights and wrongs won't come into question, sir, when this is exhibited in Court!" Mack held up a bottle triumphantly as he spoke.

The Chancellor was evidently taken at a disadvantage. As he began to splutter out his declaration that every gentleman had a right to take his own sleeping draughts, without reference to the police, and that if the small bottle, labelled with his own name, were empty it was merely because he had finished it the previous night, Mack's interruption reduced him to incoherence.

"Sergeant Tonks, in the presence of Constable Corn, found this bottle on the top of that high tallboy, hidden well out of sight, bearing your name on the label. Are gentlemen in the habit of keeping their medicine bottles in such concealment? Are they in the habit of arriving on visits with practically empty medicine bottles? Have you any statement to make about this discovery, sir, or will you insist on the presence of a solicitor? For I need not warn you that—"

"I expect Chancellor Chailly would have no objections to telling us the nature of the medicine!" Dick felt obliged to interpose—thankless as the task would be. "Surely it is very unusual for an ordinary sleeping draught to contain morphia at all? I am sure the Chancellor will let us see the prescription."

"Well, I won't," stormed the Chancellor, adding in a slightly changed voice, "because I can't! Why should I? This fellow has no more right—"

"You see, sir," broke in Dick pacifically, "this is a liquid, and the glass in Ulder's room which has gone for analysis certainly contained a sediment."

"So does this!" said Mack triumphantly, holding the bottle up to the light. "As Mr. Chailly won't help us"—he sniffed at the bottle—"we must judge for ourselves. What do you make that smell, Dick?"

"Liquorice," began Dick feebly, as the Chancellor broke into a new storm of rage. "Excuse me, sir, but surely it would be simpler to give Major Mack the prescription and explain—"

He broke off as he saw Tonks staring with meaning at the top of the tallboy. That absurd attempt at concealment hardly suggested a simple explanation.

It was not really unnatural that the old gentleman was unwilling to tell the story of his folly when at last he had calmed down enough to see that it was inevitable. It involved, indeed, so eccentric a course of action, and the truth of his tale would be very hard to prove.

"It was after my poor wife went—I couldn't sleep, and my boy was home on leave from India. He'd got hold of this stuff from a native doctor, rather a quack, I fancy. Couldn't get it made up here, because there was—well, opium in it for one thing, and our doctor wouldn't look at it. Lyall, my boy, had got a good big jorum left, and he bottled some up for me when I'd promised him only to use it in emergencies. I hadn't touched it for months, but Christmas is a trying time when you're old and alone, so I put a little into this bottle—it had cough mixture once, I fancy, and that's what the smell comes from! Packed it myself in a hurry, and the whole thing spilt!"

"Well, Soames would remember that, and might even trace the damp paper," suggested Dick to cover Mack's snort of incredulity.

"I didn't like the look of the butler and didn't let him touch my things," said the Chancellor, looking at his green baize brief bag despairingly. "I threw the damp paper in the fire myself."

"But you've got the original bottle at home, sir?" suggested Dick.

"Yes, if my housekeeper hasn't thrown it away, but she's a devil for cleaning up! My boy's got the prescription, I suppose, but he's in Quetta at the moment. And if you want to know"—he turned furiously upon Mack—"that's why I put the blasted thing up there, because I knew there'd be hell to pay in questions once you got your blasted search warrant, sir! And allow me to remind you, you have not got it, and I had no need to answer any questions at all, and why I did the devil knows!"

"Isn't it just as well, sir," suggested Dick in his unsought, unofficial role of peacemaker. "I mean, you've only got to ring up your housekeeper, and get the original bottle sent to be analysed, to prove it had no connection with the case."

"We'll do that," began Mack jealously, but had the wit to stop. No use to estrange the law still further, and the Chancellor was giving his unwilling consent to Dick.

"Though the stuff may be full of morphia for all I know, or opium may have the same effect as morphia. Certainly a quarter of the prescribed dose sent me off to sleep the clock round, and let me tell you, Major, I did not waste any of it on Ulder!"

"I'd like a talk with you, Dick," said Major Mack, pursuing his young friend, as he tried to escape down the passage. "This your room? Another of these old fancy pieces?" So Mack contemptuously designated the gay little bachelor room, with its oriel windows, rose chintzes and carved, unstained oak furniture. "All much too fancy for my taste. You should have seen Mrs. What's-her-name's room, all gilding and velvet, and reeking of Russian cigarettes and gardenia scent and violet powder! Come and have an honest pipe downstairs!"

"I must get out a bit, sir," said Dick desperately. The snow had stopped, the sun was shining, and through the open window came that deceptive scent of spring which is sometimes suggested by the purity of snow. The thaw would not last, the Chancellor, a weather prophet, had said, and there would be a gale, if not a blizzard, by night. But now the ruins lay white and gold against the purple smoke of elm trees beyond, and the primrose radiance of the sky. Bobs and Sue were standing on the terrace below, young and smiling, freed for the moment from the dark shadow of the Palace. "Don't you want me to try to get a line on Staples? He's probably in the grounds somewhere. Or will you see him yourself?"

"That little red rabbit I saw at lunch? You said you'd get his story out of him, and I'll interview him when I've had your report. We've far bigger fishes in the net!"

"I suppose," said Dick desperately, as he turned to go, "that it's no use trying to persuade you that no one you're thinking of can conceivably have murdered Ulder? You know as well as I do that the innocent behave very much as the guilty would in a shock like this. I could feel your suspicions in your interviews this morning—you could almost make me share them! But do believe me when I say that a man who's given his life to God, and served God all his life, couldn't be guilty of such a crime. Clergy may be weak, inefficient, quarrelsome, lazy, anything you like, for they're only human, but—"

"What about Ulder?" cut in Mack.

"What about him? He was bad through and through, may God have mercy on him, but the—the clergy you're thinking of have led consistent lives of piety and upright principles."

"I don't know about that," said Mack, joyfully embarking on his favourite and wholly untenable criticism of the Anglican Church. "I'm going to look into the Bishop's record at St. Blaze. Why was he asked to resign? And your Canon was little better than an unbeliever to begin with! No, I've had this out with friends before, Dick, and I hold to it that it's the danger of your Church to tamper with morals. The Catholics at least are hide-bound: they obey their Pope and priests. My Church lets each man take his stand on the Bible and its teaching of right and wrong. The Episcopal party," declared the heir of John Knox with relish, "choose what they like out of a pack of old Church Fathers, and put their ritual and party politics first and morals last. I've seen it again and again! Oh, I know you think I'm a bigoted fool," (Dick nearly acquiesced openly) "but I keep an open mind, mark you! I've got my eye on the Chancellor, in fact his behaviour and his absurd tale are the most suspicious so far, apart from that appalling young woman Judith, but I feel in my bones—oh, well, time will show—I'll see it does! You go and see this Staples and report later—and send Tonks to me—there's endless telephoning and certificates and papers to see to at once."

"I say, Bobs," said Dick, "do you think you could possibly contrive some funk hole for me? I think I shall go batty if I can't shake off Mack's conferences and enquiries and interviews and telephones, and his preposterous criticisms of our Church!"

"He does seem to have fallen for you, Dick, doesn't he, Sue?" grinned Bobs. "What's the big idea about you?"

"He's short-handed, thinks I'm honest, and I saw him bring down a stag royal fifteen years ago," returned Dick briefly. "Also I think he hopes a little detective work here will send me back to M.I., of which he thinks well, and save me from the Church, of which he thinks very poorly. What these chaps imagine we did in M.I., I can't think. I can't make him see that I came here to make my soul, not to nose out a criminal."

"Dick, who does he think did it?" Sue's face was shadowed again now and her eyes appealing, but Dick could only shake his head.

"Honestly I don't know, and if I did I couldn't talk about it. Come into the sun and let's forget it all for half an hour."

"I know just the place for you anyway if it's not too cold!" (How did Judith come to have so obedient and accommodating a stepsister? Any other girl but Sue would have plagued him with questions!) "Father's famous summer parlour, Bobs!"

"By Jove, yes! Best pick up gumboots in the garden-room first, though, for it's on the rough grass! It gave me a laugh," Bobs went on to confide aside to Dick as they stamped on tall rubbers, "considering the sort of use kings of Israel put these places to in the O.T.! It was an infernal bore when the Bishop went off there to work and pray undisturbed, for I had to bring all the notes or telephone messages across, of course."

"Well, no one's to do that for me," said Dick.

It was only by slow degrees that archaeologists had been digging up and identifying the remains of the large precincts of Evelake Palace. The ruins of the Abbey itself were in excellent order; every pillar base had been dug up, the crypt cleared, the fragments of wall and buttress, windows and tombs built up reverently, the turf mown and rolled. The east reredos, above the stone altar, was almost intact, saved probably by the high garden wall of the refectory and dormitories. The cloisters, in sun and shadow round their snow-whitened lawn, were so exquisite that the three who crossed them now exclaimed in pleasure; while seagulls, driven far inland by the storm, fluttered and swooped at their approach, as if they were the ghostly hands of monks, fluttering the scattered leaves of their vanished missals. A holly tree, rich with scarlet berries and glistening leaves, guarded a broken gate way and "Oh the rising of the sun, Oh the running of the deer," hummed Sue suddenly, as if the holy spirits of the dead had exorcised all immediate troubles for a moment. But beyond the cloisters the scene changed. The war had interrupted the work on the old Abbey kitchens and offices: elders, nettles and brambles had grown up unchecked. The outer wall here guarded the summit of a low hill, and below it the little West Country river Eve, in full spate from the moors, roared and rattled below them. A cloud obscured the sun and a gust of cold wind swept up the open arch of the old slype. Everything was grey and battered, tangled and rank, save for the little turret at one corner.

"But we'll have all these paths tidied up soon, now that the war is over," said Sue with her mother's optimism.

"The bottom part of the turret is a mess with just a wooden stair up to the Bishop's den," said Bobs, viewing the dismal little place with disfavour as he tried the handle. "Locked, of course! We must get the key from Soames."

"Come back by the shrubbery then," said Sue. "This way—"

"The shrubbery! Shades of Mr. Woodhouse! I'd forgotten this, Sue! This is the most complete place in the world; it represents every century!"

"I expect it was the Victorian bishop with a lot of children who made it," suggested Sue, "so that they could be sent off to hide in it!"

She had led them across the rubble and overgrowth, through an arch out of the ruins, where most decorously a path between laurels and rhododendrons led circuitously to the back of the Palace. At the angle of the new wing a wide door opened on to the formal garden, overlooked by the drawing-room on one side; from the other the path wound round the terrace which skirted the full length of the whole building.

"I'll go on and get the key from Soames," said Bobs, hurrying on to the door in the Bridge wing which opened into the pantry.

"What are you doing, Dick?" Sue looked round from the chocolate-cake effect of the dark earth beds beneath their snow icing, to see Dick staring up at the drawing-room windows, and at the winter jasmine bush which was making a pathetic pretence of yellow buds below.

"Oh, just geography. Is that one of the drawing-room windows?" As Sue looked up instinctively Dick jerked a bit of paper off one of the long clinging sprays and pocketed it. "You don't use that room much, do you, Sue?"

"Just for big parties in winter, lately. We haven't really been able to keep it warm. Mummy loves it, so we do often have tea there. But we don't often sit there after dinner."

"You didn't last night, I imagine, with all that was happening?"

"No one sat anywhere exactly, did they?" sighed Sue. "I expect the fire was let out there. But be careful, Dick, or I'll begin to ask questions!"

"Hang it all, the idiot's lost the key!" Bobs rejoined the two beside the jasmine, just as Dick was wishing that he could ask Sue a great many questions which would seem pointless to her. "At least he says it's in a drawer in the Bishop's room! I'll have a look there to-morrow, Dick. We ought to be going in now, I suppose?"

"There is Judith calling me," said Sue. "Did you ever know any one with such a carrying voice?"

"Luckily not," said Dick dryly. "I think I'll take a turn in the garden, Bobs. I can't quite fancy going back to Mack's Shorter Catechism yet."

The sun was low now, and the arabesque of the box-edged squares and circles, innocent of any growth but patches of sinister purple hellebore, were not particularly inviting. In this yew-hedged square the old gardener worked his own formal will, leaving the further lawns and Mrs. Broome's herbaceous borders contemptuously to his under lings. For a minute Dick reviewed it, as the sun faded, rather than sank, into the threatening clouds. For a moment he saw gloomily in it a parable of the Church, set and formal, snow and ice-bound: for a moment that simile of a hymn which haunts all ex-pupils of ancient religious foundations came to his mind—"As now the sun's declining rays," (no wonder the two short verses made it a popular choice!) "So life's brief day is sinking down"—and he thought of Ulder viewing yesterday his last sunset. Then he stretched himself, smiling suddenly at the memory of Sue's little pagan Christmas carol and its ecstasy in birth and rebirth, felt for his pipe, and returned to the jasmine bush.

"I suppose a fall of snow might have done it," he reflected, looking at the projecting stone lintel of the window above him. "It looks as if something heavy had bumped down on it recently: would snow scrape the branches apart? I'm not gardener enough to know! If it weren't for this cursed snow one might have seen footsteps, but they'd all be wiped out. Shall I put Mack on to this, and suggest the whole thing might be an outside job after all?"—But his reasons against that were pretty conclusive.

Now that he was alone Dick took out the scrap of paper which he had abstracted from the jasmine bush, but it gave him as little satisfaction as he had feared. It was only a scrap torn from a bit of ordinary azure writing-paper. They had some of this in use at the Palace, for Mrs. Broome kept a wonderful assortment of different grades of paper for her various activities, but the same was probably in use in the home of any of the house-party. There was no writing on it, the only surprising thing was that it was so clean and dry, but that was doubtless because it had been embedded so deeply in the jasmine bush. It would be valuable if it matched any tear in Ulder's papers, if and when they were discovered, but little more. And at the moment this seemed a forlorn hope indeed.

"Excuse me, sir!" Dick turned so smartly that he caught Soames unawares. The little butler's face was only just transforming itself, it seemed, from horror and dismay into its usual awkward obsequiousness. "I'm sorry about that key, and I've got one here that might fit so I thought of trying it, but the place would need tidying, and a bit of an airing, before it was fit for you."

"Oh, I don't want to use it to-night. It'll be dark soon and the snow's too thick underfoot. But the thaw's coming, I think, don't you? and a gale if I'm not mistaken." Dick's gaze strayed vaguely over his companion. Why had Soames changed out of his neat formal attire into a pretty repulsive reach-me-down of snuff-colour, and why wear a bowler hat, overcoat and carry a gampish umbrella to go down the shrubbery and try a key in the turret door?

"Yes, sir, it's unfortunate for me," said Soames, reading Dick's glance nervously. "It's my afternoon off, you see. Mrs. Broome is most considerate, and knowing I'd like to enquire at the Hospital about Mrs. Kelly, gave me leave to go into Evelake as usual and take some flowers to her, if Mr. Jay, the gardener, can spare me some."

"Mrs. Kelly?"

"Moira, that is, sir. I'd like to mark my gratitude for all the kindness and help she's given me here. *She's* one who believes in giving a man a new start and holding out a helping hand. It was she heard of me through a friend of hers, and got me the place and tipped me several winks—I mean to say—gave me every assistance in her power!"

"It's very decent of you, Soames, but I'm afraid you won't be able to go," replied Dick, remembering a saying of Mrs. Broome's long ago that Judith and men—any man—were the only people Moira got on with. "Didn't Tonks give out the Chief Constable's orders that no one was to leave the Palace to-day?"

"I took that to refer to those under suspicion, sir," retorted Soames with sudden glib impertinence.

"That covers everyone in the Palace who was anywhere near the Bridge last night," said Dick sternly. "And anyway how could you make three miles and back with snow drifts in the road?"

"I'll manage somehow on my bike, sir. I'd give the world to get out of this place for a bit," he added with sudden passion. "Oh, I know there are enquiries being made about me and all, and that I'm the only chap here who's ever been 'inside', so why not pin murder down on me and let all the swells go free? But it ain't British justice, and what had I to do with Mr. Ulder, I ask you that? What had I agin him?"

"Nothing as far as I know," said Dick severely. "We should know much more about the case if that missing bag turned up. For we know that Mr. Ulder arrived with a suit case and a hand-bag, Soames!"

That was as much, or perhaps even more, than Dick felt at liberty to give as a warning. It was evidently more than enough for Soames who broke away and hurried down the zig-zag paths, shabby and jaunty, miserable and defiant, and, from that moment, clearly an almost open enemy of Dick himself. The hope that some such challenge would lead the little man to re-place the missing bag seemed forlorn indeed. Mack should have let Dick tackle the problem at once, he reflected, instead of us-ing him as a shorthand typist in those appalling interviews! By lunch-time the butler could easily have hidden it or any con-tents he might fancy, for Soames was not the fellow to indulge in any foolish scruples about wronging the dead, or object to making use of the deceased's pyjamas, hair-brush or sponges. All that was immaterial; the vital question was what Soames would do with the papers. Would he understand them? Would he have the courage to use them for blackmail in his turn after a decent interval? Dick could hardly see Soames as heir to Ulder, but he must make Mack see how serious was the possibility.

VIII
THURSDAY AFTERNOON

MEANWHILE the stable-clock was striking half-past three and Dick had yet to interview Brian Staples, his fellow Ordina-tion candidate. It was not a job which Dick fancied, though he would certainly be a less formidable confidant than Mack for the poor little man. And luckily any consideration of the best means of approach was unnecessary, for as Dick turned out of the gardens into the avenue he saw Staples himself hurrying towards him.

"I saw you out of the window and came to catch you, Marlin," he said breathlessly. "May I have one word with you?"

"Of course! Shall we keep to the avenue or go to the library?"

"I have had a long walk already and just come in, but walls have ears." Staples' voice had a curious blur in it, but his manner was always melodramatic. "May we take refuge in your bedroom?"

"Mine is a long and sad story"—the Mock Turtle's words echoed in Dick's ears as Staples began on a history of his life which would obviously run to twenty thousand words, rather than one word. There was something of the fishy world, something watery at least, about this lank deacon, about his perpetually moist forehead and hands, dim grey eyes blurred through uncleaned spectacles, hair brushed back damply and skinny arms and legs which seemed to sway like strands of seaweed over the chair by Dick's fire. "Unstable as water thou shalt not excel"—those words about Reuben pretty well covered the long story which Mr. Staples was pouring out to Dick about his youth, his repressions and traumas! It was very difficult for Dick to attend, and turn his thoughts from a procession which was beginning to haunt his imagination unceasingly, of figure by figure of those whom he loved or revered stealing along the corridor to the Bridge, a bottle in their hands. Madness lay that way, he felt desperately. Better by far try to attend to the saga of Staples' schooldays, adolescence and his religious pilgrimage from faith to atheism and back again however tedious it was!— "My parents being Irish, you see," were the first words which caught Dick's attention—how this Irish *motif* kept recurring, and not with much credit to the nation so far!

"Your father an Ulsterman and your mother from Cork, you said, I think?" So much had reached Dick's wandering attention.

"Just so—conflict within me from the first! As I say, the effect of their quarrels was to make me determinedly English. At the Grammar School and the University in Livchester I ignored all political discussions, I refused to join any local Irish organizations. I lived for my work, and went from one scholarship to another. Then I decided to be ordained and went five years ago to Eastlake Theological College as you know—"

"And then the war interfered?"

"Yes, I felt the Church no place for me! I was a convinced pacifist, and until conscription began I endured martyrdom for my convictions but I was firm."

A certain dignity seemed to freeze the watery little man into solidity, and Dick forbore to suggest that his contemporaries had suffered worse martyrdoms in France and Gallipoli. "I avoided every kind of strife. I consorted with the English only, till I fell in love. That was my undoing for she—Bridget Malone, was Irish, and a reckless, whole-hearted Sinn-Feiner."

"Don't tell me anything that pains you!"

"I must, to explain what happened. She was suffering from diseased lungs, almost penniless, alone in Livchester. I persuaded her that my love and care would cure her if only she would go to hospital at once for treatment. Later on I discovered the reason for her refusal. She was at the centre of a desperate and criminal plot, unsuspected because of her youth and ill-health, and she would not be immured. I often said to her …"

Staples, his nerves strained, his eyes still frozen into calm, told the rest of his story with a restraint which Dick respected but for that tiresome preference for *oratio recta* to *oratio obliqua* which marks the mind that lacks a classical education. But through all the "He said" … and "I said" … Dick got a clear hold of the pitiful story easily enough. Bridget was suddenly packed off to hospital by her landlady after a haemorrhage; she sent for Staples and conveyed to him that he must take an urgent message for her by hand to her brother in London. Staples departed in all good faith, to be arrested at King's Cross.

"She had whispered to me, 'Eat the paper if they catch you', but I thought her delirious, and said to her, 'For your sake I'll be melodramatic', or words to that effect. But of course I never thought of doing so really, would you?"

Dick agreed one never expected to land up in a cheap thriller, though this Bridget might well have roused suspicions. But how should an innocent like Staples imagine the harmless paper to be a code message about the assassination of a Very Important Person. (It was just Walter Pater on Kingship, thought Dick, "poor average weak human nature thrust by the vortex of circumstances into events and tragedies too great for it".) The police had, it seemed, quickly recognized Staples as a mere helpless stool-pigeon, and investigations in Livchester confirmed the impeccability of his previous career. Through his home they traced Bridget to hospital, and took what proved to be her last confession, wholly exonerating her lover. But they were no days for those involved in any Irish affairs: the cloud on the horizon was too menacing. Staples was indeed acquitted of treason with severe reprimands, only to be imprisoned almost at once as a conscientious objector.

"And there in prison, devoid of hope or love or faith, the Chaplain found me, a wonderful fellow and a real gentleman. He led me to the light, for he said: 'Staples,' he said—"

Dick's attention wandered again. He must ask Mack to get in touch with this Chaplain, and hear his opinion of his convert. Personally Dick was inclined to believe Staples' story: he was so clearly unimaginative, and he told it so ingenuously. But there was no doubt, as Dick recalled himself to attend to Staples' monotonous voice, that the poor man had grounds enough for enmity to Ulder, if not for murder. For Staples' most inconvenient conscience had obliged him to write this whole story to Ulder, believing him still to be Head of Eastlake College. Ulder had visited him at once, sympathized with him, given him Absolution and urged him not to tell his story to the present Head of the College or any other living soul. Then, three days ago, he had written to inform Staples that, in default of the trifling payment of £10 Ulder would tell the whole story to the Bishop. "Though it is possible that this miserable Diocesan would welcome even a gaol-bird as a priest, his lordship would certainly never overlook the fact that you had not made a clean breast to him of your very curious past before you applied for Ordination at his hands," wrote Ulder. Dick himself would certainly have hastened to bash Ulder's face in at such a betrayal, but would Staples, incapable of such a step, be capable of a far blacker premeditated revenge?

"Did you know Ulder would be here?" he asked as casually as he could.

"Yes, he told me this was to be our rendezvous!"

"How did you mean to tackle him?"

"I could not tell! I passed sleepless nights—"

"Did you take any remedy for that?" asked Dick still casually. "After being so long on dope in hospital, I never can understand why people put up with insomnia."

"No, no, no!" said Staples with such energy that he had obviously realized the point of the question. "You can search every hole and corner of my room."

"Hold on!" said Dick breezily. "I wasn't making any suggestion! Tell me this, did you see Ulder that night?"

"No!" cried Staples and then, as Dick looked at him steadily, his passion died down. "You won't believe me but it's true. I tried, I confess that! After Chapel I crept to his door—there were voices inside. I sat up in my room and waited for half an hour—there were voices again. I hastened away for the butler was bringing a tray up from the pantry to the Bridge passage, and I stood at the top of the stairs above the Bridge to listen till Ulder's guest went away. Ted Parsons looked out of his room presently, and asked what the hell I was doing—no speech for one of us at this holy time, as I told him! I heard the door shut and was going down when once more it opened. Again I waited for what seemed like hours—again Parsons shouted at me. Twelve o'clock struck at last, all sounds had ceased and the house was so quiet that I felt Ulder must be alone. I was just going down when I heard his door close again, and footsteps go away down the corridor. Now at last I saw my chance, and then suddenly Parsons was upon me. He seized me and pushed me down the passage, thrust me into my room, with insolent words about putting up with my spying upon him no longer. I rebuked him but—but I felt as it was so late I must leave the whole affair for the night."

"Can you tell me who was the last visitor to Ulder whom you saw?"

"No, I could not see round the stairs, for, as you know, they take a turn. I had an impression it was a woman, for I seemed to hear a rustle, as of a woman's skirt, and a slow and halting step, but I heard no voice and no one came our way."

"Was Parsons watching you all the time you were waiting?"

"Yes, from his bed through his open door. He has some form of claustrophobia, due to shell-shock, and can only sleep with door and window wide open. That was why I forgave his violent behaviour."

"He never knew Ulder, did he?" reflected Dick.

"Never! It was through my own carelessness that Ulder ever came back into my life!"

"Well, I'm afraid you'll have to repeat this story to the police to-morrow, but I'll talk to Mack first, and put your case before him."

"There is the Chapel bell," said Staples, clearly glad of the interruption.

"I'm afraid I can't come," said Dick. "Got to see the Chief Constable."

"This is but a poor preparation for your priesthood, I fear," said Staples reprovingly.

"Oh, I don't know!" The truth was obvious and the obvious is always irritating. "Trying to get crooked paths straight, I suppose!"

"And asses out of pits," he added to himself viciously. He had just ten minutes in which to snatch an interview with the long-suffering and wakeful Ted Parsons.

"Well, come in, Dick, we must get down to work! I must get home to-night, and I can't do much more here. Tonks is to stay to keep watch and see that no one leaves the Palace. Now I've no time to ramble round and round in an argument, so I want you to sit down and discuss and tabulate our conclusions up to date. Got to see the Coroner, you know!"

"Excuse me, sir, but will you be getting help from Blacksea to-morrow?" asked Dick desperately.

"I don't know! I've rung up and they may have no one to spare there. They're mostly down with this wretched flu. Didn't give in to it in my young days!"

"Then shouldn't you get a man from the Yard? I'm glad to be of use to you, but it's not my job and I have my own job here."

"I don't call perpetual half hours in that God-box a job," said Mack ruthlessly.

"No? Well, call it preparing for the Ordination on Sunday."

"I don't know if there'll be an Ordination!"

"What do you mean by that, sir?" asked Dick, the room whirling round him.

"Oh, not what you're thinking—not as yet, at least. Leave that for the moment, and I'll tell you where we stand. I've got a promise from the police surgeon to give me the result of his examination to-morrow, but he is quite clear already that Lee can be exonerated from any question of an overdose in one tablet—couldn't be done. I rang up the Blacksea people about sending their finger-print men. Can't do these roads, and I agreed with them that there would be too many prints on the bed and the furniture to prove any thing. Corn has sent off the container and whisky glass to them already, and they'll let me know the results to-morrow too. When they come we'll have to take prints of the party here with my small apparatus. I'll bring it out to-morrow and you must get 'em." (Dick gasped.) "I've done a lot of other routine work, got to put things right with the Magistrate about that search warrant. No reply from the Chancellor's house this afternoon, so I'll try for his house keeper from my home to-night—he tells me she never sleeps out, luckily. We've sent a wire to Ulder's rectory and got no reply—shut up already, I suppose. Someone of his kin will see a notice in the *Evelake Gazette* to-morrow of Ulder's death at Evelake Palace—we put it in the ordinary Obituary. It's lucky no newspaper man has tracked us down anyhow. And I've put through some private enquiries which I needn't bother you with!"

Dick made no comment. He did not feel it necessary to repeat Judith's gay call to Sue, overheard as he left his room with Staples—"Darling, our Mack's been ringing up the Pope or Archbishop or someone to find out if darling Papa is respectable! Isn't it too sweet? I listened in at Mummy's room, and I rather think from his voice that Mack got a raspberry!"

"Now here's Tonks' report on the staff," went on Mack— "quite a good one and confirmed by Mrs. Broome who has been quite helpful, I must say. Here's the drift of it:

(1) Moira Kelly—housekeeper, 10 years with last Bishop, 15 since. Confined to room last three months with cancer—malignant growth—went off for operation to-day. She could be no help as witness unless she had heard any of the conversation from Ulder's room. Tonks and Corn tested the rooms carefully, and from her bed she could have heard nothing—even if she were not under the influence of drugs.

(2) Jane Harris—cook—15 years here and a Tartar. Never goes near that part of the house, and sees to it that her nieces, May and Muriel Hoylake (kitchen-maid and vegetable maid) have nothing to do with the gentlemen. All T.T., C. of E., G.F.S., and God knows what all.

(3) Doris Bing—parlour-maid since 1914, when footmen called up. Cousin of Tonks' wife and like an open book. Typical snob upper servant who looks down on Soames, and is going to hand in her notice to-morrow, because she thinks Soames no class at all and doesn't hold with places where they have murders.

(4) Mabel Fox—upper housemaid (36),—5 years here; London girl—no connection with neighbourhood— walking out with Tonks' nephew, so beyond reproach.

(5) Irene Hay—second housemaid (23)—3 years here, perfect references and light of G.F.S.

(6) Lilias Vere (16); the scrubbiest, most half-witted little 'tweenie Tonks ever saw. Not allowed upstairs.

"There's a list of outdoor servants too, but you needn't bother with it. All of 'em home by six last night. Gardeners, chauffeurs and all collected with their wives at the chauffeur's house to hear his new wireless. Except for gardener all fairly new to job and not from this neighbourhood. In short," said Mack triumphantly, "just the sort of well-paid, inefficient, church-going pack of parasites you'd expect to find in one of these bloated Palaces. I wonder what St. Paul would have said of all of 'em! Any comments, Dick?"

"Tonks has omitted Soames altogether, sir."

"No, but in view of your enquiries about him he's a special comment. Here we are: Only six months in job. Not up to work and no class—that's Doris—but good-natured and obliging as a rule. Cook speaks highly of him, and says she and Moira Kelly did their best to help him, because both felt 'Our Boys', who had fought for us, deserved every chance. Mrs. Broome owned that she had engaged him with a good deal of hesitation, as the Head of Evelake School had taken him without references, found him casual and unsatisfactory in his work, and admitted that there were suspicions about his honesty. Still nothing had been proved against him in the case of some missing articles of wear; no money or silver had ever been missing, and Soames had left of his own accord 'to better himself'. He was not fit for his job at the Palace, she admitted candidly, but she had no other application from the Registries or advertisements—'and what are you to do three miles from a town and these dreadful moving pictures they all rush for nowadays!' ... So you see," concluded Mack, "he's not a good character, and Scotland Yard may give us an even worse report of him, but what you've got to prove is that he had any sort of motive for doing away with Ulder. What's your case against him?"

It didn't come to much, Dick admitted. All he was convinced of was that the butler had something on his mind, but that might be his past record; that he had certainly tried to remove the tell-tale whisky glass from Ulder's room, that he had been listening at keyholes and that he, from his pantry and adjoining bedroom, had free access to Ulder's room at any hour of the night. "One thing I suspected him of was giving Ulder that glass of whisky when Ulder asked for it and being ashamed to own up. If we find there was morphia in the glass I suppose someone else was responsible. By that I mean I cannot see any motive for Soames to murder Ulder at present—we know nothing of his past life and some possible grudge, remember!"

"You can't expect such a coincidence, my good man!"

"No, you can't. But I do suspect him of making off with that bag when Ulder's death was discovered. And a man's got to be a pretty confirmed criminal to see the chance to pick up a pair of brushes and pyjamas five minutes after he's discovered a corpse. No, I can't prove he took the bag, but which of your other suspects would have done anything but remove the incriminating papers after they had given the fatal dose? The passages were full of people coming and going to all hours, and wouldn't you stare at any one carrying a black hand-bag about with him at that hour of night, except a man servant? No one would notice if he were carrying luggage with him. But my chief reason for suspecting Soames is, I admit, that he's the only man in the Palace I can conceive capable of such a crime."

"Well, Dick, we've had that out." Mack shook his head. "What did you get from Staples?"

Mr. Staples himself would have thought poorly of Dick's tabloid version of his soul's battlefield. He would have trembled indeed to hear Mack thump the table, declaring that an Irishman, a parson and a conchie was capable of any crime. But not even for the sake of dragging red herrings across the episcopal path could Dick ask Mack to believe Staples a possible murderer. "Not the guts or the morphia," Dick concluded. "And this fellow, Ted Parsons, bears out his story. He's that plump, rather bewildered-looking chap in a check change coat—a very decent sort—an ex-Guards man."

Dick repeated Staples' story and Parsons' confirmation of it, omitting indeed Parsons' forcible descriptions of Staples.

"No drugs on that floor either—Tonks searched at once! Well, I'll put him through it later. Meanwhile, here's a rough time-table made out, not that most of it is accurate!

8.30. Ulder arrives and collapses.

8.40. (or so) Dr. Lee arrives to visit patient Kelly. Ulder taken upstairs, put to bed, brought round by Dr. Lee with amyl nitrate; no morphia so far, notice. Dr. sees Kelly and leaves.

9 (or shortly after) while family in Chapel, Mrs. Broome finds Ulder in great pain. Gives him one tablet of morphia from bottle. Ulder demands visitors.

9.30 (or before Chapel over) Chancellor.

10 Bishop visits Ulder.

10.30 Canon Wye tries to give whisky but stopped by Mrs. Broome.

10.40 Mrs. Judith Mortimer, very short visit to Ulder and is dismissed by Mrs. Broome, when attempting to give him drink.

11 Mrs. Broome pays last visit to Ulder and leaves him out of pain and apparently sleepy.

11.30? (no idea) Bishop looks in but Ulder asleep. All this time, too, Soames was dancing about with trays or sweeping up glass and Staples pirouetting on the top stair. Anything to add?"

"Only Staples' and Parsons' curious tale that they heard steps much later—after twelve o'clock chimed, and thought they heard the swish of a gown on the floor," said Dick slowly.

"A woman's dress? No, might as well be a man's dressing-gown or one of these tom-fool cassocks they sport here! Now, here are my lists:

Suspect.	Motive.	Opportunity.	Suspicious Behaviour.
1. Bishop.	(1) To stop old scandal finally. (2) To protect his daughter from consequences of adultery. (*Mack believed in calling spades by their proper name.*)	Every possible chance. Visited room twice, probably last person in room at night. No guest likely to arrive with morphia but Bishop had command of every medicine chest in Palace.	(1) Objections to search. (2) Strange attitude over missing papers. (3) General demeanour. (*"Come, come!" protested Dick.*)
2. Chancellor Chailly.	(1) Fear of blackmail and serious result to his business — of exposure. (2) Realized more clearly than parsons that Ulder would never leave off threatening them from U.S.A.	Visited Ulder at about 9 o'clock or 9.30, when everyone in Chapel. Might have left whisky with drug out of sight trusting Ulder to find it later. (*"Sooner, not later, he'd have spotted it," objected Dick.*)	Dangerous drug in his possession and hidden by him. If found to contain morphia, very serious. Very thin story about empty bottle. Could have returned to Ulder's room later in evening unobserved.
3. Canon Wye.	Fear of blackmail because of: (*a*) old scandal (*b*) ruin of his career.	Visited Ulder before Chapel and at 10.30. Attempted to give him spirits against orders. Stopped by Mrs. Broome but he may have returned later.	Did not hesitate to say he rejoiced at Ulder's death. A fanatic, and has been most obstructive.
4. Mrs. Mortimer (Judith Broome).	Fear of blackmail. Intervention of King's Proctor, on Ulder's information, would stop re-marriage and render expected child illegitimate.	Could have visited Ulder during Chapel. Attempted visit after 10.30 and was preparing drink for him. Could have returned to administer it any time.	No good behaviour, at any rate.

"Well, there we are and you must add your views on Staples and Soames!"

"It's a fine time-table and list," said Dick slowly, "but, sir, do you think any coroner's jury or high-court jury could conceivably give a verdict on this? Why—" He was about to follow up the remark, but decided to leave it to Mack to think over the affair by himself. "They won't be prejudiced against the Church," he ventured to add—"quite the contrary!"

"I know," growled Mack, "twelve good and true Episcopals called by Coroner, I've no doubt. But they've got to face the fact that here in this Palace murder was done. What were you going to say?"

"Well, there's another point. I know there's not much possibility, even probability, that this can be an outside job, but I'd like to know who was responsible for locking up last night. I can count up six entrance doors apart from the back regions, and though some of the windows were shuttered last night any of us who aren't accustomed to steam-heating might have left one open. The place is a hothouse by evening."

"Too true," growled Mack, tugging his collar. "But don't let that worry you. I went into that with Mrs. Broome. As a matter of fact she told Doris to look round the old wing last night as Soames is notoriously careless. She found him herself at the drawing-room window about eleven, saying he wanted to make sure of the catch. Of course he should have done it long before—but, as she says, no method." Dick started at the remark but repressed himself. No use to bring in another side-issue just now. He would get in a question when Soames was summoned.

"There's the other point, sir! From first to last we've assumed that the morphia was in the possession of the person who administered it. Now there's a chance, I suppose, that someone might have got hold of a drug, let's say, from Mrs. Broome's medicine cupboard—"

"No morphia there! We searched it at her own request at once. A very sensible woman! And she helped Tonks to examine Moira's room—not a trace!"

"Or even the Chancellor's bottle. He may well have mentioned in the smoking-room that he had a patent paregoric and that might have suggested to someone—"

"Who do you mean?" asked Mack bluntly. "Are you accusing the Bishop now?"

"I was thinking of Soames, to tell the truth. He may merely have meant to give Ulder a specially good night and then cast an eye round his belongings. He'd feel safe to steal from Ulder, because no one would believe a word Ulder said!"

"You've got your knife into that man Soames. Well, let's have him in. Tonks is outside, I think, so just send him to produce our friend. That'll scare him to begin with!"

"There's no trace of him, sir!" Mack and Dick were still brooding over their lists when Tonks returned three minutes later. "His assistant, my niece Mabel, informs me that he has gone out."

"I warned him of your orders only an hour ago," exclaimed Dick.

"You shouldn't have let him out, Tonks." said Mack sharply.

"Excuse me, sir!" Doris appeared, settling her cuffs, and alive with importance, just as Dick had explained Soames' carefully arranged plan of action. "I thought I should just let you know that Soames must have gone off to the Hospital, for all he was ordered not to—for the flowers have gone—a beautiful sheaf of lilies he was giving, sir. Cook says to him, 'What's the hurry for Moira is too ill to care? Madam will likely let you go to-morrow, or one of us any way, her being so considerate,' but he wasn't to hold or to bind, and slipped out by the back way through the electric engine-house, which no one could watch as well as the hall, and all the back doors, without eyes all over their heads!"

"Well, that's that! I'll speak to him when I come to-morrow! You're right, Dick, he's a fishy customer." Mack rose and went to the door at last. "Hullo, young lady, have you been disobeying orders too?" Mack crossed to the vestibule as he saw Sue swing open the door, but even he could not resist a more kindly note in his voice at the sight of Sue's cheeks glowing and hair curling in the wind.

"Only to the lodge. I hope that wasn't wrong! The light is so poor to-night, and Mother fears it may fail altogether. She asked Soames to give a message to our man this morning but I suppose he forgot." At that remote date nearly every country house had its own electric light engine, kept in order, or out of order, by unskilled grooms or gardeners, and in the chronic uncertainty as to whether the engine or its manipulator were at fault, candles still remained a large item in every family's budget.

"Better if it had failed last night and kept people in their own rooms," said Mack grimly. "No, of course you may walk in your grounds, Miss Broome. I'm not such a tyrant as that! I don't enjoy my unpleasant duties, you know." (*But there you lie, my impeccable Scotsman,* thought Dick sardonically. *You've enjoyed your day of cleric hunting more than any since you got down that royal, I'll bet, though you mayn't know it.*) "Well, I'm off, Dick. Ring me up if you hear from your friend. I'm leaving Corn to keep a watch over the papers in there," he added, pointing to the study, "and you keep your eyes open for them. And go on hunting for that missing bag you set such store by, if you like," he called back over his shoulder as he and Tonks strode out through the vestibule to the car.

IX
THURSDAY EVENING

"DICK, YOU LOOK dead tired!" Sue choked back the eager questions burning on her lips. She and her mother had agreed that Judith's wild talk of Mack's suspicions with regard to her father and herself were just Judith's nonsense, that no one could dream of the Bishop being suspected for a moment, but the heavy cloud which hung over the house, and the going and coming of the police, were weighing heavily on their spirits. She had been longing to hear every thing from Dick when she could catch him, but poor Dick looked so weary and distracted that she could not worry him. "Come and have tea alone with Mummy and me in the drawing-room! Father's got the Canon and Mr. Chailly in the library, and we've hardly seen them all day. Bobs doesn't want tea, so we'll be all alone, and I promise we won't ask questions. Judith's lying down so don't be afraid of her!"

"You're an angel, Sue!" said Dick gratefully. "I'm so tired of men, do you know? At Blacksea we specialize in services and clubs and classes for men only, and yet at the moment I feel that I never want to see anything in trousers or cassock again—just womanly women who'll pet me and won't ask questions! You are so nice to be with."

"But that's what I always say about you, Dick!" cried Mrs. Broome when Sue repeated the compliment laughingly. "Are you a celibate?"

"No, I'm not," replied Dick stoutly. "I think a priest should be a whole man!"

"I've no right to ask you, of course," apologized Mrs. Broome, "but you really will make a delightful husband some day." Suddenly it struck her that her words fell into an odd conscious silence, and for almost the first time it occurred to her that Sue had really grown up in the years while Dick was away in the war. Her child hadn't been here when Dick came to them for his examination, and, of course, now the mother came to think of it, they were a young man and young woman, not just childhood's friends. In her embarrassment she forgot her earlier promise and rushed into a question.

"Dick, please tell us what the police are making of all this!"

"Oh, Mother, you promised not to ask!" Sue spoke reproachfully, but from her flushed cheeks her mother diagnosed that the interruption was welcome.

Dick looked round the room helplessly. Here in this gay, cosy little boudoir with its white panelled walls, many photos and bits of embroidery, and all the personal little relics of a happy life, it was even more impossible to tell of Mack's dark suspicions than in the more formal Palace rooms. A miniature of the Bishop, rarefied and refined, a sketch of Judith, smiling radiantly from her presentation frock, of Sue, as a funny gay little girl on a pony, all gazed at him reproachfully across the tea-table. What was the use of troubling them to-night, when Mack had gone, and who could tell what the answers to all the various enquiries winging their way by telephone and telegram over the country might be? He had no idea whether Mrs. Broome even yet realized the dangerous position of her husband and step-daughter, though from her pale face and sunken eyes he suspected the worst. Anyhow, to-morrow perhaps he should warn them, and prepare them for new terrors, but he would evade enquiries to-night.

"We should see our way more clearly," he temporized, "if we could get on the track of Ulder's missing possessions. Sue thinks he arrived with a hand-bag as well as a suitcase and, as you know, Mrs. Broome, there was not a small bag in his room this morning. The police have been hunting all day without any result. Personally I suspect Soames: I think he's a born pick-pocket. Tell me what you know about him!"

For the first time in his life probably Soames was of use, anyhow. Mrs. Broome had nothing new to tell, but she found relief in telling her old story and Dick drew from her, without obvious emphasis, the episode of the drawing-room window. There still did not seem any sense in it, to be sure! If Soames had taken the bag and, surprised by Mrs. Broome, threw it out of the drawing-room window on to the jasmine bush, he would have had to retrieve it, for after a night in a snow-storm it would be soaked and valueless. How dared he steal the bag while Ulder was alive? Only on the supposition that he himself had already given Ulder a fatal dose. But it was not credible that any one should risk the gallows to obtain possession of an old hand-bag! Anyhow, blessed be Soames and hand-bags, for they distracted the two women's thoughts.

"And I'll come and help you to look in the box-rooms, Dick," said Sue. "Do you remember our fine suite of attics running all over the old house into the Bridge wing? We went and rang all the bells there once, I remember, and the governess and Moira and the servants were so angry that we weren't allowed there again! Come on, we'll just get a candle from the pantry in case the light fails."

The pantry stood empty as the two set out on their quest, more light-heartedly than either would have imagined possible that morning. For those who have lived through a war escapism is indeed not a vice nor a fine art but a necessity.

"Soames' lair," said Dick, looking in. "Well, Tonks has been through all this."

"That's his real lair, his bedroom," said Sue, crinkling her nose disgustedly as she pointed to an inner door. "I shouldn't go in, Dick. I'm sure it's repellent!"

"Can't anyway, it's locked! Oh well, I suppose that's natural. Thieves are always suspicious!"

"Dick," Sue interrupted, "I know you'll think this dreadfully foolish but—but there was a woman fortune-teller Judith took me to who said I was psychic. I'm not, of course, except that I do always have the oddest feeling like Mummy when there's someone else in the room—perhaps everyone does—though I can't see anyone, and I feel that about that room there—" she pointed to Soames' bedroom.

"Well, you're wrong, angel! You heard the window rattling, I expect." Dick knelt and listened intently. "I am Grimm's fairy-tale man with long ears and could hear any one breathing. You're getting goosey because the light is getting worse and worse. Well, I've got my torch, so let's explore! And I'd like to begin with Moira's room!"

"Oh, must we?" Dick understood Sue's reluctance well, as they looked at the dreadful orderliness of the cold, dismal room. Moira had been so wasted by her disease that they could imagine the white counterpane was drawn over that frail worn body. Most of her possessions had gone with her, but on her bedside table lay a box decorated with cowrie-shells, a gift from Judith at Bognor long, long ago, photographs of the family and one or two books. Above them was a fretted wood cabinet, and Dick whistled as he opened it, and saw the rows of medicine bottles and ointment jars within.

"Tonks went all through these with Mother, and there was nothing. Mother never left Moira her own medicines for she was utterly casual about what dose she took and when. She adored patent medicines, and used to keep any bottle any one left behind. She used to boast that she knew every bottle in the house, and once she drank up some most expensive cleansing cream of Judith's to cure a cough. How she's hated knowing nothing of what's been going on all these months!"

"Funny she didn't take her Bible! She was very pious in the old days, wasn't she?"

"I expect she took one with a gold and purple binding which Father gave her. This is a very old one—'To Moira on her confirmation.' The surname is in pencil and I can't read it! Oh bother, the light is going very fast."

Dick picked up the book and stared closely at the pencilled name. "Almost illegible. It looks longer than Kelly but it was given to Mack as Moira Kelly, I know."

"I seem to remember she told Mother she had shortened her name long ago for convenience, under the old Bishop," said Sue vaguely, leading the way to the old wing. "We'll start first with the boxrooms—there's only old furniture in the Bridge attics." And though Dick felt the Bridge attics above the pantry were the more likely hiding-holes, still Soames was out of the way, so they could wait. He didn't mind which he looked at first, or how long he took, while he was with Sue.

The electric light was very dim and jerky now, and the candle which Sue carried flickered in the gust of wind up the twisted passage and narrow stairs which led to the attics. To grope their way was almost as much of an effort as it would have been to decipher the boxes of yellowing letters and papers which strewed the uneven floors. Cobwebs hung from great oak rafters; mice scuttled at their approach; plaster crumbled to the floor and bits of old wall-paper flapped in the fierce wind. Card-indexes of bygone years, banished roll-top desks, frowning cupboards invaded the dusty boards. This was what came of hoarding the past, thought Dick!

"We can't hunt *all* these drawers, I'm afraid," he said despairingly.

"We're nearly at the Bridge attics—look, just beyond this cistern room. Here are all the trunks and bags, you see. Dick, the gale seems worse all of a sudden."

That was obvious to her companion already. He went back and shut the door behind them, where the sound of dripping water echoed persistently in the mournful decay, but still a violent and bitter draught blew round them.

"Something's open ahead—some skylight," said Dick. "I'll be blowed—and we certainly are, Sue—if the light's not really going. Got that candle?"

"It'll never stay alight. Oh, Dick, I've got that feeling again more than ever that someone is here!"

That was not surprising. They were in a room dedicated to old luggage now, and, as she gazed at the extraordinary cliffs of old basket trunks, Gladstones, hat-boxes, dressing-cases and carpet-bags, Sue might well see a ghostly procession of men in peg-top trousers, fur-collared coats, stocks and top-hats, or women in poke bonnets and crinolines or bustled gowns and pork-pie hats vanishing into the dark corners!

"No use trying to hunt through all these with one candle!" said Dick, protecting the exiguous flame. "I shouldn't have let you come, Sue. Hullo! That draught's worse than ever! Something odd is happening! Stand back, Sue, stand back!" There was little need for the advice. As the wind volleyed round them there was a violent crash; and the door at the other end of the room, half ajar before, was flung violently open as an avalanche of old boxes and broken glass crashed down in their path.

"The window's blown in! And upset everything!" gasped Sue. "Oh, Dick, if you'd been standing below those boxes!"

"Or you, my sweet! But we weren't!" Dick grew calm. "But I don't see how it happened. Over the Bridge stair is it? I must go and have a look-see!"

"Oh no, Dick!" Sue was trembling so violently that it would have been sheer cruelty to investigate now, or to let her go back through the dark attics and stairways alone. "Let's go and look from the pantry end. Those are the stairs leading up from Moira's room—and—and Ulder's!"

"Well, let's be quick then!" No use to tell Sue that something very odd was up, and that gales seldom blew windows in at that particular angle. But there was little hope, with that one flickering candle, to retrace their steps very speedily. By the time they had bumped into boxes, groped for doors, lost their way down narrow passages to dead ends and got round to the pantry, they had lost quite ten minutes. The pantry was empty and dark but candles were laid out, and while Sue lit them Dick scanned the floor for wet foot prints. For that Soames had been here, that Soames had been following them and was somehow responsible for that broken window, Dick was certain. The storm had never brought it down: even Mack could not imagine that the Bishop, Canon or Chancellor had been prowling about the attics. And to what purpose? And what purpose indeed had Soames? And then he paused, more puzzled than ever, for above the normal pantry odours of coffee, methylated spirits and polish, he detected the scent of lilies. But Soames had surely gone off with his flowers two hours ago!

"Were you wanting anything, sir?" Soames stood before them, his snuff-coloured suit, cheap overcoat and shoes dripping, the dye from his shabby trilby hat pouring down his sallow face as he entered from the passage.

"Hullo, Soames! Wet through? Did you get to Eastlake?"

"No, sir, the snow was so bad I gave up and came back. Just got in this moment. Pitch dark it is! I steered my way to my door by your candle."

"Disappointing about those lilies of yours. They must be ruined!"

"Yes, sir, just had to bring them back with me!"

"Did you hear a crash just now?" Dick looked the butler very straight in the face.

"No, sir. I told you I just came in as you entered the pantry. Saw my way by your candle, sir, for I see that blinking electric light has failed again."

"How did those lilies fly back into your room then? I can smell them," sniffed Dick.

"Oh sir, I was only just back in a manner of speaking. I'd had time to put my things down in my room. What about this accident, sir?"

What were you to make of these clumsy lies? What importance could a bunch of flowers possess one way or the other? Beads of sweat were mingling now with the dye from his cheap hat on Soames' forehead; he knew his lie was detected, but what was its point?

"A window has crashed in in the attic. Just at the top of the second flight of stairs above, between the old and Bridge wings. You'll have to do something about it or the house will be flooded."

"Oh yes, sir!" Soames was all eagerness. "Let me see now! Yes, I've got some good strong boards in the cellar, about the size, and I'll nail one over the frame securely just to hold for the night. Leaves of an old table Mrs. Broome let me keep, for I'm very fond of carpentry, sir."

"All right. I'll help you up with a step-ladder. You'll need one for the windows are high up. But better go and sweep up some of the mess first. Hullo, Bobs! Anything up?"

"I came to see what some almighty crash was. What's happened?"

"I couldn't be more glad to see anyone!" Dick had not relished the idea of investigations on a step-ladder with Soames in his rear. "Don't ask questions yet, but give me a hand up with this step-ladder. There's a window broken in up there."

"I don't see the point of a ladder," said Bobs helping Dick with the high old-fashioned steps. "And are you intending to stuff it up with old shoe-leather? If not, why go armed with one of Soames' shoes?"

"I'll tell you later. Damn these narrow stairs! That'll do, Soames!" The butler was sweeping vigorously as rain and wind roared down the broken window, and Bobs demanded a sou'wester at least.

"You go off and get those boards, Soames. I'm going up, Bobs." As he spoke Dick put the steps to the window, his head bent with the force of the gale. "And if Soames comes round that corner send him off to fetch an umbrella for you, or a mitre or an elephant or a Family Bible or anything you like, but don't let him see me up here! I won't be a minute!"

He was indeed little more. In spite of the scurrying clouds and moon, dripping chimneys, rushing gutters and melting snows he scrambled out on to the roof and found his quest. There were two footprints in the snow and Soames' shoe fitted them exactly. There was a big smudge where he knelt on the roof; clearly he had scrambled out in a panic and accidentally or intentionally, crashed in the glass of the window or overturned the boxes as he heard Dick and Sue approach. Any fool could see what had happened, but why it had happened was as obscure as the stormy night. It was obvious by now that Soames felt Dick on his track and had something he would go to all lengths to conceal. It would be simple if he could assume that Soames was desperate enough to knock Dick out, at the very grave risk of murder. But there was an insuperable objection. When Soames climbed to the window he must have heard Sue speaking to her fellow-searcher; when once he had forced up the window and waited to crash it in with whatever instrument he had picked up haphazard, he must still have heard their voices in the distance. When Soames brought off his *coup* he must have known that Dick was at a safe distance. What in the name of Heaven and Hell was he after?

It was Bobs who suggested an explanation, but not, unfortunately, till he had dragged Dick off to his room, and they were sitting with whisky and soda on a fender stool, steaming their wet shoulders dry by a blazing fire. And because it was the first time Bobs had got Dick to himself all day he was naturally more anxious to learn of Mack's doings and attitude to the case than to make suggestions. It was a heartening conversation, for Bobs simply dismissed any question of the Bishop's guilt as fantastic: he refused to hear Judith's name in connection with Ulder. To save their reputations he was quite willing to believe that Canon Wye had seen himself as the Vengeance of God, or that the Chancellor might have doped Ulder while he got hold of his papers, and unluckily—or rather perhaps luckily—overdone it. Of Staples he said simply that any Irishman would commit any murder at any given moment, but he flung himself most whole-heartedly of course into the question of Soames' suspicious behaviour.

"Of course Soames bagged the Chancellor's dope and finished Ulder off. Why? Oh well—"

"Yes, why, why, why?" said Dick. "Don't say he was trying to save the Church or risking his life for Judith—come to that, Mack might suspect you! No, I'm sure Soames is not mixed up with murder, but I'm equally sure he stole that bag and has hidden it somewhere."

"But surely he'd destroy it!"

"What chance has he had to-day with police and guests all over the house? I'd think he threw it out of that window and retrieved it in the night, but how could he when for all he knew Ulder would wake up next morning? Sometimes I'm afraid it's the papers he was after, and the papers that he's got, and that he's meaning to set up in the blackmail business himself. But why bang windows down for that?"

"Suppose he stowed away the bag somewhere in the Bridge attics," suggested Bobs slowly. "He chose a pretty drastic way of keeping you out of that part, I admit—but effective!"

"Well, he can't get in himself now! That door's blocked up with glass and rubbish."

"But there's another door at the other end!" said Bobs unwillingly. "Hang on, Dick, this isn't a steeple-chase! I'll come with you. But I'm afraid it's too late."

If the bag had ever been in these attics it was certainly too late. The most thorough search revealed nothing in the grim, dusty skeletons of furniture and ghostly old bedsteads. And as if he feared questioning, Soames himself was invisible, and if the Palace staff were untrained, it had at least grasped one Draconian law of Good Service, that no information should be given on the doings of any servant who is, technically speaking, out.

"And I can't see that the whole thing is really so important," said Bobs reasonably. "I mean whether Soames stole this bag or not doesn't affect the—the main problem. Come on, Dick, there's the bell for Evensong! About time you joined us!"

"You're right." Dick tried to speak lightly. "So far I seem only to have been qualifying for a prison chaplain."

There are a few rare men—and far fewer women—who can shut up their thoughts and emotions into water-tight compartments. Such was Dick's usual practice, and he entered Chapel with the firm intention of attending only to his own spiritual affairs. But it was impossible. For here and now he recognized with a shock of horror how little thought he had given to the main protagonists of this ghastly duel with the Law. Yes, he admitted to himself frankly, he had been concentrating so fiercely on Soames' strange antics, just because he dared not consider other possibilities. He had refused to face the dilemma that no one in this Chapel could conceivably have committed murder and that nevertheless one of them must have done so. Every instinct told him it was impossible: he and Bobs had agreed on that with eager certainty. But what, after all, thought Dick despairingly, does one man know of the twisted convolutions of another's mind? Even his religious faith could not assure him that every man who sought and received grace from God all his life might not in time of temptation fall away. History can show only too many records of men who, never suspecting their inherent weakness or prejudices, have done wrong, terrible wrong, that good, or what they fancied good, might come of it. Let him be honest and face such possibilities in those around him, to see the real man as he was behind the Bishop's hollow face, sagging with lines of endurance, behind Canon Wye's mask of contemptuous indifference, and the Chancellor's trembling efforts to maintain his usual air of genial solemnity on these occasions.

It seemed to Dick, using the X-rays of his intelligence, as if he could watch the Bishop's influence on Dick's life, as on so many others at school and in the ministry, as an infinitely kind, sympathetic, other-worldly-minded, holy servant of God, yet dogged always by one phantom, that of Fear. Yes, he was a coward, as St. Blaze had known, and the diocese whispered. He might or might not be one physically—few had any data—but he would go to great lengths to avoid the sight of pain or suffering in others, of incurring enmity or even unfriendliness, of standing up face to face with a foe. Cowardice, so often unsuspected in the victims of inferiority complexes, is often enough the instigator of crime. Hadn't the former Emperor overturned Europe because he feared the might of England and her friendship with France? Fear of new doctrines or of devilish craft had made holy men torture heretics and witches. Fear of criticism, fear of consequences, stained the pages of the dealings of Church with dissent and free thinking through the ages, just as fear of change had led the servants of Christ to tolerate the evils of a capitalist system. Gazing at the face of the man whom he had loved all his life Dick saw, as if for the first time, those odd tiny indications of cowardice habitually concealed by the kind, dignified, welcoming, controlled mien; he noted now the drooping lip, receding chin, the hidden weariness and in-dwelling gaze of those whose imagination and self-protective instincts outrun their courage. As the Bishop knelt in his stall, his fine head propped on his long delicate hands, its outline dim by the candlelight, Dick realized despairingly that he himself, with the extrovert's lucky habit of never suspecting or meeting trouble even a quarter of the way, had not the faintest idea of the workings of the prelate's mind. As a bishop and a father he had seen Ulder as the spirit of terror and evil personified. "But the Bishop couldn't have done it," Dick's normal self reiterated, coming to life, even while his inner self reiterated: "How do you *know*?"

It was easier to imagine a case against Canon Wye! Dick knew him only slightly and he had seen him roused to passion more than once. Never would he forget a sermon long ago in which the Canon had thundered forth a picture of the pains of Hell ("So *old-world*," a curate had complained, "just like Dante

in an Underground railway!") and threatened with this probable destination not only Jews, Turks, heretics and infidels, but
any who omitted to keep every ordinance of the Church from
fasting in Lent to frequent confessions. "Yea, I hate them right
sore, even as though they were my enemies," was his view of
all outside the Anglo-Catholic world, so to what lengths would
he not go against such an enemy of God and man as Ulder?
His life of service to Heaven had made him admit his personal
ambition as a fault, but not the spirit of hatred. There he knelt
upright, disdaining hassock or pew-rest; his eyes staring bleakly
before him, black and white, a dimmed torch, but still vibrant
with passion. Might not such hatred, no less than the Bishop's
fear, have driven him to take on himself the judgment of Heav-
en when his foe lay last night at their mercy? Might not he and
the Bishop in their interviews have reasoned that Ulder was a
stricken man, probably a dying man, and that to shorten his life
mercifully by those few hours which would save them from exposure and ruin was expediently not far removed from justice?

"That's all very well, but where did they get the morphia?"
Dick silenced the voice which cried a thousand negatives to
that question. He must view this thing, like Mack, from neutral,
if less hostile, ground. It was not for him to point out to Mack
that the murderer would presumably have destroyed any tube
of morphia before the police searched the rooms, and indeed,
from a vague memory of volumes on state trials, the only reading in the hotel at Loch Echinore, Dick seemed to remember
that bottles almost always did turn up, empty or half-full alike,
as if their owners clung irresponsibly to such relics of their great
exploits. He turned his gaze to the Chancellor, for there at least
was the owner of dangerous drugs, though how dangerous only
the report next day could show. It was strange and rather terrible that, though the old gentleman looked anxious, wretched,
and ill at ease, yet it was far harder to attribute a crime to his
legal caution and habit of mind than to priests driven by fear
and hatred respectively to juggle with their own consciences.
Over Dick swept that wave of depression no honest Christian

can occasionally combat. "One could see Christ if it weren't for the Church and the clergy!" In his schooldays Dick had coined the phrase of kicking the Devil in his pants, and he took the advice metaphorically, and vigorously, now. "Working through common man Christ perforce chose for His disciples not heroes but cowards, liars and snobs," he told himself in the words of Chesterton, and joined vigorously in the not very successful hymn on which the Bishop insisted:

> *"Open to us the heavenly road*
> *And bar the way to death's abode ..."*

No, not a good escape really, for it brought a sudden vision, a youthful obsession, of a short walk at dawn blindfold, of the executioner waiting, of the despairing exultant words of the burial service. For a moment he saw the three figures before him staggering those few steps, all insignia of their professions, all dignity and respect gone. Violently he pulled himself together. "Oh come, oh come, Adonai," he almost shouted, though how had this charming medieval conception of Deity crept down into the English Hymnal? He shut his eyes to force his mind far away to those gold pillars above the Aegean, to airy gods of woods and hills, of love and laughter and Olympic heights. But that was really not of much avail, for in their glades, flower-crowned, singing, and smiling as she sang, he saw Judith, with her lovely hair alight, her white peplon floating lightly over fields of asphodel. Judith was pagan all right! She was amoral, and from nursery days would do anything to gain her ends. Was it because human nature could or would not detect real cruelty at the heart of beauty, or was it because he couldn't believe the girl had wits enough to plan murder, on an impulse, achieve it, and then not boast about it afterwards to one chosen confidante at least, that Dick could not focus his suspicions on her? Well, the service was over and much good it had done him! "The Peace of God ..." the Bishop was pronouncing, but how much peace would any one have in the Palace to-night?

Dick himself fared badly. In the room on one side of his Canon Wye was pacing up and down murmuring what might be prayers but sounded like curses. The old house with its worn panelling was a sounding board, and in the Bishop's room on the other side Dick to his surprise heard such bangs and knocks of drawers as usually attend a house removal.

"What is it, dear?" called Mrs. Broome to her husband from the adjoining bedroom to his. She was utterly worn out with the duties and terrors of the last twenty-four hours, bad news about Moira from the hospital, anxiety about her adored, sinful Judith, and most of all the unuttered suspicions of the police which haunted the house like a creeping miasma. "Aren't you in bed? Are you looking for some thing?"

"No, no!" The Bishop's denial was unnecessarily vehement.

"But, dear, you are!" Mrs. Broome got out of bed a few minutes later, to see for herself why her husband was still pulling and tugging at his drawers and wardrobe. She stared in blank amazement in the doorway when she saw him poised on the arm of a chair, feeling along the top of a very high chest.

"Mark dear! Whatever is it? Let me help you!"

"No, no, it is only my spectacles!" The Bishop, a strange, prophetic figure in his camel's hair dressing-gown, descended abruptly, and as abruptly began to search the uneven floor beneath the piece of furniture.

"But, dearest, they are on your dressing-table!"

"My other spectacles!" The Bishop moved miserably to the bureau, and opened and shut the drawers with the helpless hopelessness of those who have already searched a spot again and again.

"But there they are, on the bureau! And you should not read at night, you know, with your tired eyes! And you ought to sleep, you look worn out! Don't shake your head! Why not come to the other bed in my room and let me give you a somnerell—they are quite harmless—and let me read you to sleep?"

"No one shall ever touch sleeping draughts in my house again," declared the Bishop vehemently.

"Now, dearest, you must not let this get on your nerves!" Mrs. Broome assumed a cheerfulness which she was far from feeling. "These dreadful times pass and are forgotten, thank Heaven. Why, my old nurse used to tell us of the widow of a man who was executed and yet ended her days in a villa called Hemp View!"

But it seemed that this felicitous reminiscence brought no consolation. She had to leave the Bishop till sheer fatigue drove him to bed at last.

An hour later when the whole house seemed wrapped in slumber, more than one of those who tossed in the light sleep of anxiety seemed to remember that they heard a stealthy foot-fall creeping along the passages, and the light click of a door in the Bridge wing.

X
FRIDAY MORNING

THOUGH IT seemed incredible there was a certain slackening of tension in the Palace on Friday morning. It may be that human nature, after the strain of the shock and horror of the day before, relaxed automatically, or that the desperate appeal of the Litany and the solemnity of the following service, brought comfort. It was certainly reinforced by a telephone message from Mack that he could not reach the Palace till the afternoon, and the impression which Dick confided to Bobs that the old boy was distinctly rattled. The only orders he sent were that no one was to leave the Palace without permission from Tonks and Corn who were coming out to pursue their search for the missing bottle and missing papers. "And Corn started on the Bishop's sermons in the order of the Church year and hadn't reached the third Sunday in Advent after three hours at it," said Bobs.

The Chief Constable was one of those Scotsmen who are never so happy as when they feel overworked and meet general opposition, but he was indeed having a little too much of both. The Magistrate, a personal friend of the Bishop, had demanded an interview on Thursday evening in answer to the appeal for a search-warrant, and Mack had been obliged to leave his den, his slippers and his glass of grog to receive a few very outspoken criticisms. "Why, the man wasn't even officially dead, let alone murdered," the irate magistrate had declared, "until the police-surgeon had seen the body. We all know dear old Lee is blind and deaf, and till Surgeon Hay had given an opinion you had no official status!" Mack reached his home at eleven o'clock, to find a village Northcliffe in the hall anxious to know what line the *Evelake Courier* should take over the affair when it appeared on Saturday. Mack, imprisoned all yesterday in the snow-bound Palace, had congratulated himself on the fact that the Press would not interfere with him. He had not realized that the milkcart and butcher's van had both reached the kitchen wing through the snow, and that Tonks and Corn, however discreet, were both married men. To bristle his eyebrows and storm at the young journalist and demand discretion was useless: "I've already sent a short par. to the *Daily Wail*—it'll be in time for the second edition if not the first." Hardly had Mack turned him out than the telephone bell began to ring, first with a promise from the police surgeon to send his final report in next morning, but assuring Mack provisionally, "Morphia-poisoning, not a doubt. ..." Second, a severe message from Blacksea to say that glass, tube, and paper alike were so covered with finger-prints that they were valueless—and lastly, by a long incoherent message from a woman whom he identified with great difficulty as the Chancellor's housekeeper. She had only just got in because her nephew was taken that bad: she knew nothing about bottles and had never touched one. No, she didn't do the Chancellor's bedroom—that was the work of the daily woman who came in, and was strict T.T., and had taken the pledge and all like herself. Oh, not *that* kind of bottle! Oh, she'd seen plenty of medicine bottles and handed over a lot to a rag-and-bone man only yesterday morning. Yes, she did seem to remember young Captain Chailly having a big bottle—malt extract, was it? She couldn't remember. Oh yes, he'd other bottles, and she might have kept some of them or she might not. And what was all the fuss about anyway, for the Chancellor wasn't one to go handing his bottles about and wouldn't hurt a fly.

It seemed to Mack barely a moment before the telephone bell awakened him next morning, and from the moment he reached his office he was knee deep in reports, routine work and unsought interviews. Although the *Daily Wail*, cautious about local gossip, only referred to the sudden death of the Rev. Thomas Ulder at Evelake Palace under mysterious circumstances, which are, we understand, being investigated by the police, that was enough to rouse a storm of gossip and surmise. Then he hurried out to see the Coroner and arrange for the inquest. There would be no difficulty in collecting a jury, said the Coroner ("A churchwarden, of course, and looks it," growled Mack to himself), and it was fixed for Monday at one o'clock. "If it suits the Bishop," the Coroner added, which did nothing to improve Mack's temper. He returned to find requests for interviews from the Dean of Evelake, the Sheriff and Lord Lieutenant of the County, and an M.P., a local baronet, who was related to the Home Secretary. Nearly every one made use of the plea or implied that the demand was made in view of the indecent publicity of the case. Never again would Mack fail to recognize, or fail to impress on his subordinates, the importance of meeting with and tackling the Press! He had, since his arrival, so often heard criticisms of the Bishop, and jokes about Mrs. Broome, that it astounded him to realize how "these English" rose up as a man to defend their country, their Church, and its local chief.

There was some satisfaction in finding that Blacksea had managed to get a sergeant over, who could look after the office, and pursue enquiries about these sinister (and almost certainly imaginary) strangers. Tonks had left a report of a conversation with Canon Wye's housekeeper, a tart, austere ritualist, who said that no medicine was taken or needed at the clergyhouse, for all her gentlemen rose too early and worked too hard to bother their insides with these patent stuffs, unless it were a dose of salts! But that report could not wholly clear a man whose work often took him to London, and, moreover, in Mack's opinion, looked the most murderous of the lot.

The result of the autopsy, which arrived unexpectedly soon, cheered him considerably. The full report was to follow but provisionally Dr. Lee's verdict was confirmed—morphia-poisoning, three grains—a fatal dose.

"At last they'll all recognize that wilful murder has been done," Mack growled to the Sergeant who had been sent from Blacksea. "I've told the Magistrate in confidence it couldn't be an outside job—(though these people have been in to report sinister strangers in the local bars, of course)—or suicide—but you can see the big idea in this confounded little Church nest is to hush things up. Look at this." He rumpled his hair and eyebrows till they bristled like quills as he picked up a letter. "This is from the deceased's cousin and housekeeper and surviving relative: 'Thanks for communication re death of my cousin Ulder. Please arrange everything with his solicitors, Messrs. Bushy. Cannot attend funeral or pretend to be surprised at news. My cousin had so many enemies and indeed I often felt I could murder him myself.' There's a nice womanly woman for you! Mad, of course, like her deceased cousin, mad and bad, I expect. Still murder is murder and the Law's got to get hold of the murderer."

Three miles away at the Palace the stricken peace reigned till the arrival of the newspapers and post at an unusually late hour. After one glance at the *Daily Wail* in the hall, Bobs summoned Dick.

"Look here, you'd better get out to your hermitage as soon as you can. There'll be no peace after this!"

"They won't want me, I suppose? I mean I can't be any good."

"I don't think so. The Bishop will be kept at the end of the telephone, I expect, with messages of sympathy and condolence and the best thing for him! Mrs. Broome says he's hardly slept for two nights and he just sits in his arm chair brooding. Canon Wye's shut up over his sermon, and poor old Chailly's keeping his bed till lunch. I've got to face this music—you do a bunk. I told Soames to have the room ready for you and there he is coming from the ruins now. What shall I say to these blasted reporters?"

"Forget Alfred the Truthteller, and let them infer that the police think it's an outside job!"

"I'd he for the Bishop, let alone imply inferences," said Bobs, watching Soames as he approached.

"Good man, Bobs!" smiled Dick. "What's Soames got a bucket for? He needn't have scrubbed the room!"

"Coal, I think—I told him to try to get the fire going in the prehistoric stove there. Jove, what a little worm that chap looks among the ruins! Hullo! There's Judith!"—and "Hullo, there's Sue!" came simultaneously from the young men, as Dick stepped from the window and terrace across the lawn, and Bobs most reluctantly went off with the letters and papers to the Bishop.

The wind was still high but at the moment it was tossing the storm-clouds away from the sun, and the remaining patches of snow, the bare grey-gold stone and yew-trees, sparkling with rain drops, all seemed to shimmer and dissolve into a misty radiance round the two girls with their bare curly heads and big fur coats. Sparrows were twittering, doves were murmuring round the old dovecot, and away across the valley they could see a flight of wild duck. I don't feel much like a parson or a sleuth this morning, thought Dick. Oh dear, listen to our wild goose!

"So please understand, Soames," Judith was saying, "that when Mr. Fitzroy comes you're to bring him straight to the new wing drawing-room. Mrs. Broome says we may have it quite to ourselves, and you must send lunch and tea for us there. You're going out to Evelake for an hour or two after lunch? Oh good! Then you may bring me back a tin of verbena bath salts—why does Mother have that sickly rose now, Sue?—and two packets of invisible hair-pins—black *not* bronze—oh, and a solicitor if you see one about, because Clive will harp on that,

Sue darling! And Soames, bring out a tin of weed-killer for the Chief Constable! Come on and let's see your dugout, Dick? Oh, clumsy!"

The exclamation was indeed justified, for Dick had tripped over a very obvious stone pedestal in the grass, and knocking against Judith, in an effort to retrieve his balance, had kicked over the bucket which Soames was carrying.

"Sorry," he said. "Thanks for cleaning out the stove, Soames. Is the fire burning? Lord, what a mess!"

"But you're only making it worse!" said Judith, as Dick thoughtfully shuffled the embers into the lawn. Yes, they were warm! He thought he had seen a faint wisp of smoke in the bucket. What had Soames been burning, and why?

"Dick was quite right to knock into you and silence you!" said Sue. "You really shouldn't joke about poisons to Soames just now."

"Darling! What a perfect parson's wife you'll make some day; such a one for tact! Is this your home from home, Dick?"

The twisting gap between elders and brambles had brought them again to the outer walls of the Abbey which overlooked the little dark river in the snow, and the pleasant valley of Eve-lake below. Amid the remote, crumbling melancholy walls the newly repaired turret looked as out of place as a cake-stand in a dungeon. The interior was at first sight even less inviting, for the ground floor, half-cleared of rubble, had evidently been used as a tool-shed by the excavators of the ruins, and from it, as Bobs had said, a rickety wooden staircase led up to the floor above: the flight led from the corner where the old twisting stone steps curled upwards, blocked now with stones and rub-ble. The top step was level with the tiny rounded door of the upper room. The floor was boarded with rough deal, and the stone walls had a coat of plaster. Three slits of windows allowed a watcher to survey any comer from east, north or west. No doubt it was for the children of that prolific Bishop Main that this retreat had been thus sketchily restored, and a hideous little black stove fitted in it. Mrs. Broome's mark was to be seen in a small chintz-covered sofa and arm chair, the Bishop's in a plain deal table, a bookshelf and a prie-dieu.

"Oh, what a smell!" cried Sue, thrusting back the slender lattice windows. "Is it mould or rats, or dead monks, Dick?"

"Burnt leather, I fancy," said Dick, looking grimly at the stove. It was ready laid, and Sue was on her knees with a match to light it at once.

"I think it's rather marvellous," said Judith. "Couldn't you say your prayers indoors and let Clive and me sit here this afternoon? Goodness! I must fly to meet him in the hall, in case he meets Papa and leads the candidates into bad ways! Come along, Sue! Dick wants to tell his beads. Or do you want her to stay?"

"Well, at least she doesn't buzz," said Dick, but Sue declared, blushing a little, that she must go and do the flowers, so Dick was left to make his much needed retreat.

Very few people were in the dining-room when he entered it two hours later, save for the candidates who had evidently enjoyed a lazy, unorganized morning. The Bishop had hardly moved from his own room where, Bobs reported, he had brooded silently, save when now and again he went suddenly up to his bedroom to pace up and down, according to Mrs. Broome, refusing to answer letters or the telephone. Canon Wye strode in, ate fish at the sideboard and disappeared. The Chancellor sat sunk in silence beside his hostess, a fatigued old man. Only Doris and Mrs. Briggs waited: Soames had, it appeared, squared Tonks, and gone off on his bicycle to the Hospital. Mrs. Broome and Sue were mournful and abstracted after the Matron's answer to their enquiries on the telephone. Moira, unfortunately, had contracted a chill, and in her fragile state they feared bronchitis and pneumonia. "Some discomfort and a little homesick," the Matron said. "And one knows that means acute pain and utter misery," diagnosed Moira's mistress sadly. Dick himself had only a very sketchy meal, for he was summoned away to a telephone call from Scotland Yard.

"That you, Dick?" asked his friend, Herriot. "The Chief wants to know if your Chief Constable feller is likely to want our help? We're expecting he will!"

"He won't want it, yet I think he needs it personally."

"Stupid? Obstructive?"

"Oh no, just anti-clerical. Wants to hang a Bishop!" (With Soames safely out of the house, and everyone at luncheon, Dick felt safe on the Chaplain's telephone.)

"He won't manage that on his own responsibility, I can assure him. No end of a stir over the *Daily Wail* here, I can tell you. Well, make him see reason and ring us later. We chaps of the old brigade are laughing like mad at your having got your nose into this. Write me your impressions like a good chap, or wire in the old code to me. Meanwhile, about your questions! Your friend the butler, Edward Soames, was gaoled for petty larceny at Brighton in April 1914 on leaving some North Country Orphanage. Can't read the name! Oh yes, Dorbury! Your county— Evelake. Enlisted as private in the Larkshire Infantry in 1915, as Edward Sullivan—kept his initials, wise man!—on being given choice of enlistment or reformatory after second conviction for shop-lifting. There was some monkeying about his name then, and the army records are tracking it down for me—his new choice wasn't discovered apparently for a year or two, and they let him remain as Edward Sullivan. You know what a mess local recruiting stations were in at that time! Served on Salisbury Plain only, and not very gallantly! Owing to persistent malingering, and some noisome skin complaint, he was transferred to the R.A.S.C., and served just six weeks safely at a base near Dieppe, when he was invalided home and discharged. 1917, convicted again as Edward Soames, this time for cat burglary on a very modest scale. Prison chaplain at Blacksea helped him on discharge, and got him a new start as man-servant at Evelake Academy for Boys where there was presumably nothing to steal. Has kept straight since then and kept to name of Edward Soames. But I don't know how they dared risk him in a Palace!"

"Shortage of staff, and I fancy the Headmaster wasn't over business-like. At least I gather Soames only gave a very watered-down version of your tale to Mrs. Broome, who admits she was desperate for a man-servant. Well, Herriot, thanks a lot! I'll let you know if we want his finger-prints, but I don't think they'd be of any use in this case. I'd like to know our friend Soames'—Sullivan's—original name if you do get a report of it, just in case he's some connection with this affair. The C.C. thinks my case against him a bit bogus, but I'm pretty sure he's at his old Autolycus tricks, and I want to know how and why. Look here, I can't be bothered with codes! I think I could ring you up safely this evening at ten-thirty or eleven, home address? Love to Jane and the baby—I mean to christen it—beg pardon, him—next week."

But what would next week bring forth, Dick wondered despairingly, as he put down the receiver and turned to the vestibule. Sounds of a car in the drive had reached him during those last words, and there was Mack extracting himself from the old Humber, more bristling and purposeful than ever. The deceptive peace, the false armistice at the Palace was over indeed.

"What a morning I've had!" Mack broke out, drawing Dick into the old library. "Of all the obstructionist, high and dry Tory ritualist holes, this is the limit! Why, I might have been accusing the archangels of crime from the fuss Herne made over giving me a search warrant—chief magistrate on the bench indeed! More like a doting mother saying her blessed bairn had never done wrong in his life! I've got the inquest fixed for Monday—in the Town Hall at one o'clock, and the Coroner will do his best to pack the jury with sidesmen, you bet! Autopsy confirmed anyhow—3 grains of morphine—a fatal dose all right. And got on to Ulder's lawyers who are communicating with sole surviving relative—cousin I think—at Addsey. About time if she'd seen the *Daily Wail*. Blame myself for thinking one could escape the Press, though you'd have thought a country hole like this in a blizzard was safe enough. You might have reminded me there might be tradesmen's vans at the back, Dick! Any reporters yet?"

"The poor chaplain has been dealing with them all morning, sir. But I'm sure they got nothing out of him. In fact he may have given them an impression that you suspect an outside job!"

"Infernal cheek of you, Dick! Evelake is full of stories of sinister characters in bars and garages already—more work for the police! You know as well as I do that it was an inside job!"

"Any line on the Chancellor's bottle, sir?"

"Line! Too many lines! Last night when I got hold of the housekeeper on the telephone she was ready to say the house was a chemist's shop for medicines, and her master and his son dope-fiends. She said he threw bottles away by the cart load, and just had a good clear out. Then after a good gossip all round, I expect, she saw she'd said the wrong thing, and didn't want to lose a good place with a luxurious bachelor, so she rang up again, a solicitor at her elbow if you please, to say her master never dosed himself except with a little drop of some stuff Mr. Edgar Chailly brought back from India which couldn't hurt a fly, as she'd taken cupfuls of it herself. Every one's in league to protect their employers in this case."

"Speaks well for the employers," said Dick. "But Soames is not that type. Just a word about him! Last night—" Dick, plunging into the story of his observations yesterday, felt they were hardly convincing, and failed to attract Mack's suspicions.

"Well, well, odd, but still! Dick, how often am I to repeat to you that if you stick to motive you can't go far wrong. That chap may be up to no good, but I don't believe he is a lunatic who murders for a bit of sport. I've got reports on Staples too, and I don't think much of him. A little worm, but he seems to have told the truth all along the line. I'll let you look at the notes later. What I want to do first of all is to present my warrant and have a thorough search upstairs."

XI
FRIDAY AFTERNOON

"But this is unwarrantable," was the Bishop's first not very happy reaction to this request when Dick led Mack into his room. He was sitting, as he had done most of the day, in his armchair by the fire, dozing, writing and saying nothing, a stricken old man. "You have turned my house upside down already. Your men are still, I believe, occupied in making hay of my manuscripts; our rooms have been ransacked without proper authority—the High Sheriff rang up this morning to sympathize with my chaplain—the Lord Lieutenant proposes to call. I tell you it is unwarrantable."

"It's not that, for here's the warrant," snapped Mack, turning to the attendant Tonks. "And what, may I ask," he added, his eye caught by a long shining sports car parked below the Bishop's windows, just out of sight from the drive, "what is that car doing here? Whose is it?"

"It belongs to my—to Mr. Fitzroy, my daughter's fiancé." The Bishop stumbled a little over Clive's proper designation. "He has come here, though against my wishes, to see my daughter and, I gather, take her away to some relative, after paying a visit to the Hospital on our poor old maid."

"Hullo, where's Dick? Hullo, Bobs!" Judith's voice rang out from the hall, as the Bishop spoke. (How like that young woman to time her entrance so perfectly, thought Dick, though you bet Mack will be sticky about the exit.) "Thank you, Mabel! Thank you, Doris! Only my dressing-case, for I'm coming back in a day or two, when this house doesn't *smell* of police. Bobs, this is Clive! Isn't he perfectly sweet? And he's brought me the most surprising news, though it's made me a bit wonky somehow. I must tell Father this minute!"

"Mack's there," Bobs warned her, but Judith had already run into the library, followed by her future husband.

"And how darned good to see a layman," was Dick's unregenerate thought as he stared at Clive, the tall young guardsman. Not only the type Dick had ragged with at school, counted amongst his vast miscellany of friends at Oxford and found kinship with in France, but above all, just the type for pretty, wild Judith, he decided. Clive was no rich, vacuous nonentity: he was the huntin', fishin', shootin' young officer, who would take Judith off from her London friends and night-clubs, forget about her divorce, adore her gaiety and laugh at her follies, and in the end make an honest woman of her, with tweeds, herbaceous borders, children, dogs and all. The Bishop and Mrs. Broome had viewed him only as an enemy who had brought their Judith to Sin (all the more perhaps because it was not only his name which had figured in her divorce-suit), but it was clear that for the moment the Bishop was watching him with undisguised admiration. For Clive was no fool and knew something of the law: he was no respecter of constables—Chief or otherwise—and he was ready to speak his mind.

"Oh Father!" Judith's clear voice was a little awed and broken. "I had to come and see you! I couldn't wait any longer! Clive has brought me the—the strangest news!"

"Keep it till we're alone—" (Clive's voice of command would be very useful with Judith!) "It's this gentleman I want to see." He turned upon Mack. "I've come to ask you, sir, what you mean by your behaviour to my fiancée? It has been consistently brutal and, what's more, illegal!"

"Meaning what?" asked Mack bristling.

"You questioned her before she had an opportunity of getting her solicitor."

"Not a formal examination," snapped Mack. "Chailly was in the house anyway, if she'd asked for him."

"You searched her without a warrant."

"Oh, Clive darling, he didn't *strip* me, you know!" cried Judith brightly. "Only my cases!"

"Property of the deceased was missing," said Mack fiercely. "Every one gave us permission to hunt for it. No need of a search warrant if leave is freely given." His tone grew a trifle less bellicose as he asked himself uncomfortably if he had not omitted the formality with the girl, whom he consistently described to himself by the usual Anglo-Saxon word.

"Oh, my sweet, what a horrid fib!" cried Judith. "You just banged straight into my room and shook out my frillies! Mabel was there, you know, and she'll back me up."

"So I'm taking Judith away, sir!" Clive turned to the Bishop. "I'm sure you'd rather I got her out of the clutches of these bullying policemen, and an aunt of mine is hoping to see us both. No, you can't detain her, sir!" He turned upon Mack who was obviously on the verge of a break-out. "You've not a shred of proof against her: you've searched her things—illegally too—and I'll leave her address. Could any human being in their senses think that she went and poisoned a parson anyway?"

"Every one who was threatened by blackmail here is suspect, every one!" Mack glared at the Bishop and his daughter. "Has she acquainted you with the hold Mr. Ulder had over her and you too?"

"Nonsense! Of course I'd have paid up," said Clive with the impatience of the wealthy at the mention of a trivial debt. "And then horsewhipped him till he didn't dare to come near me again."

"Someone found a safer way to silence him. I suppose you didn't happen to visit the Palace on Wednesday night?" Mack had wholly forgotten his office now. He was speaking as a Scot to a braggart Englishman, a working man to a self assertive aristocratic idler, a hunter to a rival who was robbing him of lawful prey.

For a moment Dick thought there really would be murder in the house, and prepared unconsciously to tackle low, but Clive checked himself and laughed shortly.

"That's actionable I should think, slander and unjustifiable defamation. I was staying with my uncle, Claude Vivian, who is Member for the County, as you may know. Anyhow, you'll get a reminder when he asks a question about all this in the House."

"Indeed! And I suppose he'll produce the evidence Ulder held against you and Mrs. Mortimer. Even if we don't find

Ulder's papers and that hotel bill, the Law can follow up his evidence and make things very unpleasant for you!"

"You'd take on the job of blackmail?" sneered Clive. "I hoped you'd suggest that! What's *your* price?"

"Insults won't do you any good, sir. It would be my duty to follow up information, however received, and communicate with the King's Proctor."

Judith suddenly clapped her hands. No one present had ever seen her pale and subdued for five minutes before: that was, they were to realize, her full and unusual tribute to the past.

"Oh, Clive, I must tell him! It's too good a joke! Well, no, not a joke exactly, but—Daddy darling, Clive came here to-day, though you've never allowed it before, because the strangest thing has happened. He had a cable to say that Mike, poor old Mike, was dying of cholera in Egypt, and an hour ago a telegram came to say he'd gone! And, of course, it did make me feel—well, queer, you know, though he was pretty horrid to me, and I never loved him after the first. He wouldn't," she added with appalling candour, "hear of my having a baby, you know, and I do think that's so unfair, though I wouldn't listen to people who wanted me to go to law about it, because I do think that sort of case is so vulgar, don't you? Still, he's dead! And he did so like being alive! However, I mustn't be morbid." (No one was indeed likely to accuse Judith of this fault!) "And you may say 'all's well that ends well'. For here I am a respectable widow, and Clive's going for a special licence, and we'll be married in a day or two, quite quiet it must be, I'm afraid, but most luckily I've got a dream of a grey georgette I've never worn—you remember it, Major Mack? And the past doesn't matter a bit, Clive said—though I'd like you all to know we had separate rooms at Blacksea, darling!—why, we could book a room at the King's Proctor's without the tiniest risk now, if he takes couples in! It always sounds so like a pub, you know!"

"Much was said, little was done and an earthquake broke up the meeting." That saying of Thucydides covered the remainder of the interview pretty well, as Bobs remarked to Dick. Clive carried Judith off while Mack was still de bating whether you could or couldn't restrain the prospective bride of the Member's nephew, and Judith's last words to her family were spoken in the octagon vestibule, with Clive waiting at the car.

"Good-bye, darlings. Mummy, I'm sorry I've been a curse for I adore you. You'll let Sue come to stay with me when I'm whiter than snow, won't you? Daddy darling, I've plagued you but I worship you. I wonder if I should tell you something I did just now?" Behind very unusual but becoming tear-drops Judith's eyes sparkled now more brightly than ever. "No, perhaps not, for anyhow it's all right now!"

All right for her but not for us, thought Bobs gloomily as the light of his life (however delusive an Aurora) disappeared.

Mack strode away with his temper at boiling point. It was not assuaged when Tonks presented himself in the old library to report that he had been unable to find either Soames or Staples for those interviews which had been the first items on Mack's programme.

"Not though I searched up and down, high and low, sir," said the ex-verger with pompous resignation. "But, sir, there is a cable come for the Chancellor he told me to show to you," he added, more hopefully, "and a suspicious circumstance I should like to bring to your notice."

"Chancellor Chailly Palace Evelake. Paregoric contains opium no morphia. Forwarding prescription. Edgar."

"Oh well, that's that! Surgeon says opium would not have the same effect as morphia. Never did really think much doing about that bottle—we wouldn't have thought of it if he hadn't tried to hide it away like the old woman he is! What's the other trouble?"

"Pursuant to your orders, sir, I was keeping an eye on the inmates of the house, and noticed Canon Wye go to his bedroom at twelve o'clock this morning. Shortly after I heard the crackling of a fire, and referred to the housemaid who happened to be passing as to whether it were customary to light fires in bedrooms so early in the day, in view of the fuel shortage.

She assured me that such a course was unprecedented." ("Not on your life," had been Mabel's actual expression.) "When the Canon emerged at the luncheon gong he left the door of his room locked behind him, while he rapidly partook of some refreshment."

"Oh, get on with it, Tonks," said Mack impatiently. "You're not writing a parish magazine!"

"The Canon," pursued Tonks in a pained voice, "returned to his room, locked himself in and only half an hour ago, 3 pip emma, went down to the Chapel. On this occasion the door was unlocked and I entered to find the grate full of ashes burnt paper I would judge, and a great quantity it would seem from the—er—debris."

"Mess," suggested Mack impatiently.

"Just so, sir. I then made my way to the Chapel. The Canon knelt at his stall engaged, as you may say, in prayer. He did not notice my entrance, for I am accustomed to move about sacred edifices quietly, but continued to groan aloud, sir, uttering phrases to the effect that he had sinned most miserably against God and man. Of course, sir, we know such gentlemen may be over-conscientious, but I thought I should report these circumstances to you."

Mack followed his subordinate upstairs unwillingly enough, but as he gave a look at the Canon's fireplace he whistled loudly. Certainly a holocaust had taken place, and so thorough a one that it was impossible to trace any unscathed fragment. Well, if these were indeed the missing papers of Ulder's, for which the police had made such a hue and cry, the Canon was in a very nasty position! "A very nasty position," repeated Mack as he made his way down to the Chapel, for if there was one point which seemed incontrovertible it was that those papers could only have been abstracted safely after Ulder had been lulled into his last sleep.

"Mea culpa! Mea maxima culpa!" It was not so much the words as the heart-broken accent of the Canon's voice which arrested Mack, as, for the first time, he entered the little Pug-

inesque Chapel, sniffing disdainfully at its ornaments and flowers and a faint suggestion of incense. "Grievous to me ... the burden is intolerable!" Mack's loud cough interrupted the flow of misery from the stalls, and the Canon leapt up, even more torch-like and militant than ever in his surprise.

"You dog me here!" he cried. "You cannot even leave me alone to confess, and make my peace with God!"

"Not if it's a question for the Law, Canon. I've no wish to interrupt any one's prayers, but if there's any confession you have to make it should be made to me! And I am bound to ask you at once what exactly was the nature of those papers which you burnt in your room this morning."

"I had no right to do it!" Canon Wye suddenly quietened down and spoke almost apologetically. "I knew it, but the perusal was so bitter, so humiliating to me—"

"So it would have been to others! You were not the only one concerned!"

"You are right—they were the words of a poison pen. They have caused death, the cruellest kind of death, to the soul!"

"Look here, sir, just keep to plain language." Mack's eyes were gleaming, for now with that word poison he seemed to be on the track at last. Mad this fellow was, of course, stark, staring mad! He had killed Ulder in that very spirit in which men had burnt heretics at the stake, and "That's the sort of thing that doesn't do nowadays"—so he pursued the tenor of his thoughts aloud. "Do you stand here telling me that you murdered Ulder because of those papers, and that you've burnt the lot? Wait, you can ask for a solicitor if you want one, and if not—"

"Murdered Ulder! Ulder's letters!" said the Canon, with an outraged surprise which convinced even Mack of his sincerity. "It was my book I burnt, *The Questioner*, the book of which you heard yesterday morning. I found a copy in the Bishop's library to-day: I re-read it, and in my shame and disgust set fire to it at once!"

"Well, whyever!" This anti-climax left Mack staring almost foolishly.

"It could do, has done, far more harm than any of Ulder's foolish and wicked bids for mere money, than was done by the removal of Ulder from this world. That book may, must, have killed faith and poisoned souls. How can I ever hope for forgiveness?"

"If you ask me, Canon, you exaggerate." Mack pulled himself together to try to get some sense into this extraordinary fellow's head. "Don't suppose it was read as widely as you think—never heard of it myself! And any way, remember this. I'm a plain ordinary man and no theologian. When I read a book in defence of the Presbyterian Church I don't think it has a leg to stand on. When I read an attack on it I rise up ready to fight for every word in the Shorter Catechism. I expect this book of yours turned lots of young men to the Church, for we're all alike, Catholics, Anglicans and Presbyterians. We won't have our nests fouled by our own species and that's a fact."

This incursion into theology had a slightly mollifying effect on Mack himself, but hardly helped to advance the case. He must have a chat with Dick over this absurd episode, and he would waste no more time with the Canon, who seemed inclined to start an argument on the probability or improbability of his book buttressing the faith of its readers.

"You just think over your sins, and a bit more quietly," was Mack's advice as he turned to cut the Canon's answer short. "And if you'll excuse me just think over the sixth commandment and make sure you didn't murder Ulder!"

But Mack could only feel, as he returned upstairs to find Tonks, that both the Chancellor and Canon were not really likely suspects. He'd never believed it of Chailly, he told himself and, whether Wye were mad or no, no man who was taken up with this book of his and felt it so appalling a lapse in his past, could readily dismiss a crime like murder so lightly. And besides—always Mack returned to this point—was Wye likely to have come prepared with morphia, and if not, where could he have got it? Meanwhile, slightly at a loss for occupation, the constable determined to use his search-warrant on a thorough search upstairs.

"Dick! I want to speak to you!" Dick and Sue and Bobs had fingered gossiping in the hall after Judith's departure, and Dick was about to make for his turret retreat when the Bishop called him into his room. "I want to see you. Ah yes, my boy, I have been telling myself that in all this turmoil I have not seen as much of my candidates as usual, but I must indeed hear your thoughts and schemes sometime. You will be a brave and faithful soldier of the Cross, I know, not such as I, not such as I. Dick, I can bear this no longer—I can speak to no one else, involved as we all are in this terrible business. I—I have a terrible confession to make."

"My lord!" Dick's brain whirled as he told himself the Bishop was suffering from delusions—delirium, self-hypnotism. "I don't think you should talk! I think you should rest."

"Rest!" The Bishop strode up and down the room. "As if I had any rest day or night since that awful disclosure yesterday. No, Dick, I must speak or I shall go mad. Let me begin by owning to you what no human being has hitherto suspected, not even I myself, that I am a coward!"

Dick said nothing. He only hoped that his attempt at surprise and polite protest covered his sudden memories of the St. Blaze estimate of Dithers.

"Imagination breeds cowardice," the Bishop went on, as if by generalizations he hoped to avoid his main theme. "I suffer from the acutest, yes, even absurd apprehensions for those I love. And now in this ghastly tragedy in the Palace I see myself suspected, arrested, brought to justice. No doubt you will assure me that Mack's insulting manner and questions to me, from the first, are due to his prejudice against our Church and its servants. To me it has seemed more, and I have been afraid, I own it. In my few snatches of sleep, Dick, I have seen the condemned cell, the last walk, heard the last prayers!"

"My lord!" Dick sprang forward as the Bishop swayed on his feet, groaning, and helped him into his chair. "Indeed you are torturing yourself wrongly! The only unfortunate circumstance in this case for you is that you, like others, had a motive for wishing Ulder—well, out of your way! But no man is brought to trial when motive is the only plea—that you know yourself in your sober senses. You have let your imagination run away with you—" (And what candidate for the priesthood, wondered Dick desperately, had ever so spoken to his Father in God in the past?)

"Listen, my boy!" The Bishop shaded his face with his hand, and Dick saw the long fine fingers grip the amethyst ring in anguish. "That is not all! I—I have withheld a certain piece of information from the police."

Then the Bishop had somehow got hold of Ulder's papers—or at least those which related to Judith! That could be the only meaning of such a confession, but how and when had he managed it? Not that Thursday morning: the door had been locked on him. Could he, fantastic as the idea seemed, be in some sort of collaboration with Soames? But after all the question of what the Bishop had withheld, and how or why, mattered not at all compared with the urgent necessity of persuading him to own his error, his stupid, even fatal error, to Mack himself. Stammering in his earnestness Dick set himself to the task, using every conceivable variation of the old theme that honesty is the best policy, but the Bishop not only gave him no answer, but made no apparent attempt to attend to him. He sat back with his face still hidden in his hand, his body huddled so helplessly in his chair that it almost seemed as if his fatigue had overwhelmed him and he was asleep. But he must not sleep yet on any account, not yet!

"If you would tell me, my lord, if you would trust me!" Dick switched on the electric lamp beside him so as to arouse the Bishop. "If you would let me break this—this piece of information to Mack for you—"

Suddenly the Bishop sat up and held up his hand, listening. "That is Mack!" he said with dilated eyes. "What has he been doing? Where has he been searching? What has he found?"

"But, my lord, if you've any evidence, any papers, you have surely hidden them or kept them on your person!" Dick was at sea now indeed, and a very stormy sea.

"I mislaid it—I could not find it. It had disappeared."

There was a knock at the door and Mack entered, followed by the cowed and miserable Tonks. Why had Dick unluckily turned on the light just at this minute, for if ever a model was wanted for a picture of a convicted and guilty criminal discovered in the act, one was provided at that moment by the Bishop of Evelake.

"Bishop, I have come to ask you a question!" By the restraint in Mack's manner Dick realized the importance of his discovery. "Would you like to have Chancellor Chailly here as your legal representative, for I am bound to tell you that anything you say may be used in evidence."

"No, no! Do not fetch him!" the Bishop muttered, as Dick sprang up. "No one else must know my weakness, except Bobs. Bobs," he called through the intervening door, "come here! Let me tell you, Major Mack, that I have just been admitting it to Mr. Marling here and was about, by his advice, to confess my oversight to you!"

"Then you know what I've found?" asked Mack grimly, while Bobs exchanged questioning glances of surprise and dismay with Dick.

"I think so, I think so, though how or where I cannot imagine. I could not find it myself in its usual hiding-place!"

"But you recognize it all right?"

Dick could hardly restrain a cry of horror as Mack displayed, carefully wrapped in a handkerchief, a thin, tiny tube covered with a paper label. The print was very small, but, as it lay beneath the light, Dick clearly made out the words printed in red on a folding label—"Poison—Morphine."

"Yes, yes, I do. But I kept it always in the secret drawer of my bureau, in the right-hand side wall behind the well of the writing-table. I have searched there again and again, and-there was nothing."

"Nothing on the right hand but this was on the left—the top drawer—rolled under a bit of loosened paper, very cleverly concealed. Perhaps you would like to tell me why you did not inform us of this tube when we were hunting the house for poisons yesterday?"

"Because I could not find it," repeated the Bishop almost stupidly.

"All the more reason to tell us. We should have assumed then, said Mack with great emphasis on the last word, "that someone else had got hold of it and hunted him down. Such secrecy is open to the gravest construction, as you can see for yourself."

"No one could have got hold of it!" If the Bishop were a criminal, Bobs thought passionately, he was an amateur at the job, for surely he should see for himself that he should allow Mack to believe that others had access to his secret! "My wife knew nothing of it."

"Could Soames have found it when he was valeting your clothes?" broke in Dick, disregarding Mack's frown. "He has a passion for spying and picking and stealing, as we all know."

"He was never allowed near my room," replied the Bishop, ignoring Dick's life-line. "As he came to us with none too good a character my wife arranged that Doris should have complete charge of brushing my clothes, keeping my drawers, packing, unpacking, and so on. It is most improbable that so honest and superior a woman would pry her way into the secret drawers of my bureau, and she has no conceivable connection with Mr. Ulder."

"Could old Moira have got hold of it when her pains began, before she owned up to them? Isn't that just possible?"

"No, indeed. She would never have taken any property of another on any provocation. She had too an almost morbid horror of drugs. I remember that my wife and Dr. Lee had great difficulty in persuading her to have her first injection though the poor soul was in torments. Besides, she had been bedridden for weeks and it was only last night that I missed it."

"We have only your word for that," said Mack, eyeing the Bishop curiously. "Would you care to tell us how it came into your possession, and what use you made of it?"

"It—it's a story of my weakness," said the Bishop slowly, to Dick rather than Mack. "I was in London when war broke out in 1914, and the stories of invasion, rapine, and this new and terrible air weapon of the Germans alarmed me. Not for myself so much, I humbly trust, as the thought of my wife and daughters at the mercy of invaders or trapped in our old home's ruins! I appealed to my old friend, Hartley Head, a brilliant surgeon, lost to us here now alas, and he gave me a small tube containing just such small morphia tablets as my wife was given by Dr. Lee. I put them away safely in a secret hiding-place and as you know there was no such use for them as I had imagined. But when this memory came to me my horror was too great for words. Major Mack, I could see you had suspected me from the first. You would like a Bishop to be guilty of crime—oh yes, I know it! I was sure that your two clumsy minions would never find my cache, but I did not dare to go near it till they were all safely out of the house and my wife occupied. Then I went to the secret drawer of my bureau, intent on destroying it with no more ado, for I knew I had never had such recourse to it as you would imagine. And it was gone, Dick, gone!"

"So that's your story," said Mack, rolling the little bottle in the handkerchief under the light. "Well, no doubt your cloth makes a difference but I can't see any jury finding it very convincing, Bishop. Your memory has played such odd tricks it would seem—you forgot you had it on Thursday morning, remembered it, and concealed your knowledge from us, found the bottle mislaid from its usual drawer (but in another close by, close by mark you!) forgot to mention all this to the police, and ask us to accept your information. I should be glad if you would refresh your memory and answer my next question very carefully. You say you alone knew of this drug and that no one else can have obtained possession of it."

"My lord, you should send for Mr. Chailly." Bobs had kept silence by the Bishop's wish till now, but he could not restrain himself. But the Bishop spoke with sudden vehemence.

"I should only be told that I arouse more suspicion! No! I am telling the truth and shall continue to do so. I could do no more if the whole Bench were here. What do you want to know, sir?"

"This, Bishop. Has this case been opened and how many tablets were in it?"

"Well, let me see!" Bobs and Dick exchanged horrified glances as the Bishop hesitated and stammered like one pre-varicating. "I will tell you the truth. I never had through the mercy of God to use the morphine for the purpose for which it was intended. But of late years I have suffered at times from gall-stones, and I can only hope you may never know the agony caused by that complaint. On the first occasion I was alone, my wife was speaking to some society at Blacksea, and I was terri-fied. I took one of those tablets and got relief. When I consulted the doctor, he disapproved strongly, and temporarily he cured me. But I lived in terror of that pain attacking me when I was staying in some far, lonely rectory for a Confirmation service, and made a rule to take it with me—"

(Did Mack notice, thought Dick miserably, that only a little while ago the Bishop said he had never thought of the tube for years?)

"—Twice I was forced to use it, and neither my wife nor the doctor discovered that I had done so, so it can have done no harm. Recently I have had an operation and fear the trouble no longer. So you may find three of the tablets missing."

"Three!" said Mack, "oblige me by a glance at the label—ten pellets, each containing half a grain!" He emptied the bottle gently over the handkerchief, and before their eyes lay only one tiny tablet. It was then that the cowardice which had darkened his spirit swept in a wave over the poor prelate, leading him to stammer out the most unwise and unavailing prevarication of his life.

"I—I do not understand. Perhaps it was more often—I rec-ollect, I think, another time at Compton Wyck."

"It is what happened to those other three tablets on Wednes-day night that we wish to hear about," said Mack.

"Bobs, help me!" The Bishop rose and staggered as he did so. "Help me to my wife's room. God pity her! Bobs, help me to my wife."

To Dick's surprise Mack made no objection as the old man dragged himself heavily away on the Chaplain's arm. But Mack made no move save to close the door behind them. Then he turned upon Dick and said doggedly—"Well, you can see for yourself, Dick, there's only one course open to me. I must arrest the Bishop."

XII
FRIDAY EVENING

Dick had served in the Yeomanry in Flanders in the darkest hours of 1914 and 1915: he was to spend the rest of his life in war against the Devil and his angels, but he often told him-self that he had never fought a tougher engagement than that against Mack, in the half-hour which followed.

"Why should I delay?" repeated Mack. "It's all clear against the Bishop now—motive—opportunity—weapon. If he were a labourer or a shop-keeper you wouldn't ask me to hesitate. It's my duty to arrest the Bishop!"

"The whole argument is wrong—the facts don't tally: half the business is still unexplained. I'd say as much for an old lag," urged Dick, "not because we're speaking of a man who has served God and never harmed his neighbour all his life, and not because he's a Bishop! Give me till to-morrow anyhow. Do nothing to-day! Give me till to-morrow evening."

"Leave him till to-morrow to make a get-away!"

"He won't! Listen, sir, how do you account for his keeping the bottle if he'd done the murder? Why on earth didn't he throw it away? No one would have discovered it."

"He was keeping what was left to finish himself off with if he were found out! He can't get at it now anyway!" Mack fingered his handkerchief.

"Someone may have known of it, realized the danger and hidden the morphia, and then replaced it. Someone may have taken it and used it—it's been there for years, the Bishop admits. You're no nearer proving that he gave the poison!"

"He had every motive and every opportunity, and he had morphia in his possession," repeated Mack stubbornly. "He got it for use in a possible Zeppelin raid: he never was in one. Do you ask me to believe a sane man would ever dose himself with the stuff without doctor's orders?"

"Soames could have taken it!" suggested Dick hurriedly. "You haven't even examined him yet."

"I shall examine him about his pilfering, but again I ask you why on earth should he risk his life to murder Ulder? He didn't stand to gain or lose a penny by it. Ulder wasn't bullying him about his past!"

"Wait till to-morrow!" Wait till you've consulted higher authorities was what Dick tried to imply, and probably the memory of his morning had some effect on Mack. For just when Dick had almost given up hope he said brusquely:

"Very well, I'll take no steps till to-morrow evening. It can't be later, for how can a murderer take this service of yours at the Cathedral? Do you want to be ordained priest or whatever you call it by a murderer?"

"If he were one it's the office not the man who matters," was Dick's rapid verdict.

"And suppose it's this Chancellor in the end? Would his legal stuff be valid?"

"Oh yes, in virtue of his office."

"And suppose, though mark you I doubt it, that Canon Wye had got hold of the stuff and stood up to preach to you before he went to the gallows?"

"We'd still have respect for his office!"

"Damned bureaucracy I call it!" puffed Mack. "Well, till to-morrow evening then. Send Soames here and then Staples! Heaven pity 'em if they're not in yet!"

"Telephone for you, Dick. From Scotland Yard." Bobs gave the message in the doorway, glaring at Mack.

"I'll take it in your room if I may, Bobs!" Dick's one idea was to escape alone, but he owed Bobs the relief of conversation first. "Just watch that Soames doesn't listen in from the hall!"

"Tell Tonks to find him and send him here first!" growled Mack.

"That you, Dick?" (How cool, how detached, how carefree the lucky Herriot sounded on the telephone!) "That name's just come in and I'm off on duty in a minute so here it is—Edward Kilkelly—yes, KILKELLY—Kilkelly. That all right? You all right? Your Bishop hasn't murdered you yet? Good! So long!"

Dick looked round sharply as Soames emerged from the Bishop's room. "Just pulling down the curtains and making up the fire," he volunteered, quite unnecessarily, and then darted down the servants' passage in that eel-like way of his. Damn all the Palace extensions! The butler had clearly been listening in, and heard what was probably his own name, and certainly knew now of the width of Dick's net around his past. Well, it couldn't be helped! Tonks would presumably drag Soames from his pantry lair next: the policeman was escorting Staples across the hall to Mack now, and if ever a fellow wore the guise of a convicted criminal it was the poor little red-haired parson. There was Canon Wye rustling towards the stairs in his cassock on his way from Chapel, looking like a murderous saint or a saintly murderer. The Palace might be a Dartmoor convict gang as far as looks were concerned!

Bobs at least did not look a criminal as he awaited Dick at the door of his room. But his pleasant boyish face was so pale and miserable that Dick forced himself to go in and begin the weary round of discussion again. It was only fair to give Bobs a complete picture of the situation, and there was some comfort in Bob's reiteration, in such happy contrast with Mack's, for:

"He didn't do it! He couldn't have done it!" was his cry. Only as Dick's voice died away Bobs suddenly burst out, in anguish. "Dick, why don't you say more? You don't think—?"

"No, no, I don't think of anything at all. I must get away for a bit, Bobs, or I'll go mad! I'll go out to my turret just for an hour—don't stop me, like a good fellow."

"In the dark? Oh, all right! Soames has been mending the steps—went out there I noticed as soon as he saw the police car. And remember, Dick, the Bishop isn't going to tell Mrs. Broome or Sue this story or the whole of it! He can't help knowing Mack suspects him."

"Oh, my God!" groaned Dick, as he went out into the icy darkness and across the lawns as if pursued by fiends. The gale was getting up again: snow still lay in unexpected corners for the unwary, but without hesitation he plunged on through the ruins, and, missing the narrow path, crashed through the undergrowth to the summer parlour. As he lit a match at the bottom of the wooden steps he noticed that some work had evidently been done on them, for one board had been renewed. Still he walked up gingerly in the howling wind, let himself in and lit the candle which Soames had left. Thoughtful of the little wretch—and then Dick stopped suddenly. Wasn't it rather odd that he had brought a half used candle? The Palace ménage under Mrs. Broome was not at all a home of carelessness or economy. Had Soames brought a used candle, or had he burnt one here before—last night or the night before?

Dick threw himself down on the dumpy old schoolroom sofa, staring at the plaster walls in their flickering light, and the black narrow windows. He had got to think, and think hard. So many things had happened to-day, one on the top of each other, that he had not been able to sort anything out, and he must do it now. He must put aside all thought of the Bishop for the moment. A brief review was enough to reassure him that Mack's case was weak, and any defending counsel would have no trouble in getting an acquittal if it got as far as that. What was it which he and Mack had missed altogether in their hurried discussion just now? Why, Judith, of course! Wasn't it more than probable she was mixed up in it? But then if she had got at the Bishop's morphia she could not have replaced it before the police were all over the house and the rooms guarded. Every one up to that point had heard only of a suspicion of suicide. And if she 1 had taken it, surely her natural instinct would have been to hide it in her dressing-case—and Mack himself had searched that! Why should she have kept it at all? Why not throw it away? The answer to that might be, he supposed, that there is always difficulty in disposing of glass. It does not necessarily burn, its fragments may reappear. Why not throw it away in the ruins or among the bushes or shrubs, or dig it into the earth? Because apparently someone—whoever it was—wished to keep the remaining morphia tablets. That didn't seem like Judith. It was her nature to give away everything or throw away everything, old clothes or jewellery, position, respectability or a good man's love. And never certainly, even to defend herself, would she have replaced the morphia in the desk to incriminate her father.

But someone had taken it and replaced it, if the Bishop's story were true. Dick had read murder trials enough to realize that hardly any poisoners seemed able to part entirely with their chosen destroyer, or to dispose of it finally even if they tried. Well, it was no use going round and round in a cage like this. He would ring up Judith to-morrow, on the chance of her being at the bottom of it all—as she was indeed at the bottom of most of the trouble, and God pity poor Clive, and thanks be that Bobs had sighed for her in vain!

Well, he must do something or he'd go mad, for by now fantastic images were beginning to form in his brain. Couldn't Staples have got down in the night in spite of Parsons, (But how did he get hold of morphia?) No one had suspected Mrs. Broome from first to last? Why? Well, the answer to that was really Mrs. Broome herself, for by all accounts she was not Ulder's last visitor. But if Judith had intervened for her father's sake why not his wife, Sue, Bobs, Dick himself? Come, this was sheer lunacy! He must stop and turn his mind to Soames. Suppose the butler took the bag overnight and, alarmed by footsteps, scuttled to hide it in the disused drawing-room, because he felt it a safe temporary hiding-place, and then, suddenly discovered there, dropped it on to the jasmine bush. Next morning (or that night indeed) he had retrieved it and put it in the attics. Alarmed there again by Dick's search he had brought it to the disused summer parlour, only to find, at Dick's request, that this cache too was to be disturbed. Well, it was easy for Soames to pretend he had lost the key, easy to imagine that early this morning he had examined the bag here at leisure, and, despairing of keeping it, abstracted what contents he desired and burnt the bag itself. Dick could swear there were bits of burnt leather among those still warm embers this morning. But no! It didn't work! Soames would never have taken the bag on Wednesday night while Ulder was still alive, and for all he knew would wake next morning to demand it. But then suppose—Dick gave a start—suppose Soames knew that Ulder would never wake again? But here again was a dead end. No one, and specially not that cringing little sneak thief, could murder Ulder for the sake of an old black bag containing a few toilet necessities! But did he know of the papers—did he murder Ulder so as to become heir to his trade of blackmail? Then why did he not abstract the papers and leave the bag? Had he reason to suppose there was something in the bag which he could not find at once and feared to destroy? But what, in Heaven's name, could he hope for, when he had known nothing of Ulder as far as Dick could gauge; when he could not have foreseen Ulder's arrival, for no one had expected the parson; when he could not have heard Dr. Lee's instruction about Ulder's dose at any of his beloved key-holes, for Ulder's door had been half open, Dick stood near it and saw no one in the passage at the time. Would Soames have dared, if he could have acquired the knowledge, to go from room to room while Mrs. Broome, servants and guests were all about the passages, collect the Chancellor's bottle (which was now proved harmless!) and morphia from the Bishop's room, which was so emphatically Doris' province and forbidden ground to him?

No, it didn't make sense and yet! Every one knows when they work at a difficult jigsaw how they com plain that some pieces must be missing, but in the end make a complete whole of the pieces before them all along. So the pieces of this jigsaw must all be here, if only Dick could fit them together. The room was growing very cold and the candle was burning low. It was not worth lighting the fire, for it was after seven o'clock now, and he could hardly retreat here after dinner. Unless he cut Chapel—for how could he think there among the tortured faces of Mack's suspects? No, he must go back to the Palace now, and he must promise himself to turn away from all thoughts of the murder and possess his own soul, which was indeed in no state for the Ordination. But at one glance at the stove, to see if it was laid, all his detective instincts revived. It was laid but it had not been thoroughly cleared out. There were still ashes beneath paper and sticks. These last were removed in a minute, and Dick eagerly yet carefully poked among the debris below. Just ashes he was telling himself, nothing save ashes. And then, pulling out the iron of the stove, he felt a catch. There was something left, something which kept the damper from pulling out properly. Soames had probably not been thorough enough, in his haste over his holocaust this morning, to do more than rake out the embers above and below, leaving the iron in its place. Dick pulled very cautiously and drew out a crumpled, browned slip of card board with a red circular hole. A half was burnt, string was missing, but here clearly was a luggage label. He turned over the scrap with peering eyes to read:

Rev. Th. Uld … Add

In a moment he was up and stuffing the slip into his note case—no, safer still in that ticket pocket which tailors always make and no man ever uses. He hadn't a moment to lose for he must catch Mack with this final proof of Soames' theft before the police car left. He strode across and tugged at the door. It was abominably stiff and the wind blew out his candle at once, raging against him as if witches rode it to the rescue of Soames.

But it gave at last, Dick pushed through it, and clattered out on to the steps impatiently. He had only taken one when there was a rending noise, the snapping of wood. His feet gave beneath him, the steps collapsed with a violent crack. And the crack was followed by a heavy thud, because Dick had fallen with the wreckage and lay stunned on the rough floor below.

Dick was not unconscious for long, it appeared after wards, though naturally he had no way of knowing what time had elapsed when he fought his way out of a confused dream in which his head was a bomb bursting in a snow field, being kicked about ignominiously by a soccer team. His head was in a drift all right, was his first conscious thought; snow had no doubt drifted into the turret with the wind, and softened his fall perhaps on the uneven stones, but it was cruelly, cold. He tried to move himself very cautiously. Men who have played rugger all their youth, and spent their first manhood among the wounded on the fields of Flanders, come to assess their own injuries pretty accurately. His left ankle was hurting ferociously—a strain if not a break, probably. His left arm and shoulder were so badly bruised that they felt numb, but with luck it was bruises not breaks. Yes, he could just shift a little, so probably he'd be able to get up and drag himself back soon, but he'd give himself a few minutes more in spite of this confounded cold, before he faced the torture of the attempt. It was no use to shout for help probably: the Palace windows, twinkling with restored electricity to-night, seemed infinitely far away. Someone seemed to be closing shutters and curtains, so he did essay a shout, for the loss of those lights would somehow make everything worse, but no sound came. There was a chance, of course, that someone might have heard the crash when the staircase fell, but in stormy weather it was no unusual thing to hear the thud of a stone falling from a roof, or the collapse of an arch, and the crash might rouse no interest. No, he had just decided that he must make the attempt alone and was trying to roll to his comparatively unhurt left side when, to his infinite relief, he heard light footsteps and saw the flash of a torch. And then, relief changed at once into an almost sick apprehension, for the newcomer was Soames.

Dick's thoughts raced in his racking confused brain. In spite of his pain he recognized clearly that here was a chance to see what the butler's intentions really were. Had Soames come, knowing nothing of Dick's presence, to this hiding-hole of his, or had he heard the noise and come to give aid to one who was injured? Or was he hoping, having seen Dick's destination, to find him involved in some accident and finish him off? At all risks he must find out, thought Dick. He would shut his eyes and keep quiet. If the butler tried any funny stuff over Dick's prostrate form, well, here was his left arm as good as ever, ready with a punch which would knock the starveling out! But he had to confess that the moment in which Soames padded up to him and bent over his prostrate form was not among the most pleasant of his life. At least the butler wasn't coming up behind with a blunt instrument to bang his head and finish the job! It was only very dubiously that he knelt down by Dick's side and j fumbled through his waistcoat to feel his heart: even in his pain and apprehension Dick nearly smiled when Soames proceeded to pull out his notecase from its pocket; for so clearly was the ex-thief considering if it was worth the risk of discovery to steal a parson's slender store. With a sigh Soames replaced it. "Ah, that's lucky, for I nearly put something in it just now, and what was it, what on earth was it?" groaned Dick to himself. He must be going mad or light-headed, he decided next minute, for surely he was not seeing Soames aright. What on earth was the fellow doing?

He was apparently taking no further interest in Dick. He stood instead, staring at the broken steps, picked one up to examine it closely by his torch, and then began to hunt on the ground beneath, sweeping up the wreck age, as far as Dick could judge. But what on earth did that matter? Why was he throwing his light on a broken tread and regarding it with such satisfaction? Should Dick end this farce and startle the idiot by a sudden groan or question?

And then Soames suddenly started and swung round vi-olently, and as he turned Dick saw another torch flash in the butler's face, heard light footsteps and a voice calling, and it was Sue's voice.

"Soames! What has happened? What was that noise. I was afraid there must have been an accident! Oh! Oh! Dick. Soames, is he hurt? What are you doing fiddling with those bits of wood? Are you mad? Oh, Dick!" Sue was sobbing in an agony of fear and fury. "Don't you see Mr. Marlin lying here? Run to the house for help at once. Mr. Borderer! Mr. Parsons! A stretcher!"

"You run, miss, and I'll 'old his head up for him, and make him more comfy," muttered Soames, with chattering teeth.

"No!" Dick achieved speech at last with a great effort.

"You stay, Sue!"

"Oh Dick, you can speak!" Sue suddenly pulled herself to-gether in a wholly commendable way. "You're not dead! Are you terribly hurt? I can see you are! Look, here's my coat un-der your poor wet head. No, don't try to talk or tell me what's happened!"

Dick wanted to talk, for the shock and chill together were making him a little feverish, and his brain began to work with the clarity of a rising temperature. If only it wasn't so difficult to think or see straight or speak at all. But he got out his de-mand at last.

"Sue! Flash your torch on that step, will you? The step which Soames was looking at just now."

"Why on earth—oh, never mind!" Sue, true to her stoical principles about not asking questions, did as he asked. Light shone through the gathering mist in Dick's brain as he stared. The outer ends of the step which had broken into two halves showed the signs of ordinary fractured wood. But at the broken centre were marks clearly made by a crosscut saw, cut up to about an eighth of an inch from the upper surface. Now, too, he could see the little heap which Soames had swept together: they were not made of the splinters produced by an ordinary breakage, but of clear clean sawdust. Soames was a clever devil! Under pretence of mending the stairs he had framed these fractures on the under side of the top step, on the chance that the hasty tread of a heavy man would break it and precipitate the victim below. Well, that was the plot, and a pretty simple and effective one, but why was Soames trying to get rid of him? Why not Mack, Tonks, any one in authority? What did he think Dick knew which made him so desperate? The flowers? His absence? The attics? No, he had not seemed unduly upset then. It must be something which had happened to-day, something which Dick had done or said which Soames had overheard. At some keyhole or on the telephone? And then with a wave of sudden gathering force Dick began to understand. Soames had been in the old library when Dick was taking Herriot's message in the hall. Not much of a message, just a name and what was the name? What was it?

But before memory aided him again he and Sue saw lights and heard voices, and in the torture of being hoisted on to an amateur stretcher, Dick lost consciousness in good earnest.

XIII
SATURDAY MORNING

"WELL, LUCKY it's not a successful murder this time!" These cheerful, if hardly tactful, words of Dr. Lee were the first to which Dick attached any importance. "You're in luck! Slight concussion … you'll be sick presently and feel much better! That's a nasty sprain but I don't think any of the ankle bones are broken. Shoulder hurt you most? They're nasty bruises but no more. You've got to keep your bed till Monday, Dick, and I'll expect to find you nicely put together by then!"

"But I must—" Dick stopped. Experience had taught him not to argue with doctors.

"Mrs. Broome, dear," he said persuasively, when they were alone together. "There are just two people I want to see, only two!"

"The doctor said no one and, Dick, it's no use asking to see the Bishop!" Mrs. Broome sat back in her chair so wan and haggard that Dick's heart ached. "This is no moment to talk to you about such things but he is at the end of his tether and—though I don't know how to tell it, he thinks that dreadful Mack believes—and expects the worst!" Most unusual tears ran down the plump lined cheeks suddenly, but she checked herself. "I must not speak of all this. It can't be true! It is all some terrible nightmare!"

"You don't think I'm going to be here while all this is happening, do you?" asked Dick. Dr. Lee was right and he would be sick soon but he must get his way first. "Of course I shan't and I've a clue—I know I had a clue, which will come back when my head's clearer. There was something I heard or found. I know there was. But I'd never dream of bothering the Bishop. It was Mack I wanted to see!"

"He's gone and a good riddance!" replied his hostess in a voice more like her own.

"Oh damn—sorry! Well, can I see Bobs, and then I do want to see Sue for just a minute. I want to ask her to do something for me! Oh good, here's Bobs! I've a job for him!"

"By Jove, it's true what Lee said!" volunteered Dick five minutes later, "I do feel clearer. I'm glad it was you here for this show." Bobs, removing traces of sickness, was not so sure that he was glad, but it was a relief to see Dick less far away and spent on his pillows. "Bobs, this is all more hanky-panky of Soames, I am sure! He didn't go to tighten up the treads of those stairs but to loosen them and let me down. As I lay on my back, because I couldn't get up just then, I thought I saw how he'd done it—a cut on the under side of the top treads with a saw—nothing to show but a certain break under my weight. Have a look first thing, will you, and ring up Mack afterwards and tell him that Mr. Soames is behaving more strangely than ever. You couldn't call it attempted murder, for the drop wasn't big enough."

"Might have killed you—then it would have been the drop for him," said Bobs fiercely.

"Very difficult to prove! But I want to give Soames a good fright, so spread it far and near that I'm in very bad case, will you? I want to be off the map to-morrow. I don't feel I can quite explain why with this blasted head—indeed I can't quite remember yet, but I had a big idea, and it may come back!"

It was such a pale and subdued Sue who crept into the room presently that Dick had to smile and thus dispel her worst fears at once.

"Sue, I'm almost as glad to see you now as I was an hour—or whatever it was—ago, and that's saying a lot."

"I was glad I came," replied Sue simply. "Soames didn't seem to be helping you! Is he mad?"

"I expect so—anyway bad. Sue, angel, will you take me a motor drive to-morrow? Don't humour the invalid by saying you can't drive, because I know you had to learn when your last chauffeur was called up so as to take the Bishop about! Besides you drove me here!"

"Yes, and I got very tired of all Confirmation sermons—the parsons never would let me stay in the car and read a book. Don't be a Bishop, Dick! You'll get so that when you hear 'Soldiers of Christ, arise!' you'll want to sit down for the rest of your life! But I won't take you anywhere to-morrow. You've got to stay in bed, and you'll miss Sunday, I'm afraid."

"Just as well—*'non sum dignus'* indeed. But I must go out to-morrow. Have you heard that things look pretty bad here? For your father, I mean. Oh no, don't look like that! Of course he's as innocent as triplets unborn, and Mack can't prove a thing, I promise you, but the Bishop made—one mistake let's call it—which may lead Mack to—to make things very unpleasant for him. I've the ghost of the ghost of a hope I might be able to get on another line if I paid one or two distant visits to-morrow. I can hop down to the car and sit up all right, you see, and my head's all right—this bandage is only eyewash. And I shall probably go mad if I lie here doing nothing."

"But—but—Dick, Mother—the doctor—everyone will prevent you!"

"Not if we sneak out when they're mostly in Chapel. I heard Mrs. Broome order my breakfast at eight—she's afraid to leave invalids too long, after poor Ulder, I expect! Could you have a snack with your early tea, sneak out and get the car and smuggle me down? I don't want anyone to know that we've gone—that's important—no one, none of the servants—just leave a note for Mrs. Broome—we should be back by tea. Be a sport, Sue!"

That childhood's appeal, combined with the unknown horrors hanging over the house was too much for Sue. She was not the maternal type which fusses to protect men from themselves, but the super-maternal which sits back while men make fools of themselves, waiting to pick up the bits.

"Unless you're very feverish to-morrow," was her only proviso, "and Mother sends for Dr. Lee again!"

"I won't be! Then two more things, Sue, and one will seem idiotic. Could you go to Moira's room and find out the name written in pencil under Moira? In the Bible we were looking at when the light went back on us, and don't ask me why for my head's so muddled I can't quite remember, but I know I meant to look."

"I'll get it if you don't bother your poor head about anything till to-morrow! Promise!"

"All right. Look here, write it on a bit of paper and I swear I won't look at it till to-morrow. My head is a bit muzzy!"

His brain was curiously dull and stupid indeed, though now and again sudden flashes of illumination seemed to strike across it, only in such uncorrelated glimpses that they made no sense. Never mind, he told himself, the good old subconscious will get to work on it! But not yet, not till Sue came.

"There you are, Dick!" She was in the room. "I'll put it by your bed. I don't believe you could read it anyway!"

"See any one while you were in there?" Dick forced the question from the waves of sleep sweeping over him.

"Only Soames, snooping about as usual!"

"Oh!" The waves receded for a moment. "Sue, will you please lock my door behind you and keep the key or give it to your mother. Please!"

He was asleep almost before she left the room, secure in the knowledge that Sue was perhaps the only woman in the world who would do what she was asked without questions.

Did Soames pay him any further attentions that night? That was of course Dick's fear, though the butler's schemes and methods were still inexplicable. If he did, he only over reached himself, and unknowingly did Dick, a service. For when Dick heard, or fancied he heard, a stealthy pull at the door handle and a creak of woodwork he switched on his bed lamp, thankful that he was protected by the lock against intrusion. Beneath the lamp lay Sue's bit of paper and he picked it up and read it. Though the letters seemed to dance about a bit, it read certainly … Kilkelly … Kilkelly … where had he heard that name recently? Yes, yes, it was coming back! Now he remembered! It was the name which Herriot had given him on the telephone, the name which confirmed the vague suspicions he had felt for some time about the strange tie between the superior house keeper and the inefficient, offensive little butler. Now indeed he could go to sleep.

He awoke next morning, when Mrs. Broome stole in with a cup of tea, with an extraordinary sense of lightheartedness, quite unjustified by the pains and aches of his body. A wedding bouquet on a hearse I feel like, he thought, even while Mrs. Broome was telling him how he must lie quiet all day and not dream of getting up. Evidently she was relieved not to receive a grand remonstrance, and left him lying with his eyes dutifully closed in apparent obedience.

But as soon as she had gone Dick rolled over very gingerly and as he put it to himself, told all his bones. Head much better, shoulder still hurting like fun but not crippling. His ankle was decidedly not too good, but then the latest treatment for sprained ankles was to walk on them at once: he could just manage to get himself into old grey bags and a loose tweed coat, and as for his head, well, fresh air and Sue's company would do wonders for that, and the old brain seemed to be functioning all right.

"But it's mad, Dick, mad," said Sue anxiously when she saw him limping down the main staircase. The house was very still save for that faint sound of chanting which Dick had come to look upon as Ulder's funeral dirge. The hall dark and mysterious with its overwhelming scents of azalea and hyacinths, might suggest a mourning procession of flowers in some crowded cemetery chapel, but the octagon vestibule was full of sunshine and the two truants stepped out into a world where the gale had hushed itself into a soft west wind, and, if spring were very far away, red holly berries in wet, sharp, sparkling leaves and golden yews mocked winter gloom; where sparrows twittered and robins sang as if they could hold their own orchestra without waiting for any faraway migrant birds.

"It's rather a long drive, I'm afraid, chauffeur," said Dick when he had mastered the considerable pain of getting into the car. "Have you ever been to Dorbury? I want to go to the Orphanage there!"

"Oh!" Sue was evidently surprised but asked no question, after a glance at her companion. "It's a good thing I filled my tank up and took spare tins. Fifty miles and I expect the roads over the hills will be under snow still! You'd better fill up Dick! There's a flask of brandy just in front of you and I've got a thermos and sandwiches for lunch."

I wish, thought Dick, I could tell her that she's better than any brandy! It was precisely at that moment he realized that Sue was the one essential person in the world to him and that he could never let her go. Unmanned by pain, that's what I am, he told himself. Nearly proposing to a girl when I'm (a) crippled, (b) on the job of saving her father from arrest, and (c) acting as if love sprang up from her sound ideas of food and drink, (d) just going to be ordained priest and work on twopence a year, (e) realizing that she deserves a king at least, though I expect most of them are dull dogs!

"What are you thinking about, Dick?" asked Sue, catching his odd grimace in the driving mirror.

"You," answered Dick simply. Sue made no reply but the car swerved so violently that there must clearly be no more sentiment on this important expedition. He must not look at Sue. He must not even try to enjoy the patchwork of the winter countryside, the black, silver-fringed hedges, the red earth of ploughed land, the purple tangled mats of frosted roots in fields, the rust gold of fallen beech leaves, the sad green clumps of plantations. He must not look up to the line of glinting chalk hills which they approached, or the faint hyacinth blue of the freshly washed sky. He must close his eyes and do some really hard thinking.

There are days when everything goes wrong, when human nature and inanimate things seem equally to combine against us. After a full experience of this at the Palace, Dick realized triumphantly that nothing would or could go wrong to-day, that this was a sample of the opposite number, one of those rare delightful days when everything goes right. What did it matter if he felt like a badly set jelly in an earthquake? Everything would be all right because Sue was with him.

He was justified in this optimism in their first call at the Orphanage at Dorbury.

He had left a note asking Bobs to ring up and fix an interview at twelve, but how easily the car might have broken down, the head of the establishment been absent on business or, worst of all, that it had been run on such unbusinesslike lines that any work of research would be out of the question! But his luck held good in every respect. Sue drew the car up to the building which looked like a barracks outside, but sounded like a jolly nursery party within, punctually at twelve o'clock. The Head's wife carried Sue off to a cup of tea while the Head took Dick to his office, and waved proudly to neat rows of car indexes.

"About 1895 you think? Here is the register. You are not sure of the name under which the child was entered—that happens only too often in the case of an illegitimate union. Boy or girl? Excuse me, the boys are this side. The name might be Soames—Sullivan—Kelly or Kilkelly you think? A wide choice but they are all in strictly alphabetical order. Kilkelly! I have heard the name recently!"

"You must do a wonderful work here, sir." Dick was glad to let loose a flood of description and reminiscence, partly because he really wished to please this kind old gentleman with the huge beard and small twinkling eyes, partly because he preferred to work unaided. Though he could not forget his bruises and sprains they hardly seemed to matter in his excitement. There was no luck among the Soames and Sullivans—he hadn't expected it. He grew anxious when the Kellys were no more rewarding. But he was rather excited than surprised when the Head waved to him from an old index marked K.

"Yes, this is the case. Someone was enquiring about it, that is why it struck a chord in my memory!"

"Was that only yesterday, sir?"

"No, no, a few weeks ago I should say. Some lawyer or detective agent I fancy—filling up some dossier. I did not enquire for of course this entry was here before my time. I fear my predecessor was not business-like. Here you see is all he wrote: Kilkelly—Edward—1895. Sept. 1st—two years old. Unmarried mother Moira Kilkelly. Father's name withheld. Birth registered Addsey, 1893. Left 1910 aged 17—not satisfactory. No more than that! You will find under my entries weight, height, colouring, history of parents and wherever possible in these cases the name of the putative father."

"Splendid!" said Dick heartily. "I'd have given a lot for that last in this case. No more in the Addsey register either, I expect?"

"No, I formed the impression, but only the impression, mark you, that the enquiry was being instigated by the father's side, but I could not pursue enquiries as Kilkelly had not been in my care."

"And you know no more of him?"

"Let me see! If there is anything it will be on the back of the card. Ah yes—applications for references 1912, 1913, 1914—too many for a good character I fear. And those crosses refer, alas, to short-term sentences in prison. But we must trust he made good in the army, poor fellow. We do what we can for our charges, and are often richly rewarded, but one sometimes feels that the secrecy and hatred and shame which surround such a child's birth live on in him. Ah, by the way, here is a last entry which will interest you." It was all Dick could do not to tear the bit of pasteboard from the Head's hands. "'Enquiry from Army Records Office on enlistment 1916. … Enlisted as Edward Sullivan—Sent full details—unacknowledged.' Yes, yes, of course I remember. I had much correspondence over more than one of my pupils, and I cannot say they gave me a high respect for the organization of that army department!"

"Dick, did you get what you wanted?" asked Sue. Bidding farewell and tucking Dick back into the car had been a lengthy business, and they had only evaded a pressing invitation to the children's dinner with difficulty, but as Sue looked at her companion, now that they were on the road again at last, she knew he was rewarded.

"Did you have a good time?" countered Dick.

"Yes, indeed, the sweetest, happiest children, and the nicest Mrs. Head and Matron—but terribly strong sugary tea, I admit. But about your job—no, I won't ask! Where are we to go? Straight home?"

"No, Sue, please to Addsey! I wasn't going to break it to you till we saw a cross-roads, but that's well to our east."

"Addsey! Well, we'll stop and have lunch soon anyway, because it'll be fifteen miles through ugly flat mining country. Here's a nice stretch and we can park by this bridge. Addsey! Oh dear! 'Childe Roland to the dark tower came,' Dick!" Sue implored as she busied herself with sandwiches and cups— "You can tell me just a little, I suppose? Have you found what you want?"

"Yes, I have, and I'll tell you this, because you've been such an angel—and also everyone will know it soon. Sue, did you ever guess that Moira was Soames' mother?"

"Oh Dick! Soames' mother! I can't believe it! When—why—how—what made you think of it? It can't be true!" And yet because Sue already believed, and would believe in the future, that Dick was always right, she exhausted such comments reasonably soon, "Though how you thought of it or found out, Dick!"

"I didn't think of it till we looked at Moira's Bible, and then Herriot gave me Soames' original name. We hadn't deciphered Moira's name, so it was only your remark about her shortening her name long ago and then the slip of paper which made me hopeful. I'd meant to go to Dorbury in the hope of any sidelines on Soames and it would have been an utter flop if that name had never reached the Orphanage. But I wondered at the connection between Soames and Moira from the first. Why did a first-class old-fashioned servant like Moira ever suggest him to your mother, and how could she tolerate him when he came? That story about 'Our Boys' was pretty thin when you think of our Soames' career! And would a little pip-squeak like that show such real attachment to a funny, strict old housekeeper? For I do believe he was and is really anxious and unhappy about her, and I'm sure it's a relief to think the little wretch has some natural feelings!"

"It's almost harder for me to think Moira ever had a past or a child, or could care for him now or any one but Judith," meditated Sue. "I wonder if the old Bishop knew all that his wife would, I suppose, but she was dead, and Mummy was only too glad to take Moira on with the Palace as housekeeper! Not that she kept house much at first, for she made herself into Ju's nurse, Mother says. My nurse adored me and hated Judith, you remember?"

"Naturally! She was and is what nurses call a madam!"

"Moira wouldn't let you say so. And what was odder still Judith adored her. I think she liked to feel there was some one she could tell everything to—"

"I didn't ever notice that she was sparing of her confidences!" put in Dick.

"No, but she'd talk to shock or amuse people, but with Moira she'd just pour out everything, knowing Moira would applaud her all the time and always take her side. That first evening she went up to tell Moira all about Mr. Ulder's seeing her at that hotel and blackmailing her, and about well, everything else—" said Sue with a pre-war blush. "And then after dinner, to describe Ulder's arrival and his fit and all the rest of it. When Mummy and I tried to talk when Moira's pain was bad she'd hardly listen, but she'd have come back from the grave to listen to Judith!

"Moira must have taken a poor view of the Rev. Thomas Ulder!"

"She did indeed! You know she's often been rather queer with her dreadful pain—illusions the doctor calls it—and Ju said she used the most awful language about him and prayed Heaven to curse him. Rather dreadful, when she was so ill and going away to this dreadful operation."

"Any good news of her? Has she had it yet?"

"Oh no indeed! Mummy rang up first thing. She has bronchitis still and they evidently expect pneumonia and can't possibly operate. And Mummy told me straight out that they don't expect the poor dear to get through!"

"Better not," said Dick sombrely.

"I suppose so, with that operation before her! But, Dick, what has this to do with Addsey?"

"Because Moira's illegitimate baby was born there. She may have gone into service at some house or farm, near there when she first came over from Ireland, but of course that's thirty years ago. I don't suppose we'll find out much, but I'd like to make sure of the register and pick up any gossip we can."

Sue drove in silence as they left the clear stream in sun shine and travelled steadily into thick dull clouds and the blackened countryside which surrounds mining neighbour hoods. Whether she had arrived at his own suspicions about Soames' parentage Dick could not tell. He was tired and aching and could not rouse himself to try to disentangle the skein of this knotted story. So far he had only untwisted the thread and pulled it a little way before another cross-thread intervened. And whatever the end of the quest might be it seemed as if it must lead some human creature, however criminal, that hated road to the gallows.

"Two miles to Addsey!" said Sue reading a sign-post. "Do you want to go to the Rectory, Dick?"

"I believe it's almost the only house there; it's just a ham let; we've only to find the Church and that's up the hill before us."

"Shall I go to the Church and look at the register and leave you at the Rectory? Though I don't see how it can help you!"

"No, I don't suppose we'd find any one to show the register to us. The police can ring up about that to-morrow. You stay with me, Sue! But don't be afraid of dark towers. I don't think it's an historic old house. Ulder's father, a local manufacturer, built and endowed the Church and kept the advowson for his precious son. It's more likely pepper-pot Gothic in decay—the ancestral seat of papa Ulder, of the same date, is a reformatory now, I believe—a little ironic!"

But the suppositions of both Sue and Dick were wrong. They had left the dark patch of coal pits behind for a dull, treeless, flat countryside, bare alike of trees and cottages: even the hedges were dwarf and there was no difficulty in locating the low small church with its squat tower. Opposite it, standing just back from the road behind a golden privet hedge, was a prim square bow-windowed house with clean windows and well-polished brass. It must be the Rectory, for a few huddled cottages composed the rest of the hamlet, but it was hard to believe it was the sinister Ulder's home.

But the surprising contrast was forgotten as Sue stood before the front door and rang the bell. It was fitting, perhaps, that the house, like Ulder, should present a respectable façade to the world. But when, after strange sounds of scraping, shuffling and dragging, the door opened at last, there could be no question but that something of him remained in his former lair. No woman, thought Sue, could have lived with Mr. Ulder without becoming bad or mad, and his cousin, Miss Ulder, had clearly chosen the latter alternative. She was small and emaciated: her dark dress was neat though shabby: her iron-grey hair plastered back stiffly. That was, as it were, the substructure of her original self. But everything else about her was eccentric to the verge, if not over the verge, of madness. It was not only that wild yet cunning eyes avoided theirs, that her hands were filthy, her old boots torn and plastered in the mud of weeks. In startling contrast she wore, floating round her, two or three gay flowered scarfs of shot tissue, a cheap gilt belt and so large and varied a store of old-fashioned jewellery that the total effect was that of a grandmother's trinket-box, worn, torn and faded, exhibiting its store of pinchbeck, of cameos and onyx brooches, sets of jet and amber, massive gold lockets, silver filigree bracelets, coral ear-rings, rings and bracelets of hair mounted in gold, silver serpents entwined round the wrist, small garnets and sapphires deeply embedded in gold. In the place of honour on her bosom lay, however, in contrast, one of those gunmetal watches which had been fashionable some twenty years before.

"If you're reporters you can go away!" A thin, precise voice rapped out the words. "If you're police you can go away! If you're the removers you can take a look round. If you are the valuers for the auction you can come in!"

"Well, we're none of them really," said Dick with his friendly smile. "As a matter of fact we've come from the Palace—this is Miss Broome, the Bishop's daughter. We have all felt so much sympathy for you in this dreadful shock and—and loss."

Dick faltered over the last words, for Miss Ulder, eyeing him closely, burst into a shrill laugh.

"Sympathy! From the Palace! My good young people, I imagine they feel at the Palace what I feel here, free at last!"

"Still—it has been a very sudden blow for you," put in Sue, seeing Dick wholly at a loss for once.

"Why? I'd told him I wouldn't stay with him any longer, and he was going to America, he said. Across half the earth or under it doesn't make much difference. Who murdered him? Quite a choice, I expect, and I don't blame them. I do believe in seeing things *straight*, don't you?"

"We do hope, at least," ventured Sue, feeling it simplest to take no notice of this merciless candour, "that it hasn't put you in an awkward financial position. My father is always so worried about any of the relatives of his incumbents when they sustain a very sudden loss." (Good for you! thought Dick, admiring Sue's diversion.)

"Very kind of your papa, I'm sure. I hope it's not what they call conscience money." She laughed more heartily at her joke than her companions. "Tell the Bishop I'm in clover! Thomas speculated away all my money years ago. I had to stay with him and keep house for him for I hadn't a penny or crust of my own, though indeed," suddenly she began to whimper, "my father kept his own pony cart!"

"You have all that lovely jewellery anyhow," put in Sue swiftly, for the thin face had puckered, the wild eyes dimmed so desperately.

"Yes, my dear! Isn't it nice!" Miss Ulder cheered up at once. "A little excessive for a quiet day in the country, you may say, but I have never dared to wear any since I found he always managed to get hold of it and sell or pawn it. My dear father's silver half-hunter watch, my aunt's seed-pearls! Oh dear, oh dear! But he can't steal any more now! He meant to, you know!"—she lowered her voice to a confidential whisper. "Come in, for that poor young man has a bad foot and we'll see if we can find a chair and I'll tell you all about it. There is no one I can talk to in this village, as I always said to my cousin, not our class, not our class at all!"

It was not at all easy to find a chair in the crowded sitting-room into which the pathetic, repulsive little elderly woman led them. One was evidently the throne of an honoured cat; another piled with old clothes, another with boots and shoes, and another with books. And over chairs, table and floor alike spread an avalanche of papers.

"All his things! I'm going to make a bonfire of them when the snow's melted. I know the village thinks I'll hand them round, but let his goods perish with him, and his heritage let no man take! The lawyer who came to see me yesterday, on seeing the news, said 'Look through his papers,' but I told him, 'No,' I'd destroy every trace of him!'"

The room was so unbearably stuffy, with the odour of foul tobacco, stuffy clothing and the kipper with which the cat was toying that Dick's head ached unbearably, and though his sense of urgency remained he hardly knew what it was he had hoped to find. Some paper to trace the connection he was sure of had been his aim, but he felt like nothing now but Rider Haggard's travellers trapped to death in the diamond cave. The riches of Ulder's past records were all around him but how could he make use of them? But Sue, at his appealing glance, put in a quick question to their companion:

"You were saying he meant to cheat you, but everything is all right, I hope?"

"Yes, yes, he died intestate, so I inherit his money and furniture—not much, though he told me he was coming into a fortune, but quite enough for me! Oh yes, he meant to cheat me of it. He told me when I said I must leave him (for really a scandal in this village was too much, and such a *common* woman!) that he would cut me out of his will. And then he told his lawyer (so I heard yesterday) to track down all his—my dear, you are only a girl, I don't know if I should tell you!—well, let us say all the women he had any connection with and their children, and let them know he would remember them. I don't think the lawyer had got very far, for every woman who had ever known my cousin had no desire ever to see him again—it's one thing to be hard and another mean—but to be *both*, you know! And this shows you what he was like! He was to raise their hopes as he used to raise mine, and then his last instructions were for the lawyer to draw up a will leaving everything he possessed to a home for fallen women. Dear me, how I laughed when the lawyer told me! I'm afraid the good man must have thought I was just a little *odd*, you know. Thomas meant to sign that will on Friday morning, but he didn't, and his old one was destroyed and he died intestate, so I get everything!"

"Then he never married?" asked Dick.

"No, no indeed! Not *married* if you take me!" She turned her back on Sue and winked vigorously at Dick. "The lawyer asked that so I said: 'No; if you like to look through my cousin's diaries—40 years of them—you'll see the kind of man he was, for he wrote everything down, everything. He gloated on his wickedness! But not one word of marriage!' The lawyer looked through one or two and gave it up—there they are, you see, in that corner behind Adam, his cat. Adam got cream while I had skim milk, so I'm not sure that Adam shan't go into the bonfire too!"

"Oh no, you couldn't be so cruel!" Sue's pretty voice calmed the little woman strangely, and as Sue bravely patted the dirty ringed hand Miss Ulder smiled and the mad hatred died down. "You see, it wasn't Adam's *fault* that he got the cream!" added Sue.

"No, no, how well you put things! My dear, would you like some tea?"

"No, no, thank you!" However badly she needed it the thought of anything prepared in this house was impossible. "I'd like—I'd like to see the other pretty things you have upstairs. I see you have lost a jet ear-ring, haven't you? I believe my mother has an old set, left her by a governess, which she never wears, so perhaps I could match it for you ..."

"How did you know I wanted to be left alone downstairs?" asked Dick when, half an hour later, the two escaped and, flinging open the car windows, welcomed every breath of the fierce winds as they drove away.

"How could I help it when I saw you eyeing those diaries? Have you got what you want?"

"Yes, I have, the last link."

"Then Moira was—"

"Yes, it's all here—1892—I took it away with me. Why not, if it was going into that bonfire? I won't let you see it if you don't mind, Sue. A bonfire's the place for it, later!"

"Moira! Moira!" repeated Sue in horrified surprise. "Then Soames is—"

"Yes, Ulder's son. And he must have known it. That lawyer's envelope which she pointed to was the only other paper I looked at. He'd traced Soames all right—he must have been the other person who'd been enquiring at the Orphanage. I suppose he let the Army Records know later."

"Then—then—if Soames knew it was his father who'd wronged him and his mother—and might leave him money when he died! Oh Dick!" Sue suddenly stopped the car dead and, laying her head on the wheel, shook with sudden sobs. "I—I can't believe there's all this wickedness in the world. You think that Soames—"

"I don't think things happened as you imagine them," said Dick cryptically. He himself was white and tense with the effort to sift his evidence rightly, but all he could think of was how to console Sue. "Listen, dear Sue, I'd better tell you. All this seems grim, and worse even than you imagine, I fear, but Mack was hot on a false trail which would have hurt you infinitely more!"

"Did he think it was Judith? I sometimes worried a little, though it's too awful to say so. She was on some warpath of her own, I'm sure, and I knew it wouldn't be she who—who killed him, but—but the awful part was that *someone* did didn't they?"

"Well, love, here's a post office and telephone in this village. Will you stop and I'll manage to get out because I must do some telephoning and it's urgent. Ah, it's got a tea-shop behind. Tea for two, and you go and sit down and begin, Sue, and I'll tell you this to make you forget the rest; Mack's Favourite run-

ner-up was—your father! Yes, just as well you weren't driving
when I said that! Be a good girl and keep some tea for me."

Dick was lucky with his calls. He got through to the Hospital and spoke to the matron and the doctor. He got through to
Mack and wondered if the village telephone would ever recover
from the grunts, oaths, queries and remonstrances with which
Mack heard the story of Dick's theory, his quest, and some of
its results. But if he were only half or a quarter convinced he
agreed to fall in with Dick's plans, recognizing their urgency.

"Then you'll be with Soames at Evelake Hospital at six
o'clock," ended Dick. "There's a chance of getting the truth,
though it's only a chance. They give her a few hours at most."

Then he rejoined Sue and to his relief found her laughing
helplessly. "I can't stop myself," she said, handing him a crumpet
and filling up his cup. "It—it just seems so ridiculously funny
to arrest a Bishop!"

"Doesn't it!" said Dick, but inwardly he felt that funny hardly described the experiences of the last two days.

XIV
SATURDAY AFTERNOON

"WELL, DICK, I've done what you asked in your extraordinary
message on the telephone an hour ago. Seen the matron and
made all arrangements and got that fellow Soames here. But
what on earth it's all about you've still to explain! Why trouble that poor old soul who's dying by inches? Why should she
know the worst?"

Mack stood puzzled and angry in a small bare waiting-room
in Evelake Hospital, where Dick, flushed and jaded, limped in
to join him when darkness had fallen and the building was
echoing with the sound of trolleys carrying round suppers and
running taps for night ablutions in the wards.

"I'd better explain a bit later, Mack! Didn't the sister say we
haven't any time to lose if we're to see Moira, and it's imperative
that we should."

"Trouble her when she's dying?" asked Mack angrily. Scotsmen think little of Bishops but much of mothers, said that imp in Dick's brain which whispers such remarks to most of us in the most inappropriate moments. "Why not let the poor soul go in peace without knowing that her son's a murderer?"

"You'll understand if only she can still speak. I can't help it; a life depends on it!"

"It isn't pneumonia," said Mack. "I asked Matron."

"Bronchitis, but the sister has just said the strain of the cough is terrible, and each fit of coughing may be the last. Don't waste any more time, sir! Is Tonks there? He must be in the room to take notes. Where is Soames?"

"In with his mother. Dick, it's cruel, it's abominable, it's not necessary!"

"Sorry, Major." Dick was so nearly at the end of his tether that he hailed the sight of the nurse with infinite relief. To get this dreadful affair over was all he could hope for now. "Yes, Nurse, we're coming!"

At the end of a long corridor Tonks stood waiting outside a door. Dick had vaguely imagined a ward, and a bed screened only by a curtain, so it was a real relief to see that Moira was alone in a room for her few last hours.

"You'd better come away now, dear!" said the nurse persuasively to someone within.

"No, I'm not going to leave her now!"

It was Judith who spoke and as she confronted the little party who filed in, Dick had an odd memory of some Flemish glass window where St. Michael, wide-eyed and unafraid in shining armour, trampled down the old dragon. Behind her radiance the poor bare little dusky room faded into grey insignificance; two narrow beds were empty; on the third, so wasted that her form scarcely showed under the sheet Moira lay, propped up with pillows. By her side was a chest with glass, books, and a vase of half-faded lilies, as sallow and drooping as the emaciated face of the old woman. Dick remembered Moira only as a pleasant, middle-aged, buxom woman who had, it would seem, disguised the outspoken merry ruler of the nursery under the pose of the high-class servant downstairs. Now that disease had worn away her body and pain her spirit, he found nothing to remind him of the past, till Moira opened her eyes. Those grey, dark-rimmed pupils and the murmur in a hoarse voice which had yet a lilt of the old sing-song Irish belonged to the Moira whom he remembered.

"Don't go, my darling!" Those eyes, dulled with drugs, sunk in the hollow face, could still shine, as in old days with passionate tenderness for Judith, and then they turned to the dark corner where Soames was standing, half-crouching over a radiator, and in them shone all the baffled, thwarted love of the saints and angels who would save mankind from itself, if only they could. "I'll speak better if she's near me."

Dick looked at Mack, who only shrugged his shoulders and nodded, as if he had lost all control of this monstrous, unorthodox situation. He sat down heavily on a chair at the foot of the bed as Dick approached.

"Remember," whispered the nurse, behind Judith's chair, "she can't speak for more than a few moments at a time. Please don't say anything to agitate her if you can help it!"

But those were not instructions which Dick could obey.

"Moira," he said, "we know now who stole Mr. Ulder's bag and we have traced the missing morphine which killed him. Your son Edward is in grave peril, others you love are in some peril of being arrested for poisoning Thomas Ulder. Have you anything to tell us about it?"

Soames gave a strangled shriek of anguish and moved towards the bed. But before Dick could silence him Moira spoke in the puzzled querulous voice of weakness and detachment.

"Why, yes, it was I gave him that morphia. I got out of my bed that night, I that hadn't for weeks, and went to plead with him for my son and for Miss Judith and all. He wouldn't listen so I put the poison into whisky and went back and made an end of it all."

"Will you tell us how you got the morphia? Was it from the Bishop's room?"

"Why yes!" The faint ghost of a smile suddenly, unbelievably, crossed her face. "Him and his secret drawers indeed!"

"You'd never miss a thing in spring-cleaning, darling!" Judith tried to speak as lightly and gaily as usual but there were tears in her eyes.

"How did you manage to get it that night? Or had you taken it before?"

"I'm no thief!" Moira's cough began to shake her in her indignation, but she choked it back to add: "She"—gazing at Judith—"got it me that night. I said for my own pain—the doctor was that cruel, starving me of his injections ... but I thought I'd need it for that man all along!"

"Why did you do it?" Mack had to raise his voice for the cough was getting beyond control.

"Don't make her speak!" cried Judith. "I'll tell them, Moira, and then they must go! It was partly because Ulder had threatened me, and partly because he'd recognized Soames, and Moira knew he'd tell Mrs. Broome about Soames' bad ways and send him away, just when poor Moira was trying to get him straight. That was why you killed him, wasn't it, Moira darling? And I don't blame you one bit!"

"He'd ruined me ... he took my boy away ... my poor Edward had no chance like ... I wouldn't let him hurt my Judith ... and her child that's to be ..."

"And meanwhile you exposed your son and Mrs. Mortimer, the Bishop himself and others in a less degree, to the grave danger of being tried and hanged for murder!" Dick' could hardly wonder at Mack's outburst, for indeed the faint ghostly triumph in Moira's eyes and Judith's casual approval could only be an abomination in the eyes of the Law. But as he laid his arm on Mack's to suggest that they should withdraw, Judith looked up at the Chief Constable, with the angry contempt of an avenging angel.

"How could she tell, bottled up in this place? Do you suppose when we visited her and she was hardly conscious, that we woke her up to say: 'Dear Moira, we're all going to swing for murder?' I didn't know she'd done it till just now! I thought that—well someone else had got hold of that bottle. What does it matter? She did it for love, didn't you, Moira? Nurse, please, please, send them away!"

"You'd better go too, dear," whispered the nurse. "I've pressed the bell and Sister will come with an injection. She won't come round again, I fancy!"

"No, I'll stay with her. You go, Soames! It's no use crying or fainting, and she'll only want me if she does—come back again!"

Was Mack wondering, as Dick wondered, at this strange display in this fly-by-night, will-o'-the-wisp, light-of-love Judith—of a devotion and courage which knew no criticism of her old nurse's life, or fear of death? Dick could not tell, but he did recognize then and remembered always, that the facets of love are endless and set at very different angles, and only when some unnoticed brilliant comes to light do we see the reflection of the perfect sun of Love. Only he did not put it to himself like that then: "Judith's got a heart after all," was the sum of that odd impression. "Every one has got a heart somewhere, and my job will be to help God to find it!"

"Well," said Mack, when they were back in the waiting-room after a long pause, "what next? I imagine I should have this fellow arrested as accessory to the crime," he added, pointing to Soames, but speaking in a whisper, "but not till the poor old woman's gone!"

"Not at all, sir! It's an odd place and time for questioning but why not hear his story now? He'll feel worse still when it's all over in there, and it would be cruel to take him away."

"I'd nothing to do with it, sir, nothing!" Soames wailed. "I guessed she had, so I couldn't speak out. I haven't known what to do, sir. I've been almost out of my mind."

"So you concentrated on trying to murder Mr. Marlin," snapped Mack, as he began to piece the story of the last two days together in his mind. "How was that to help you?"

"Oh never, sir, not murder! I've the greatest respect for Mr. Marlin, almost one of the family, as Doris says! But I knew he was on my track, and that if he went on nosing round he'd soon find out I was Mr. Ulder's son and had taken his bag and all, and then it'd be the long drop for me as things were—or for my mother if she got better and heard of all the goings-on and owned up. A gentleman like Mr. Marlin, a Rugby player and all, couldn't be killed by my little contrivance in the turret—just got out of the way for a little, till things blew over a bit, if you take me!"

"That attic window might have finished me all right though!" The long day and excitement, pain and intense fatigue were sending Dick's temperature up again and he found himself unable to regard Soames as anything but a joke ("though not in the best of taste", Doris would have added primly).

"Oh, sir!" Soames seemed genuinely shocked. "That wasn't meant for you—that was only to keep you out of my attics—all I could think of in a hurry. I'd gone up in the first place to listen to what you were both saying. You did seem so 'ot on my trail, as one might say—I don't know how you did it and how you found out first one thing and then another. That's why I didn't dare go out on Thursday and leave you!"

"I know how you found out everything," retorted Dick, "listening at keyholes and listening in on the telephone switches, quite a fine art of yours."

"Well, let him speak up and tell us the whole tale," said Mack impatiently. "It's more than time we had the truth at last!"

"Well, sir, it was like this. Mr. Marlin knows my record, and that it wasn't too good, but when I was last 'in', the prison chaplain wrote to my mother and said I was repentant and all, and what about her helping me to a new start? I did try at the Academy and then she got me to the Palace. I did try, sir, that I did; never picked up as much as a back-stud that didn't belong to me and began a savings book. And Mother did her best to 'elp me though, of course, I were a disappointment to her. That Ulder had forced her to give me up to that Orphanage, and she never forgave him, for she said it was there I was led into bad ways."

"Why on earth didn't she tell Mrs. Broome you were her son? In her position, after years of service——"

"Mother'd die rather than own herself not respectable," said Soames stiffly.

"Thinks murder respectable, I suppose," growled Mack under his breath. "Well, go ahead! I suppose when Ulder came he recognized you and you him. But how?"

"He'd been making enquiries about me, sir. Seems a fellow can't keep himself to himself when once he's been 'in'," reflected Soames aggrievedly. "He said nothing in the hall, of course, and I popped up straight to Mother in a terrible way to tell her he'd come! And next thing we heard while we was talking was 'im being carried up next door to her."

"Did Ulder know your mother was in the house?"

"Not he! He hadn't enquired after her seemingly. But he'd put an agent on to find me saying he was going to remember his—well—as you might say his bastards in his will. That was all I'd heard of him and though it had raised my hopes like, I got the wind up proper when I heard Dr. Lee and you, Mr. Marlin, sir, begin to suspect murder!"

"How did you hear?" asked Dick sharply.

"Up agin the partition wall, sir! I did have a laugh when the cops tried acoustics as they called it from Mother's bed to next door and all. Stands to reason you couldn't hear there!"

"Seems to me you'd hear pretty well anywhere. So you thought the next thing would be a lawyer's letter telling you were Ulder's heir and that your motive for finishing him would be clear enough?"

"I'm afraid," put in Dick as Soames nodded assent gloomily to Mack, "that you mustn't hope for anything from Ulder's enquiries. I saw his cousin to-day. He was playing tricks on you to rouse your hopes because he was angry with her—he never meant to leave you a thing."

"Dirty swine!" said Soames malevolently. "Not that I'd have touched a penny of his filthy money." This noble sentiment was obviously only an afterthought however. "A blackmailer! That's what he was. Worse than a murderer, says my poor old mother. My hands may be poor but they're clean—" ("Not at the moment, however," murmured Dick's imp.) "That's why I hung on to that blinking bag, in case I'd find a will or something in it."

"Now I want the truth, Soames!" Mack spoke so sternly and eyed Soames so severely that the poor little man nearly collapsed to the floor. "What did you do with the other papers, those papers which he was going to use for black mail on certain people in the Palace? For I suppose you'd discovered that?"

"Mother had, sir. At least about Mrs. Mortimer, for Mrs. Mortimer came straight up and told her all about it. A very free-and-easy lady, Mrs. Mortimer, but a kind heart!" Soames suddenly stared at the door as if the memory that even now his mother might be coughing her life away overwhelmed him. Dick longed to end the enquiry but dared not suggest it, for who knew but that further evidence might be needed from Moira at some point, and that soon she would be silent for ever. Mack, however, appeared to feel no sentiment.

"Better own up your whole story from the beginning," he said gruffly.

"Well, sir!" As Soames pulled himself together and began his story Dick realized that the odd little fellow's relief on coming into the open, and his sense of drama, were loosening his tongue effectively. "Well, to begin with, Ma sent for me that Wednesday evening in a proper taking and says I've to get hold of Mr. Ulder's bag and bring it to her as soon as ever his room is quiet. 'Get me those papers of his against my Miss Judith and I'll slip in and coax him round later,' she says. 'Why, Ma, you'll never get to his room and you bed-ridden for weeks,' I says. 'I've been out of my bed and about my room this evening,' she said. 'Dr. Lee's given me no injection to-day and I'm restless-like!'"

"But you've got some of his stuff there, haven't you?' I says, seeing a little tube on her table, and she just nods and says she's something if she needs it and I thought no more of it then. I went and fair crept into Mr. Ulder's room to see to the fire, as Mrs. Broome had said something about leaving it low and crept back to Ma with the bag in my hand, Mr. Ulder seeming asleep. 'Quick and let me put it back,' I says, but what did we find but that it was locked! I was fair upset but Ma never turns a hair. 'Just hide the thing somewhere and we'll search it to-morrow,' says she. 'But he'll miss it any minute!' says I. 'You leave it to me,' she says, as cool as a cucumber!"

"What time was all this?" asked Dick.

"Well, getting on for eleven I suppose, sir; I'd heard Canon Wye leave Mr. Ulder, and Miss Judith came after him, but Mrs. Broome soon walked her off to her room and gave me the chance to slip in as I told you. Next thing was we heard Mrs. Broome coming back, so I slipped away from Ma's room and off down the new wing in case Mrs. Broome should see me. There was someone on the stairs above, but the drawing-room was all quiet and empty and it came to me that it wouldn't be a bad plan to leave the bag there behind the sofa till morning. That room is Mrs. Briggs' province and she never comes up till nine o'clock. The maids are all over the rest of the house and that Doris always snooping about my bedroom and my pantry. And then I hears Mrs. Broome coming along to the draw-ing-room, and at that hour—like a 'unted 'art I felt, sir, and so I opened the window—"

"And dropped the bag on the jasmine bush. Yes, we've got back to that, but what did you do with it afterwards?"

"I slipped out to bring it in when the house was quiet at last and then all of a sudden I thought of that there summer parlour and nipped over there with its key, and with the bag and a torch. And first thing I saw was a light in Doris' bedroom window, so I knew she'd see my torch if I stayed in the turret and wouldn't Miss Nosey be asking questions next day! So I left the bag there, fair sick of it all I was, and went back thinking I'd be up at dawn and try my bunch of keys on it and get those papers to Mother and the bag back in the gentleman's room and thankful to be done with it all. But I was that worn out with all the fuss and bother and fourteen in the house party too, that I went to sleep like a log, and first thing I heard was Doris knocking on my door saying it was nine o'clock and I was a lazy hound and to take Mr. Ulder's tray up at once. So I tumbled into my things anyhow and took the tray, and on my way looked in on Ma to tell her I still hadn't got those cursed papers she was after. Like death she looked but never turned a hair. 'Just get them this morning and bring them to me in the Hospital,' she says. 'Let's see, yes, you get a nice bunch of flowers from Mr. Jay and wrap the flowers up with the papers. No one will suspect that and I'll keep them safe.' 'But he'll be asking for his bag and hunting for them!' I says. 'You go on, it'll be all right,' she says, and after I remembers that but I was in such a state I just took the tray in and hoped for the best—"

Dick and Mack exchanged glances. From that moment in the artless tale each recognized that Soames was clearly free of suspicion from any share in the murder itself. The narrative style of the butler might be open to criticism but his sequence was convincing.

"So I went into Mr. Ulder's room and put on the bed-light, and then!" Soames gasped and, choking feebly, pointed upward with the same gesture which Mabel had employed in the Chapel. It was to be hoped, thought Dick, his mind confused with pain and fatigue, that the judgments of Heaven were as merciful to Mr. Ulder as those of the Palace domestic staff.

"But you'd no reason to suspect your mother then?"

"No, sir, but, well, she was queer and no denying. She'd heard the news when I screamed and the maids came running and sent for me again. But all she'd to say was: 'Keep your ears open and hear what they're all saying about this!' Well, I thought, after all she'd been his wife in the sight of Heaven as you may say and I was his son and that was all she had to say: 'Keep your ears open!' And then I got a nasty shock when I sees the glass in Mr. Ulder's room when you called me in. It hadn't been there when I took the bag, Mrs. Broome wouldn't have given him drink. Ma must have done it, I thinks, and she shouldn't have. And then I listened by the window on the pantry stair which is very conveniently placed, sir, for the window to Mr. Ulder's room and heard of suicide and how you weren't sure if it was suicide at all. My head was going round and round and I felt I must see Ma again, but there was Miss Judith leaving her room and Mrs. Broome taking the doctor in, so all I could do was just to walk in and pick up her breakfast tray and carry it off. I couldn't say a word to her but she just followed me with her eyes and they frightened me. And then I looked at her table and noticed that the tube which had been there the night before had gone, and then—"

"Then you began to suspect?"

"I don't know exactly, sir, I was more afraid people would suspect me! And I'd never time to think things out before I got a fresh fright. For there you were telephoning about me to Scotland Yard, Mr. Marlin, after all your questions to me, and then the house upset and the police coming and the silver to do and fourteen to lay for and on top of it all your asking for the key of the summer parlour. Well, I just made off at that, and changed my kit and got into the turret, burst the lock, undid that blighted bag and took out a long envelope labelled 'Palace Business', then I made off to get Ma's flowers from Mr. Jay. I took the bag and sneaked it up to the attics on my way. I'd heard Mr. Tonks say they'd leave the box-rooms till next morning, so it seemed safer there than in my bedroom with Doris next door in my pantry."

"But why on earth didn't you destroy it at once?"

"Well, sir, there was that question of the bequest," said Soames reluctantly. "I'd no time to go through all the letters in the thing and then there was always the chance of finding some stuff belonging to Mr. Ulder—morphia or such, with which he might have overdosed himself and finished himself. You said he couldn't have finished himself off because the bag had gone, but I was, as you may say, more in the know about that!"

"It would have been a bit tricky to explain how you got hold of it!" To Dick, in his pain and exhaustion the butler's tale had varied dizzily between comedy and tragedy and Soames' air of injured innocence was now comic relief.

"There were difficulties of course, sir." It was odd to see how Soames, scenting ridicule at that remark, assumed his model butler manner. "But had any one been unjustly arrested I should not have hesitated to produce my evidence."

"Brave Butler defends Bishop," muttered Dick to himself. "Well, go on. Did you go to the Hospital or not that afternoon?"

"Punctured half-way and came back," said Soames gloomily. "I got in through my bedroom window because I wanted the staff to think me out. Doris and Mrs. Briggs were washing up tea-things and gossiping and so the next thing I heard was that you were to hunt the attics. Always on my trail you were, sir! I was beginning fairly to hate you I must own! Doris and Briggs dawdled on so that I'd only just time when they'd cleared off to rush up to the attics and hear you and Miss Sue upstairs already. So I opened the window and put the bag outside—the roof is flat there, you see—and knocked over all that there mountain of boxes to give you a good fright and block your way a bit!

"But, of course, I could see you suspected me, sir, and I guessed you been on the roof spying after me. All I could do was to slip out in the small hours that night, turn that bag inside out and all and then burn it in the stove, and thought I was quit of it till I saw you looking at those embers and poking them on the lawn and knew you was on my track again. And then I heard you telephoning to Scotland Yard, sir, and so then I decided on my little ruse with those turret steps, sir! Just to get you knocked out as it were, and keep you quiet with luck for a day or two till I could talk to Ma and see how we stood. I got the flowers and papers to her early Friday afternoon but wasn't allowed to see her and the reports were cruel bad as you know. It seemed as if all the world was against her and me, and specially you, Mr. Marlin, sir, and I had to rid myself of you!"

"What you really wanted to do was to save your own skin," suggested Mack unkindly.

"Well, I was in a predicament, sir. It looked like me or Mother, didn't it? and her dying too. I don't know what would have come of it all if Mr. Marlin hadn't arranged all these interviews. But I can say, sir, that I don't think I could have been through a worse time if I'd been arrested and hanged straight out. It 'as," concluded Soames with absolute sincerity, "been just fair b——y Hell!"

"You may have more of it too if Mr. Marlin likes to summon you for assault and intent to do bodily harm," declared Mack with a sad lack of sympathy. "I only held him, Dick, and waited to arrest him after hearing of your accident from the Chaplain this morning. I thought we might as well learn first from your enquiries about the fellow's real parentage. I still think you should summons him, Dick. And throughout he was obstructing justice, what's more, leading us to entertain groundless, though," emphasized Mack, "wholly justifiable suspicions! Well, I suppose the next thing to do is to apply for a formal arrest for that poor old soul, but I must own it goes against the grain, Dick."

But before Dick could reply, or Soames could babble out his protests, there was a knock at the door and one look at the Sister's face showed them that the other fell sergeant, Death, was taking Moira to a higher Court.

"She wants you, Mr. Marlin—she—she feels she did wrong, Mrs. Mortimer has made out from her whispers. She wants a priest, she thinks. Yes, you'd better come, Mr. Soames."

Mack and Tonks were left alone staring at each other, each visualizing in his own way the scene in that room down the corridor. "Funny job, a parson's," volunteered Mack once, and "A priest's is a very high calling, sir," replied Tonks solemnly, "for I suppose in view of the emergency Mr. Marlin will venture on his full spiritual responsibilities before to-morrow." That remark was not quite intelligible to Mack, but later Sue understood very well Judith's one confidence to her, or to any one, about the strange moments of Moira's passing. "She just knew, just understood, I think—he did all the talking for her. Your Dick is a darling, Sue! I'm pretty hard-boiled, as you know, but he made me keep on thinking of our old nursery hymn—'Tender Shepherd'. I'd rather live with Clive, darling, I'm not your sort, but I'd like to die with Dick around!" Cook was the only other to hear of the scene from Soames, and his comment, if less suggestive, was as whole-hearted in its praise. "A true Christian, Mr. Marlin, and a perfect gentleman!" was his solemn verdict.

Mack had gathered his hat and coat and stick together when the oddly assorted party returned, leaving Moira to peace at last. He was in a state of such perturbation that his eyebrows and hair were entangled in the hearth rug, Judith was to report later.

"I knew I'd an urgent appointment! Must go at once! And, by Jove, do you know what it is? Slipped my memory in all this! It's to meet this fellow from Scotland Yard! Scotland Yard! What'll he say I'd like to know when we've nothing for him to do! Why did you make me send for him, Dick?"

"I didn't, sir! You weren't thinking of it yesterday!"

"Well, I only decided on it last night when I thought I must arrest—you know what I thought. When you rang me up with that tale about Soames' birth and parentage and all the rest of it I still thought we'd keep him busy making out the case against this fellow here! And there's nothing to clear up but all this business about the morphia. Mrs. Mortimer has still to do that. Look here, you come and meet the Yard chap with me, Dick!"

"He'll do nothing of the sort," said Judith decidedly. "He'll just drive back to the Palace with me and go straight to bed, and I'll tell him bed-time stories about my business with the bottles! But I'll just tell you here and now, Major Mack!" Judith's mercurial spirits leapt upwards suddenly. "Guess where the tube was all the time you were searching me and my room! In this hat, this very hat! D'you see this nice wide flat bow?"

She pulled off the small chic hat delightedly. "Wrapped in a bit of tissue paper but winking at you all the time, I'm sure!"

It was certainly as well that Mack was obliged to hurry off at once before he could find a suitable reproof for this crowning insult. "But I'll never really like this hat or wear it again," was Judith's last comment as they got into the car. "I think I shall give it to Mrs. Mack!"

XV
SUNDAY ENDING

BUT THE BED-TIME fairy-tales had to be postponed. When the strange small party reached the house it was to find Dr. Lee's car at the door. The Bishop had collapsed altogether after the strain of Friday's interview and lain awake all night preparing for his arrest. Now he lay in bed, on the verge of "what we'd have called in old days brain fever," said Dr. Lee. "A bad nervous breakdown and no Cathedral for him to-morrow or for weeks to come." He found great pleasure in making the same pronouncement to Dick whom he met limping upstairs, and scolded well for his disobedience and folly. Poor Bobs was left to telephone and wire hopelessly for some leisured prelate to take the Ordination, to enquire when, if, and how long it might be postponed, to deal with the enquiries of candidates, excited reporters, the Cathedral authorities and the sympathetic questions of personal friends. It was not till Sunday evening that Dick persuaded Mrs. Broome to let the girls and Bobs come to his room. He couldn't sleep, he explained, till he had heard Judith's story and he would sleep much better when he had seen Sue. Probably he felt that he deserved such a treat, when Mrs. Broome said that if he could possibly limp just along the passage for a few minutes the Bishop would be very thankful to see him.

Dick could not refuse but had little pleasure in the prospect. He had no wish to tell the whole tangled story again: he was ashamed to look one whom he had ventured to suspect, even for one moment, in the face: he did not feel well enough, or at any time qualified, to justify the ways of God to man, or indeed man to man, as the Bishop often loved to do.

But he returned to his room in a very different mood. For the Bishop asked for no details save for one or two of these points which Mrs. Broome had naturally failed to make clear, and indulged in no reflections on how good came out of evil, but lay there, a tired, sad, yet serene old man, who had sinned and repented and was sure of forgiveness.

"It may be my duty to resign my bishopric, Dick, I don't know. I see now how mixed my motives were in hushing up the old scandal: it was for my sake more than for my Church. Ulder had raked up a very old indiscretion of my College days—no need to worry you with it now! I have spoken of it to my wife. I sinned indeed in persuading myself that all I did was for the sake of the Church."

"But, sir, it was the general opinion!"

"Not yours, Dick. You only acted as mediator for us with Ulder, by our request and against your real judgement, I know. I was a coward in my dealings with my Judith, too. She was all that was left me when my wife died, and I feared to alienate her affections if I thwarted her. So she grew up unbridled, and she has paid a heavy price. Yes, very nearly were bread and tears her portion to eat and drink!" (But they never were the portion of the Judiths of this world, thought Dick.) "I was a coward to demand that morphine when war began, a coward to dose myself later, a coward when I dared not confess. I tell you this, not because you will ever share my temptation, but because I wish to tell one whom I love almost as if he were my own son, that, however we may deceive ourselves, however far we may wander from true self-knowledge, we are not left in our darkness, if all our lives we have tried to turn our faces to the light. We may seem to have dwelt in Plato's cavern of shadows, but we are given grace to turn and see absolute truth and beauty if we have tried to keep faith."

"May I come in, my lord?" Canon Wye had knocked so quietly at the door and entered so gently that the Bishop and Dick alike looked up in surprise. Nor was it fancy that the hard, gem-like eyes were lit by a kindlier, more human flame, and his voice lowered to a gentler note.

"You are going, my dear Canon? Sit down for a little."

"I am only allowed, my lord, by Mrs. Broome's orders to say good-bye and no more, but I must thank you for all your kindness—and for all you have done, Marlin, too! We all owe you our thanks!"

"It has been a strange time, a strange testing time," said the Bishop. "I have been telling Dick that such trials must be sent us to help us in that wearisome life-long lesson of knowing our true selves."

"You are right, my lord. I have taught little to the candidates, but I carry away the knowledge that I must learn humility, that I must distinguish, as I have never done, between my zeal for the Church and my pride, yes, personal pride as a priest! Humility—that fair forsaken Christian virtue—"

"And I must even at my age struggle for the Christian—and pagan—virtue of courage! But I have been trying to encourage our young friend here, as he considers our failings, to reflect that we can and do discover them. Our faith gives us a perfect standard, so that we may acknowledge our weakness. There surely we have the advantage over agnostics, for how lenient one would be to any departure from an ethical standard of one's own! When our lamps flicker we know that we have failed to trim them."

"But what of our example to others—those who see sins we have failed to rid ourselves of and judge the Church by the clergy? Can Marlin here feel that we can hand on the torch, however unworthily, to him and those like him, on the threshold of the priesthood?"

"I looked up Evelake once," said Dick, avoiding the question with embarrassment. "The name comes in Malory's *Morte d'Arthur*, you know. Evelake was a king and all his knights rode into battle with veiled shields. But when they conquered and removed the veils in triumph, the shield bore the likeness of Our Lord and His Apostles. Whatever we may seem to the outer world I like to think that we have this behind the veil." (Having missed my ordination, usurped priest's Orders and served as a policeman, I now seem to be giving a short address to my superiors! he reflected in horror.) But the two men smiled as if pleased.

"*In exitu Israeli!* I thank you, Canon. I thank you, my dear Dick, and hope to see you again."

But if Dick crept back into bed touched to the heart and anxious for his old friend's health he was after all young and at the end of an ugly adventure, and he had a great new hope in life springing up before him. His spirits rose as Mrs. Broome and her daughters came on their visit after tea. Sue was sitting near him in a green frock that suggested spring, her pretty smile always ready to meet his, and Judith was her own absurd disgraceful, delightful self again.

"Well, Lucasta Messalina Borgia, tell us all about it," said Dick. "I go all in a huddle when I try to work out just what you did with that tube of morphine!"

"It was quite simple, really," said Judith airily, sitting on a tabouret against the arm of her mother's chair, the fire light making a mystery of her naughty eyes, and lighting up the exquisite lines of her head and neck. "Moira, poor darling, should have been told nothing that night; that was the whole trouble and I began it too! I let out to her about Ulder's threats before he arrived, and then I told her when he was taken ill. She'd been so restless without her usual injections that I just told her anything that came into my head!"

"So unlike your usual discretion, darling!" put in Sue ironically.

"I wouldn't call Ju really *discreet*," said dear literal Mrs. Broome.

"Well, I wasn't discreet anyway about the morphia! But I did think it so cruel of Dr. Lee to leave her like that, for all night as far as we knew, just because they might or might not operate next day. So when, after suddenly lying quite still a bit and thinking, she asked me to get some medicine from Daddy's secret drawer, I went like a shot. It was something he took for a bad pain he had sometimes, she told me—"

"How did she know about it when even I didn't?" asked Mrs. Broome.

"Darling, you don't spring-clean the house as she does. I don't know how she knew about his pains—perhaps Soames inherited the keyhole habit from her—you know she always did know everything. She said she'd keep the stuff and only take it if the pain were very bad and that I must put it back next day—'For your poor papa might be taken bad.' Then when I went in for a last good night she asked for some whisky—which was most unlike her, but I know invalids have odd fancies. I'll soon be asking for green apricots like the Duchess of Malfi, shan't I? That was when you saw me, Mamma! I'd taken Moira's drink and I suppose that wretch next door heard the happy sound of a gurgling siphon for he called out for some, and I thought all of a sudden I might get him tight, and coax him not to be a blackguard."

"There, Judith love, you did over-estimate your charms, I think," said Dick.

"Well, anyhow, I left Moira quite jolly with her drink and her dope. I'd no idea it was morphine or any sort of poison you know, and I never looked at that silly little label! It wasn't till all the fun and games began next morning—"

"Judith *dear*," protested Mrs. Broome.

"Sorry! I mean the sad tragedy, that I had any qualm about it all, for Moira herself was all right you see. And then Moira told me to listen at the partition wall to hear what it was all about, and I heard Dr. Lee and you, Dick, talking about an overdose of morphine. I didn't think of Moira's having anything to do with it for a minute, but I did hop to her bedside and look at the tube and saw it was morphine, so I felt it was best out of the way, and put it back in Daddy's drawer. Dr. Lee gave Moira

206 | WINIFRED PECK

an injection then, you remember, because he wasn't sure if the
ambulance was coming, so she didn't know what I was doing.
The person who got the fright of his life was poor old Soames,
I gather. He'd seen the morphine tube by Moira's bed when he
went in late to say good night while you were all at Chapel, and
I'd gone to try to get the one hot bath of the season. I do hope
Clive's home has a better hot-water system than ours! Moira
told Soames then that she was going to try to persuade Ulder
to leave me alone—preserve my fair fame sort of thing, I suppose—and persuade him not to expose Soames and the truth
about him. Would you really have minded so much if you'd
known he was her son, Mummy?"

"Well, dear, it would have been a great shock, but as a matter
of fact," admitted Mrs. Broome truthfully, "I'd have engaged
almost anyone then, fathers or no fathers!"

"I said so that night, but I don't think she could bear you
ever to know she wasn't what she called respectable. 'Aren't we
a nice pair!' I said to cheer her up, you know, but she didn't
rise! I suppose she told him then to take the bag when Ulder
was asleep and bring the papers to her, so that she could look
through them and destroy them, and that Soames was to put
the bag back when he called Ulder next morning, I imagine.
Well, by the time Soames managed to sneak in and hook out
the bag he failed to find its key and they couldn't get out the
papers. They didn't know what to do, so they decided to hide
the bag till next day—oh yes, you all know all that, and then
next day Soames went in to call Ulder, and found he'd never
have a next day at all. If Soames had had the sense of a rabbit
he'd have burnt the lock somehow, taken the bag back without the papers, but of course he was rattled by seeing the glass
of whisky by Ulder's bed, and then noticing that the tube of
morphine wasn't in Moira's room any longer. But you know
his part in it all. I knew nothing about bags or papers, of course,
but I was worried about Papa's dope, so I went to Moira's room
and listened again when Mack came, but don't worry, darlings!
I shan't adopt the keyhole habit because I'm sure one's hair

would catch terribly! When you agreed that some one else must have provided the dope I was a bit worried and when the search began I really felt quite frantic—just like being late for one's dentist, you know. I couldn't get into Daddy's room because the maids were doing it and then Mack came up with Tonks and Corn, just like God in a thunderstorm, muttering about a search. I was petrified! I was sure he'd nose out secret drawers even if Tonks didn't—how could you be a posh copper and miss a thing like that? But luckily he started with me and I managed to nip into Daddy's room through yours—you were lying down, Mum my, you remember?—and take the thing and put it in my hat—wasn't our Mack's face a dream when I told him about that? I do pity the next young woman he suspects, for he'll strip her from cover to cover."

"Well, it's a tangled tale, all right," said Dick. "But why on earth, Ju, didn't you throw the thing away or take it away with you? Why put it back?"

"I'd promised Moira," said Judith simply. "And you see later on I'd seen Tonks and Corn shaking out Daddy's aprons and gaiters, and having much more quiet fun over it than Mack had over my frillies. I never thought any one would go near his room again. And I couldn't tell Father about it without giving Moira away, you see."

"Did you suspect Moira all along?"

"As soon as I heard of the whisky with morphine sediment at the bottom. I expect you know she really did try to persuade him first, and then only went back with the morphia because there wasn't any other way."

"Well, dear," said Mrs. Broome miserably, "she always spoilt you and saw you got what you wanted, but I never thought she would go to such lengths as that!"

"She was glad about me all right. You know, Mummy, she had sort of delusions, hadn't she? And I think she wasn't quite sane really. She sometimes seemed to mix up Soames and my future family as Ulder's victims, and I really couldn't bear to have a baby like Soames!"

"Dear Judith!" protested Mrs. Broome.

"We didn't talk obstetrics when the little stranger came," quoted Sue, obviously a little vague about Mr. Kipling's exact meaning.

"My dearest Sue, I am horrified!" With her own daughter Mrs. Broome could still make a stand.

"I say, may I come in?" said Bobs' voice from the door. "We've got through chapel somehow, and there's still half an hour before dinner. Are you all sitting round listening to the great sleuth explaining his methods?"

"I must say," said Mrs. Broome, roused apparently after her former effort to reprove the rising generation, "that I do feel you all forget there have been two deaths in the house—well, practically in the house—since Thursday. Now in my young days—"

"I suppose it's the War," murmured Sue. "I mean death doesn't seem so—so far away to us as it did to you."

"And anyhow those two are better dead!" cried Judith. "I—I minded dreadfully when Moira was so ill, but I felt triumphant, yes really that, when death kept her from suffering any more. And it's no good pretending that the world isn't a better place without Ulder. I'm sorry for poor little Soames, though. Doris will never let you keep him now, Mummy. I wonder if Clive and I should take him as butler, and convert him!"

"How rude we all are," said Dick at the shout of laughter which greeted this suggestion. "But don't let him try any amateur carpentry for you, Judith."

"But, Dick, tell us how you found out such a lot," pleaded Sue. "I shall always think of you as Conan now, though I like Dick better!"

"Sherlock would think very poorly of me or of Mack! And rightly, because we did what none of the best detectives in books nor, I suppose, in real life, ever do—we each started with a prejudice. Mack had a strongly marked one against parsons and specially bishops. I simply felt that there wasn't a soul in the Palace who could have committed a crime except Soames!"

"Not even me, Dick?" asked Judith, a little hurt.

"Not that crime, but any other. Mack said once you were the murderous type, though."

"Like Mary, Queen of Scots, I suppose! How sweet of him," said Judith, deeply gratified.

"Then," continued Dick, "Soames did his best to oblige me in my suspicions by his extraordinary behaviour. He really is the clumsiest little plotter, only so clumsy that no intelligent person could make sense of it! If he'd made booby traps for Mack and Tonks and all, he might have got away with it, but by Thursday night it was quite clear that it was me he was afraid of. That could only be because I knew most about him through Herriot, and because, I imagine, he'd picked up enough with those keyhole ears of his to know that Mack was after bigger game, and that I was the danger. But though I fancy he'd planned out that stair dodge when first he was sent to open the summer parlour, he only brought it off after Herriot's second telephone message. Why had that driven him into a panic? You remember it was after that message that I got my bump, and I'd hardly time to think of it. Then I began saying to myself Kilkelly, and it still didn't mean anything much. But when I came round, the good old subconscious had been hard at work, and suddenly I saw Moira's Bible again—you remember, Sue, how the light failed as we looked at it, and I wasn't specially interested then in her maiden name. But I was afraid I was wishfully thinking it, till I got Sue to refer to the Bible and write the name for me, and there it was when I woke—Kilkelly, Soames' name, changed to Kelly by Moira to wipe out her past rather than for convenience, I expect. So then I only had to pay those visits with Sue to make sure that Soames was the son of Moira. I found that at Dorbury—and that Ulder was his father—that's in Ulder's diary, Bobs, but the Church Register will confirm it, if it's ever needed, I suppose."

"But, Dick, that didn't prove that Moira had murdered Ulder!"

"No, of course not, but it proved there was someone almost as anxious to get him out of the way—someone with all the grievances of a lifetime to repay, and the future of her son and of Judith endangered. There were lots of side-lines, too. The Bishop said no one would look in his drawers, but I remember Moira was always noted for thoroughness. The Bishop said she had a horror of drugs, but she was said to collect medicine bottles of every kind and try them out. She knew something about morphia, too, and she had made Judith listen to and repeat all Dr. Lee said. I couldn't see Soames carefully choosing out a suitable jorum or getting hold of the stuff that night without being suspected. But the chief point was one which Mack would only twist to his theories, that Staples insisted he heard a door open and a rustle like a skirt and a faint voice saying 'Good night' in the distance. Mack dismissed that at once as a rustling cassock or a man's dressing-gown—the Canon or the Bishop, you see. He didn't even think of yours, Judith, by the way!"

"Oh no, Clive frightened him, I'm sure," said Judith complacently. "Darling Clive! I did adore him when he fell upon old Mack!"

"I'd have thought of you all right, Judith, but for your telephone chat at lunch on Friday! I simply didn't believe you could have put up such a good act. You'd have been far more likely to say, 'Oh, Clive sweet, I've poisoned someone. Do come and take me away!' Well, the only other conceivable woman was old Moira, and when once I'd found out her connection with Ulder, it all seemed to fit in. She knew all the circumstances, she could get hold of morphia more easily than anyone else: she wouldn't be suspected because it was only that day, when she was so restless with pain, that she got out of bed at all. But it couldn't be proved. Nearly everything that incriminated her incriminated Soames as well. The only hope was to get her confession."

"What if she hadn't been dying?" asked Bobs.

"I just couldn't say. I didn't have to decide about that, because when I rang up the Hospital from the road yesterday they said she couldn't last the night. No, I don't think I've done anything to be proud of from first to last, except that I did keep Mack in check a bit. You see, I knew he had a vague dream—I'd almost say hope—of entering the Palace with a warrant and saying—" began Judith—"Oh no, that's quite another form of prayer, isn't it? Sue darling, why are you blushing? Darling Clive went off to buy a special licence yesterday from the Archbishop, so I'll be first! I do hope the Archbishop isn't a criminal too!"

"Judith!" Mrs. Broome raised her unheeded reproof. "I think it's time we all got ready for supper as people are coming."

"A party?" asked Dick in surprise.

"Well," admitted Mrs. Broome a little shamefacedly, "I did feel it was the least I could do for that poor Major Mack after his having this special man down from Scotland Yard in vain, and after such an unpleasant time here, and Judith so rude to him, so I asked him and his Yard friend and Mrs. Mack to supper quietly here to-night, not dinner, and we wouldn't dress, I said."

"With two deaths in the house so recently too," said Judith dreamily. "Now in my young days—!"

"Well, it isn't as if we'd any of us enjoy ourselves very much," said Mrs. Broome with cheerful candour. "And I thought I'd get over the invitation while your father was upstairs. I should have asked the Macks long ago, but I do feel your father won't care to meet him for quite a long time—"

"Mamma darling, you are the best joke in the world," said Sue.

"Isn't she?" agreed Judith. "I wish I'd got just a little arsenic to put in Mack's port, because you see however much he suspected us he could really hardly come hanging round trying to arrest us again so soon."

"Not port, darling," said Mrs. Broome who was not attending, as Dick's tray was at the door. "Never on Sunday night, so as to let the servants clear away early, you know—and Doris and Mrs. Briggs will be alone as poor Soames is out to-night."

"That's a pity! He'd have loved dropping plates of hot soup and carving knives on Mack's head," said Sue. "Have you got everything, Dick?"

Dick's guests were leaving the room, but at Sue's question he eagerly called her back.

"No, no, just one thing!" He waited till the voices died down the corridor. "Sue, you know what Judith was saying just now about arrest the Bishop. I wish you'd try it another way—just try it—I, Susan, take thee, Richard—just once!"

"Oh, Dick, to hang round your neck till you're dead," protested Sue, half laughing, half crying.

"No, to have and to hold! Sue, promise to think whether you can't say it some day soon!"

"Oh, Dick, stop!" Sue was kneeling by the bedside when Judith's step came lightly down the passage. "What—what is it, Ju?"

"What—what is it, Sue?" mimicked Judith. "Bless you, darlings, I guessed it from the first. But, Sue, you must come. Mack is here, saying he must see Dick for a talk after dinner, but we won't let him. Mamma told him he couldn't, and he was beginning to bristle, but I think I calmed him! I just said: 'But, of course, darling'—you should have seen Mrs. Mack's face—'of course you shall come upstairs and arrest the Bishop'."

THE END

41673020R00126

Made in the USA
San Bernardino, CA
18 November 2016